FURTHER CoNFESSIoNS
oF GEoRGIA NICoLSoN

LOUISE RENNISON

FURTHER CONFESSIONS OF GEORGIA NICOLSON

VOLUME 3: KNOCKED OUT BY MY NUNGA-NUNGAS

VOLUME 4: DANCING IN MY NUDDY-PANTS

AVON BOOKS

An Imprint of HarperCollins*Publishers*

Library of Congress Cataloging-in-Publication Data
Rennison, Louise.
    Further Confessions of Georgia Nicolson / by Louise Rennison.
    p. cm.
    New edition of two novels previously published separately: New York :
HarperTempest, 2002 and 2003 respectively.
    Contents: Knocked out by my nunga-nungas — Dancing in my nuddy-pants.
    ISBN 0-06-059007-6 (pbk.)
    [1. Diaries—Fiction. 2. Humorous stories. 3. England—Fiction.] I. Rennison,
Louise. Knocked out by my nunga-nungas. 2002. II. Rennison, Louise. Dancing in
my nuddy-pants. 2003. III. Title.
PZ7.R29114Fu 2004   2004041107
[Fic]—22

First Avon edition, 2004
Originally published by Piccadilly Press Ltd.,
5 Castle Road, London NWI 8PR

AVON TRADEMARK REG. U.S. PAT. OFF. AND IN OTHER COUNTRIES,
MARCA REGISTRADA, HECHO EN U.S.A.

❖

Visit us on the World Wide Web!
www.harpercollins.com
www.georgianicolson.com

KNOCKED OUT BY MY NUNGA-NUNGAS

To my lovely family and fab mates. You know who you are
and it is useless to beg me not to mention you in public. Come on,
you know you are proud!!! Yes you are . . . Mutti, Vati, Kimbo,
Sophie, John, Eduardo, Honor, Libbs, Millie and Arrow, Apee,
Francesbirginia and family, Salty Dog, Jools and the Mogul, big Fat
Bob, Jimjams, Elton, Jeddbox, Phil and Ruth, Lozzer, Mrs. H, Geoff
"Oh is that champagne?" Thompson, Mizz Morgan, Alan
"It's not a perm" Davies, Roge the Dodge, Jenks the Pen, Tony the
Frock, Kim and Sandy, the fab St. Nicolas crew, Fanny Fanshawe,
Black Dog the Captain, Downie trousers, the Ace mob from
Parklands, Caroline, cock of the North and family, to the English
team of magnificence—Brenda, Jude, Emma and Clare and
Gillon. And to all the lovely, lovely Hamburger-a-gogo types who
have written to me to tell me they love my books. Thank you.
Finally a very huge ginormous thank you to the marvy
HarperCollins family and in particular to the MARVY
beyond Marvydom Alix Reid.

A NOTE FROM GEORGIA

Dear tiny American chums,

It is I! Georgia, your English pal, writing to you from the exciting organ that is my mind.

Here is the third part of my diary. I hope you *aime* it a lot, as much as *Angus, Thongs + FFS* and *On the Bright Side, I'm Now the Girlfriend of a Sex God*. Hey, guess what, do you know that in England the second book is called *It's OK, I'm Wearing Really Big Knickers*?

The title was changed because apparently you don't wear knickers in Hamburger-a-gogo land. At first I thought that meant that you were all in the nuddy-pants under your skirts, but no, it means that you call knickers "panties." I don't know why when they are clearly knickers. But have it your own way. At least you are not as bonkers as people in Germany. My first book there is called *Frontal Knutschen,* which is German for full-frontal snogging. Frankly I will not be *knutsch*ing anyone in Germany.

Anyway as usual in the interests of world diplomacy I have agreed to do a glossary AGAIN, in the back of this book, for words that you might not understand.

You'll laugh at this. . . . I was told that you wouldn't even know what nunga-nungas are!!!!!! I said, "They're not thick, you know, Americans, just because they don't talk properly."

Anyway, pip pip for now.

Lots of luuuuuuurve,

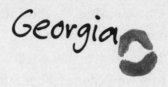

Georgia

P.S. You don't know what nunga-nungas are, do you?

P.P.S. Oh good grief.

P.P.P.S. You know I love you all though, don't you? Even though you are so dim.

oCTOBER
RETURN oF THE LooNLEADER

thursday october 21st
my room
1:00 p.m.
Looking out of my bedroom window, counting my unblessings. Raining. A lot. It's like living fully dressed in a pond.

And I am the prisoner of whatsit.

I have to stay in my room pretending to have tummy lurgy so that Dad will not know I am an ostracized leper banned from Stalag 14 (i.e., suspended from school). I'm not alone in my room, though, because my cat, Angus, is also under house arrest for his love romps with Naomi the Burmese sex kitten.

2:00 p.m.
They'll be doing P.E. now.

I never thought the day would come when I would long to hear Miss Stamp (Sports Oberführer and part-time lesbian) say, "Right, girls, into your P.E. knickers!"

But it has.

3:30 p.m.

All the ace gang will be thinking about the walk home from school. Applying a touch of lippy. A hint of nail polish. Maybe even mascara because it is R.E. and Miss Wilson can't even control her tragic seventies hairdo let alone a class. Rosie said she was going to test Miss Wilson's sanity by giving herself a face mask in class and seeing if Miss Wilson had a nervy spaz.

Jas will be practicing her pouting in case she bumps into Tom.

3:50 p.m.

How come Jas got off with cloakroom duty and I got banned? I am a whatsit . . . a scapethingy.

4:10 p.m.

Robbie the Sex God (MY NEW BOYFRIEND!!! Yesss and three times yesss!!!!!) will be going home now. Walking along in a Sex Goddy sort of way. A walking snogging machine.

4:30 p.m.

Mutti came in. "Right, you can start making your startling recovery now, Georgia."

Oh cheers. Thanks a lot. Good night.

Just because Elvis Attwood, school caretaker from the Planet of the Loons, tripped over his own wheelbarrow (when I told him Jas was on fire), I am banned from school.

Mutti rambled on, although she makes very little sense since Vati got home. "It's your own fault. You antagonize him and now you are paying the price."

Yeah, yeah, rave on.

4:45 p.m.

Phoned Jas.

"Jas."

"Oh hi, Gee."

"Why didn't you phone me?"

"You're phoning me. I would have got the engaged tone."

"Jas, please don't annoy me. I've only been speaking to you for two seconds."

"I'm not annoying you."

"Wrong."

"Well, I've only said about two words to you."

"That's enough."

Silence.

"Jas."

Silence.

"Jas, what are you doing?"

"I'm not annoying you."

She drives me to the brink of madnosity. Still, I really needed to speak to her so I went on, "It's really crap at home. I almost wish I hadn't been banned from school. How was Stalag fourteen? Any goss?"

"No, just the usual. Nauseating P. Green smashed a chair to smithereens and back."

"Really?! Was she fighting with it?"

"No, she was sitting on it having her lunch. It was the jumbo-sized Mars bar that did it. Everyone was killing themselves laughing. The Bummer Twins started singing 'Who ate all the pies' to her, but Slim, our beloved headmistress, heard them and gave us a lecture about mocking the unfortunate."

"Were her chins going all jelloid?"

"Yeah. In fact, it was Chin City."

"Fantastic. Are you all missing me? Did anyone talk about me or anything?"

4

"No, not really."

Charming. Jas has a lot of good qualities though, qualities you need in a bestest pal. Qualities like, for instance, going out with the brother of a Sex God. I said, "Has Hunky, I mean, Tom, mentioned anything that Robbie has said about me?"

"Erm . . . let me think."

Then there was this slurp-slurp noise.

She was making slurping noises.

"Jas, what are you eating?"

"I'm sucking my pen top so I can think better."

Sacré bloody *bleu*, I have got *le* idiot for a pal. Forty-nine centuries of pen sucking later she said, "No, he hasn't said anything."

7:00 p.m.

Why hasn't Robbie mentioned me? Hasn't he got snogging withdrawal?

8:00 p.m.

I can hear Vati singing "If I Ruled the World." Good Lord. I have only just recovered from a very bad bout of pretend lurgy. He has no consideration for others.

8:05 p.m.

The worsterosity of it is that the Loonleader (my vati) has returned from Kiwi-a-gogo land and I thought he would be there for ages. But sadly life was against me and he has returned. Not content with that, he has insisted we all go to Och Aye land to "bond" on a family holiday.

However . . . nananana and who-gives-two-short-flying-pigs'-botties? Because I live in Love Heaven.

Lalalalalalala.

I am the girlfriend of a Sex God!!

8:15 p.m.

The Sex God said I should phone him when I get back from Scotland. But there is a fly in his ointment . . . I am not going to Scotland!!! My plan is this, everyone else goes to Scotland and . . . I don't! Simple enough, I think, for anyone to understand.

operation explain-brilliant-not-going-to-scotland plan to mutti and vati
8:30 p.m.

The olds were slumped in front of the TV canoodling

and drinking wine. They are so childish. I had to leave the room in the end because Dad did this really disgusting thing. They were laughing and grappling about on the sofa and they did number five on the snogging scale (open-mouth kissing). Honestly. I mean it. There might even have been a suggestion of six (tongues). Erlack a pongoes!!!! Libby was there as well. Laughing along. It can't be healthy for a toddler to be exposed to porn.

I'm sure other people's parents don't do this sort of thing. In fact, some of my mates are lucky enough to have parents that are split up. I've never really seen Jas's dad. He is usually upstairs or in his shed doing some DIY. He just appears now and again to give Jas her pocket money.

That is a proper dad.

11:00 p.m.
Before I went to bed I explained to the elderly snoggers (from outside the door just in case they were touching each other) that I will not in a zillion years be going on the family excursion to Scotland tomorrow and said good night.

friday october 22nd
scotland
raining
10:30 p.m.

I have come on holiday by mistake.

This is the gorgeous diary of my fantastic family holiday in Och Aye land. Five hundred years driving with a madman at the wheel (Dad) and another two mad things in a basket (Angus and Libby). After two hours of trying to find the cottage and listening to Vati ramble on about the "wonderful countryside," I was ready to pull his head off, steal the car and drive, drive like the wind. The fact that I can't drive stopped me, but actually I'm sure that once behind the wheel I could pick it up. How difficult can it be anyway? All Dad does is swear at other cars and put his foot down on some pedal thing.

Finally arrived at some crap cottage in the middle of nowhere. The nearest shop is twelve hundred miles away (well, a fifteen-minute walk). The only person younger than one hundred and eighty is a half-witted boy (Jock McThick) who hangs around the village on his pushbike (!)

In the end out of sheer desperadoes I went outside after supper and asked Jock McThick what him and his mates did at nights. (Even though I couldn't give two short flying sporrans.) He said, "Och." (Honestly he said that.) "We go awa' doon to Alldays, you ken." (I don't know why he called me Ken but that is the mystery of the Scottish folk.) It was like being in that film *Braveheart*. In fact, in order to inject a bit of hilariosity into an otherwise tragic situation I said when we first saw the cottage, "You can tak our lives, but you cannae tak our freedom!!"

1:15 a.m.

It's a nightmare of noise in this place, hooting, yowling, snuffling . . . and that's just Vati! No, it's the great Scottish wildlife. Bats and badgers and so on . . . Haven't they got homes to go to? Why do creatures wake up at night? Do they do it deliberately to annoy me? At least Angus is happy here, now that he is not under house arrest. It was about one A.M. before he came in and curled up in his luxurious cat headquarters (my bed).

saturday october 23rd
10:30 a.m.

Vati back as Loonleader with a vengeance. He came barging into "my" (hahahahahaha) room at pre-dawn, waggling his new beard about. I was sleeping with cucumber slices on my eyes for beautosity purposes so at first I thought I had gone blind in the night. I nearly did go blind when he ripped open my curtains and said, "Gidday, gidday, me little darlin'" in a ludicrous Kiwi-a-gogo twang.

I wonder if he has finally snapped? He was very nearly bonkers before he went to Kiwi-a-gogo land and having his shoes blown off by a rogue bore can't have helped. But hey, El Beardo is, after all, my vati and that also makes him vati of the girl-friend of a Sex God. So I said quite kindly, "*Guten Morgen*, vati. Could you please go away now? Thank you."

I think his beard may have grown into his ears however, because he ignored me and opened the window. He was leaning out, breathing in and out and flapping his arms round like a loon. His bottom is not tiny. If a very small pensioner was acciden-tally walking along behind him they might think there had been an eclipse of the sun.

"Aahh, smell that air, Georgie. Makes you feel good to be alive, doesn't it?"

I pulled my duvet round me. "I won't be alive for much longer if that freezing air gets into my lungs."

He came and sat on the bed. Oh God, he wasn't going to hug me, was he? Fortunately Mutti yelled up the stairs, "Bob, breakfast is ready!" and he lumbered off. Breakfast is ready? Has everyone gone mad? When was the last time Mum made breakfast?

Anyway, ho hum pig's bum, I could snuggle down in my comfy holiday bed and do dreamy-dreamy about snogging the Sex God in peace now.

10:32 a.m.
Wrong.

Clank, clank. "Gergy! Gingey!! It's me!!"

Oh Blimey O'Reilly's trousers, it was Libby, mad toddler from the Planet of the Loons. When my adorable little sister came in I couldn't help noticing that although she was wearing her holiday sunglasses she wasn't wearing anything else. She was also carrying a pan. I said, "Libby, don't bring the pan into . . . "

But she ignored me and clambered up into my bed, shoving me aside to make room. She has got hefty little arms for a child of four. She said, "Move up, bad boy. Mr. Pan tired."

Then she and Mr. Pan snuggled up against me. I almost shot out of bed, her bottom was so cold . . . and sticky . . . urghh.

What is it with my room? You would think that at least on holiday I might be able to close my door and have a bit of privacy to do my holiday project (fantasy snogging), but oh no. There will probably be a coachload of German tourists in lederhosen looking round my room in a minute.

I'm going to go and find the local locksmith (Hamish McLocksmith) and get two huge bolts for my door and you can only get in by appointment.

Which I will never make.

11:00 a.m.

Libby has clanked off with Mr. Pan, thank the Lord. I don't like to be near her naked botty for long, as something always lurks out of it.

I think Mum and Dad are playing catch downstairs. I can hear them running up and down and giggling, "Gotcha," and so on. *Sacré* bloody *bleu*.

Très pathetico. Vati's only been back for eighty-nine hours and I feel more than a touch of the sheer desperadoes coming on.

11:10 a.m.

Still, who cares about his parentosity and beardiness? Who cares about being dragged to the crappest, most freezing place known to humanity? I, Georgia Nicolson, offspring of loons, am, in fact, the GIRLFRIEND OF A SEX GOD. Yessssss!!!! Fab and treble marvelloso. I have finally trapped a Sex God. He is mine, miney, mine, mine. There is a song in my heart and do you know what it is? It is that well-known chart topper "Robbie, oh Robbie, I . . . er . . . Lobbie You!!! I Do I Do!!!"

1:00 p.m.

Hung around sitting on the gate watching the world go by. Unfortunately, it didn't. All that went by were some loons talking gibberish (Scottish) and a ferret.

Then Jock McThick or whatever his name is loomed up on his bike. He has an unfortunate similarity to Spotty Norman, i.e., acne of the head.

This is not enhanced by him being a ginger nob. Jock said, "Me and the other lads meet oop at aboot nine just ootside Alldays. Mebbe see you later."

Yeah right, see you in the next life, don't be late. Nothing is going to make me sadly go and hang out with Jock and his mates.

8:59 p.m.
Vati suggested we have a singsong round the piano tonight and started off with "New York, New York."

9:00 p.m.
I took Angus for a walk to check out the nightlife that Jock McThick told me about. Angus is the only good thing about this trip. He's really perked up. I know he longs for Naomi the sex kitten in his furry inside brain, but he is putting a brave face on it. In fact, he is strutting around like he owns Scotland. This is, after all, his birthplace. He can probably hear the call of the Scottish Highlands quite clearly here. The call that says, "Kill everything that moves." There were four voles all lined up on the doorstep this morning. Mum said she found a dead mouse in her tights. I didn't ask

where she had left them. If I ask her anything she just giggles and goes stupid. Since Dad came home her brain has fallen out.

Angus has made a new furry chum. None of the other local cats will come near our cottage. I think there was a duffing-up challenge last night. The black-and-white cat I saw in the lane yesterday has quite a bit of its ears missing now. Angus's new mate is a retired sheepdog called Arrow. I say he is retired, but sadly he is too barmy and old to know that he is retired, so he keeps rounding things up anyway. Not usually sheep though . . . things like chickens, passing cars . . . old Scottish people doing their haggis shopping. Angus hangs out with Arrow and they generally terrorize the neighborhood and lay waste to the wildlife.

9:30 p.m.
It's quite sweet and groovy walking along with Angus and Arrow. They pad along behind me. At least I have got some intelligent company in this lonely Sex Godless hellhole.

When the three of us got to Alldays, Scotland's premier nightspot, I couldn't believe it.

Alldays turns out to be a tiny twenty-four-hour supermarket.

Not a club or anything.

A bloody shop.

And all the "youth" (four Jock McThicks on bikes) just go WILD there. They hang around in the aisles in the shop, listening to the piped music! Or hang about outside on their pushbikes and go in the shop now and again to buy Coca-Cola or "Irn-bru"!

Sacré bloody *bleu* and *quel dommage*.

midnight

That was it. The premier nightspot of Scotland.

I said to Mutti, "Have you noticed how exceptionally crap it is here?"

And she said, "You have to make your own fun in places like this. You have to make things happen. Anyway, you do exaggerate."

12:30 a.m.

Hoot hoot. Scuffle scuffle. Root root. Hey, Mutti is right, it is FANTASTIC fun here!! There's an all-night party going on right outside my window!!! I would join in, but sadly I am not a badger.

sunday october 24th

10:20 a.m.

Still in Och Aye land. Tartan trousers for as far as the eye can see.

10:31 a.m.

How many hours has it been since I saw Robbie now? Hmmm, ninety hours and thirty-six minutes.

11:00 a.m.

How many minutes is that?

11:34 a.m.

Oh God, I don't know. I can't do multiplication very well: it's too jangly for my brain. I've tried to explain this to Miss Stamp, our maths Oberführer (and part-time lesbian). It is not, as she stupidly suggests, that I am too busy writing notes to my mates or polishing my nails to concentrate. It is just that some numbers give me the mental droop.

Eight, for instance.

It's the same in German. As I pointed out to Herr Kamyer, there are too many letters in German words. The German types say *goosegott* in the morning: how normal is that? In fact, how can you take a language like that seriously? Well, you can't, which is why I only got sixty percent on my last German exam.

11:50 a.m.
I'm just going to lie in bed conserving my strength for a snogging extravaganza when I get home.

midday
Mutti came into my room with a tray of sandwiches. I said, "*Goosegott in Himmel*, Mutti, have you gone mad? Food? For me? No, no, I'll just have my usual bit of old sausage."

She still kept smiling. It was a bit eerie actually. She was all dreamy. Wafting around in a see-through nightie. Good Lord.

"Are you having a nice time, Gee? It's gorgeous here, isn't it?"

I looked at her ironically.

She raved on, "It's fun though, isn't it?"

"Mum, it's the best fun I've had since . . . er . . . since Libby dropped my makeup into the loo."

She tutted, but not even in her usual violent tutting way. Just like, nice tutting.

Even though I started reading my *Don't Sweat the Small Stuff for Teens* book she still kept raving on. About how great it was to be a "family" again. I wish she would cover herself up a bit more. Other people's mothers wear nice elegant old-peoples' wear, and she just lets her basoomas and so on poke out willy-nilly. And they certainly do poke out willy-nilly. They are GIGANTIC.

She said, "We thought we might go to the pencil-making factory this afternoon."

I didn't even bother saying anything to that.

"It will be a laugh."

"No, it won't, when did we last have a laugh as a family? Apart from when Grandad's false teeth went down that woman's bra?"

1:00 p.m.
The lovebirds went off to the pencil factory. They only got Libby to go with them because she thinks they are going to go see the pencil people. And I do mean pencil people. Not people who make pencils. Pencil people. People who are pencils. She'll go ballistic when she finds out it's just some Scottish blokes making pencils.

Oh, I am SO bored. Hours and hours of wasted snogging opportunities.

1:20 p.m.
I'd go out but there is nothing to look at. It just goes trees, trees, water, hill, trees, trees, Jock McTavish, Jock McTavish. What is the point of that?

On the plus side, I am going out with a SEX GOD!

1:36 p.m.
Oh *Gott in Himmel*! What is the point of going out with a Sex God if no one knows?

4:00 p.m.
I wonder if I should phone him.

4:05 p.m.
Not to speak to him as such. Just to remind him that I am his girlfriend.

4:10 p.m.
No one here knows that I am the secret girlfriend of a Sex God.

5:00 p.m.

No one at home knows I am the secret girlfriend of a Sex God.

5:15 p.m.

I am like a mirage. In a frock.

7:00 p.m.

Forced to go and sit in the pub with the elderly loons to "celebrate." Libby is being baby-sat by Jock McThick's parents. I hope they have fastened her nighttime nappy securely; otherwise their cottage will not be a poo-free zone. The pub was full of Ye Olde Scottish People (i.e., loads of loonies like my grandad, only wearing kilts). Yippeee. This is the life (not). I asked Vati for a Tía María on the rocks with just a hint of crème de menthe, but he pretended not to hear me. Typico. On the way home M and D were linked up, singing "Donald, Where's Your Trousers?" whilst I skulked along behind them. It was incredibly dark, no streetlamps or anything. As we tramped along the "grown-ups" were laughing and crashing about (and in Dad's case farting) when this awful thing happened.

I felt something touch my basooma. I thought it was the Old Man of the Loch and I leapt back like a leaping banana. Jock McThick spoke from out of the darkness, "Och, I'm sorry. I couldnae see a thing in the dark. I was just like . . . you know . . . feeling my way hame." And he scuttled off.

Hame? Why was he calling me Hame? He used to call me Ken.

11:30 p.m.

Feeling his way? Feeling his way to where? My other basooma?

This was disgusting.

11:45 p.m.

Molesting my nunga-nungas.

Nunga-nunga molester.

11:48 p.m.

Despite the incredible crapness of my life, my nunga-nungas have made me laugh. *Nunga-nungas* is what Ellen's brother and his mates call girls' basoomas. He says it is because if you pull out a girl's breast and let it go . . . it goes *nunga-nunga-nunga*. He is obviously a touch on the mental side.

11:50 p.m.
But quite funny though.

11:55 p.m.
Perhaps I could make some nunga-nunga protectors by electrifying my sports bra with a battery type thing. That would give Jock McThick or any other nunga-nunga marauders a shock.

midnight
But it would also give me a shock, which is *la mouche* in the ointment.

12:10 a.m.
Angus has rediscovered his Scottish roots. Apparently they are in the middle of some bog because he had bits of horrible slimy stuff in his whiskers. He came into my bed purring and all damp and muddy. He soon got nice and dry by wiping himself on my T-shirt.

God, he smells disgusting. I think he's been

rolling in fox poo again. He thinks it's like a sort of really attractive aftershave.

1:00 a.m.
It isn't.

monday october 25th
10:10 a.m.
Why oh why oh why has the SG not called me? Oh hang on, I know why he hasn't. It's because we haven't got a phone in our fantastic cottage. I couldn't believe it when we first arrived. I said to Mutti, "There has been some mistake. I'm afraid we must go back to civilization immediately. I'll drive."

Dad raved on about "tranquility" and the simple life.

I said, "Vati, you can be as simple as you like, but I want to talk to my mates."

He grumbled on about my constant demands. As I pointed out to him, if he would buy me a mobile phone like everyone else on the planet I wouldn't have to bother speaking to him at all.

2:00 p.m.

I can't stand much more of this. The rest of my "family" has gone on a forced march. Well, Vati called it "a little walk in the woods." But I know about his little walks. It will end in tears, but this time they will not be mine. I know exactly what will happen. The Loonleader will be all bossy and "interested" in stuff like cuckoo spit. Then he'll lose the way and argue with Mutti about the right way home, fall over something and be attacked by sheep. And that will only be the high spots.

I pretended I had a headache.

Vati said to me as I lay in my pretend bed of pain, "You've probably given yourself eyestrain looking in that bloody mirror all the time."

I said, "If I develop a brain tumor you will be the first person I will come to because of your great kindness and sympathosity."

4:20 p.m.

On the edge of sheer desperadoes. Decided to go for a walk.

Arrow tried to round me up as I came out of the gate. So to make him happy I let him herd me into a hedge for a bit. Then I set off down the lane. Ho hum. Birds singing, ferrets ferretting, Jock McThicks McThicking around. Good grief. Then I came across a phone box.

A phone box!!!

A link to the real world!!! It wasn't even a tartan phone box!!

I skipped inside and dialed Jas, my very bestest mate in the universe.

"Jas, it's me!!!! God, it's good to speak to you. What's been happening???"

"Er . . . well . . . I got this fab new foundation. It's got gold bits in it that make you . . ."

It is like talking to the very, very stupid. (In fact, it IS talking to the very stupid.) I had forgotten how annoying she is. Not for long though. She rambled on, "Tom is thinking about doing Environmental Studies."

I nearly said, "Who cares." But you have to be careful with Jas because she can turn nasty if she thinks you are not interested in her. I tried to think of something to say. "Oh . . . er . . . yeah . . . the environment . . . er, that's great, erm, there's a lot of, er . . . environment here; in fact, that is all there is." Then I told her about the Jock McThick fandango. She said, "Erlack a pongoes. Did you encourage him? Maybe you gave out the wrong signals."

"Jas, I was not in the nuddy-pants."

"Well, I'm just saying, Jock must have thought he could rest his hand on your basooma. Why is that? He has never rested his hand on my basoomas, for instance."

"Jas, you are three hundred miles away. You would have to have nunga-nungas the size of France for Jock to be able to rest his hand on them."

"Yes, well . . . I'm just saying, even if I was, you know, in Och Aye land, next to Jock, well, even then, you know . . ."

"What are you rambling on about?"

"I'm just saying, this is not the first time this has happened to you, is it? There was Mark, the Big Gob. . . ."

"Yeah, but . . ."

"You say it just happened. That just out of the blue he put his hand on your basooma. No one else was there so we will never really know for sure."

"I didn't . . . it was . . ."

"Perhaps Jock has heard about your reputation. Perhaps he thinks it's alright to fondle your basoomas."

I hate Jas. I slammed the phone down. I will never be talking to her again. I don't forget things. Once my mind is made up, that is it. The friendship is finito. I would rather eat one of Libby's nighttime nappies than talk to Jas again.

She is an ex–best mate. Dead to me. Deaddy dead dead. Forever.

4:22 p.m.
Phoned Jas.

"Jas, are you suggesting I am an easy fond-leree?"

"I don't know. I might be."

"What do you mean 'you might be'?"

"Well, I might be . . . but I don't know what a fondleree is."

It is like talking to the very, very backward.

I explained to her as patiently as I could. "Well, it's like dumping. If you dump someone you are the dumper. And they are the dumpee."

"What has that got to do with fondling?"

28

"Jas, concentrate. The verb is 'to fondle.' I fondle, you fondle, he, she, it fondles, etc. But I am the recipient of the fondle, so that makes me the fondleree."

She wasn't really concentrating though. She was probably looking at herself in the mirror they have in their hall . . . imagining she is Claudia Schiffer. Just because some absolute prat told her she looked a bit like Claudia. Yeah. Claudia with a stupid fringe.

Walked back to Crap Cottage.

in my room
6:00 p.m.

Brilliant. Miles away from civilization and my so-called mate says I am an easy fondleree. Still, she is mad as a badger; everyone knows that.

9:00 p.m.

Sitting around in the tartan lounge in Crap Cottage. My breasts are making me a mockery of a sham. They are like two sticky-out beacons attracting all the sadsacks in the universe.

11:00 p.m.

Mutti came into my bedroom to get Libby out of my wardrobe. She's made a sort of nest in there that she says is a treehouse.

Over the shouting and biting I said to Mutti, "Do you think you could ask Dad if you and he could club together to let me have some money for breast reduction surgery?"

It took her about a year to stop laughing.

It's pointless asking for money. I can't even get a fiver out of Dad for some decent lip gloss. He would never give me the money. Even if my breasts were so big that I had to have two servants called Carlos and Juan to carry them around for me.

tuesday october 26th
10:00 a.m.

The postman came this morning. He didn't have any post, he just said, "Good morning to ye. It's nice to have a good-looking lassie round the place."

He was quite groovy-looking. A bit like a young Sean Connery. But with more hair on his head. And quite nice lips.

10:15 a.m.

Oh Blimey O'Reilly's pantaloons, I think I have got general snoggosity syndrome.

11:00 a.m.

Maybe Jas is right. I have become an easy fondleree because of my pent-up snogging deprivation.

Oh Robbie, where are you now? Rescue me from this valley of the loons.

4:29 p.m.

Accidentally found myself next to the phone box.

Uh-oh. Temptation.

The phone box was saying to me, "Come in and use me. You know you want to."

I have been practicing maturiosity by not phoning the Sex God. It seems like a lifetime since he last snogged me. My lips have definitely got snog withdrawal. I found myself trying out kissing techniques on scuba-diving Barbie last night. Which is truly sad. I must pass by the phone box with complete determinosity.

4:30 p.m.

Brring brring.

Please don't let it be Robbie's mum or dad. Please don't let me have to be normal. Oh thank goodness SG answered the phone. Jellyknickers all round.

He said "Hello" in a Sex Goddy sort of a way. Wow!!

Then he said "Hello" again.

Wow.

Then I realized that normally when you phone someone up you are supposed to say something. And that something is NOT "I love you, I love you" or "Ngyunghf." So I took the bullet by the horns and said, "Hi . . . Robbie . . . it's me. Georgia." (Very good, I had even said the right name!!!) He sounded like he was really pleased to hear from me. "Gee! How are you, gorgeous?"

Gorgeous. He, me called, gorgeous. Me, I. Georgia to brain! Georgia to brain! Shut up shut up shut up!!!!!

He said, "Gee, are you there? Are you having a good time?"

"Fantastic, if you like being bored beyond the Valley of Boredom and into the Universe of the Very Dull."

He laughed. (Hurrah!!!) Oh, it was so dreamy

to talk to him. I told him about everything. (Well, apart from being molested by Jock McThick.) He says some talent scouts are coming to see the next Stiff Dylans gig on November 6th at the Buddha Lounge!! My first official outing as an OG (official girlfriend). What shall I wear, what shall I wear? I noticed he hadn't really said anything for a bit whilst I had been rummaging through my mental wardrobe. He was not *le official grand bouche* like some people (Jas). I thought I would entertain him with an intelligent story, but all I could think of telling him about was my nunga-nunga protectors idea. Just in the knickers of time I didn't. Why couldn't I be normal with him?

Fortunately he said something. "Look, Gee, I'm really sorry but I have to go. I could talk to you all day, but I have to go off to a rehearsal. I'm late now."

Ho hum. Well I suppose this is the price I must pay for being the GIRLFRIEND OF A SEX GOD POPSTAR!!! YESSS!!!

He said, in his groovy voice full of gorgeosity, "See you later. I'd like to snog you to within an inch of your life. I'll phone you when you get back."

Ooohhhhhh.

After he had put the phone down I stroked my T-shirt with the receiver pretending it was him. But then I saw that Jock McTavish was waiting outside the telephone box looking at me, so I had to pretend I was cleaning the receiver.

5:00 p.m.
Phew.

To make Jock go away, I have said I will go to Alldays later. Which I will not. Jock seemed to believe me because he said, "Awa the noo hoots akimbo" or something.

9:00 p.m.
How soon can I get them to set off for home tomorrow? If we set off at dawn we could be back in Normal Land by about four P.M.

9:30 p.m.
I wonder if the ace gang might arrange a surprise welcome home party for me. It's half term now, so I am no longer an ostracized leper on my own. So ha-di-haha. She who laughs the last laughs, erm, a lot. Slim thought she was banning me for a week but she was banning me for two weeks!!!

10:00 p.m.

In "my" bed, with the usual crowd. Libby and the entire contents of her traveling toybox: scuba-diving Barbie, one-eyed Teddy, Pantalitzer, Panda the Punk (Libby shaved his head). The only difference is that to celebrate our holiday in Tartan-a-gogo Libby has replaced Charlie Horse with Jimmy. Jimmy is a haggis with a scarf on. Don't even ask. Libby made him this afternoon and she "lobes" him.

I am sleeping in a bed with a stuffed sheep's stomach. With a scarf on.

wednesday october 27th

6:00 a.m.

Up and packed. I tried to get Mutti and Vati to get up and make an early start, but when I went into their bedroom Vati threw his slipper at me.

9:00 a.m.

At last! Escape!!!! Soon I will be back in the arms of my Sex God. At last, at last. Thank the Lord!!! I love you, Jesus, really, really I do. Good-bye Och Aye land!!! I sat in the back of the car daydreaming of my return as OG. But as they say, "Every silver cloud has a dark lining," because Vati decided to wear his ridiculous souvenir bagpipe hat as we eventually got into the loonmobile. I got down as low as I could in the back of the car so that no one would see me. I wish I could have an inflatable dad, like in that old film *Airplane!* where there is an inflatable pilot. Still, with a bit of luck I need never see him again when I get my freedom back. Arrow looked all mournfully at Angus when we left. He will miss his furry partner in crime. Angus and Arrow, *los dos amigos bonkeros*. Angus didn't even look back. He just shot into the car and started wrestling with the car rug.

11:00 a.m.
Meanwhile in my fabulous life, another eighty-five years of my parents' company in the car going home.

Libby has insisted on bringing Jimmy the haggis home with us.

1:00 p.m.
Oh good grief. Angus ate half of Jimmy when Libby had to be taken to the piddly diddly department

at the service station. She went ballisticisimus when she found out. She hit Angus over the head with scuba-diving Barbie. I don't think he even noticed—well, he didn't stop purring. I nodded off for the whole of the Midlands because Dad started telling us about his hopes for the future. When I woke up I noticed that both Libby and Angus were nibbling away at Jimmy.

They are disgusting.

I sooooo hope that Robbie rings when I get home.

6:00 p.m.

Home!!!! Oh, thank you, thank you, Baby Jesus. I am SOOOO happy. I will never complain about my dear little home again.

6:15 p.m.

God, it's so boring here. Nothing is happening.

6:30 p.m.

No phone calls.

All my so-called mates forgot to remember that I am not dead. Don't they even wonder where I have been for the last five days?

7:55 p.m.

Jas, Jools, Ellen, Rosie, Mabs, and Soph are ALL out. They've all gone to the cinema together. The Fab Gang but without one of the fab. People can be so self-obsessed. Right, well, I am going to eat the souvenirs that I brought back from Och Aye land for them.

8:25 p.m.

Lying down.

Urgh, I feel sick. I may never eat Ye Olde Shortbreaddy again as long as I live.

9:00 p.m.

Tucked up in bed. I have made a barrier with my bedside table so that no one can get in my room.

Now I really have got snogging withdrawal BADLY!!

9:05 p.m.

I must see him. I must.

10:00 p.m.

Undid my barricade and went downstairs. I am so restless.

Angus is driving everyone insane!!! He is not allowed out at night until he learns his lesson vis-à-vis Naomi the sex kitten. He has to be kept away from her; otherwise he is in for the big chop. Although I would like to see the vet that could do the job and still have both arms.

Angus keeps yowling and scratching at the door. He is supposed to go to the piddly diddly department and poo parlor division in the laundry room. But he won't go in. He just hangs round the front door trying to get out, whining and scratching and occasionally licking his bottom.

Libby said, "C'mon, big pussy, I'll show you," and went and had a piddly diddly on his tray. Oh marvelous. Now we'll never get her to go to the ordinary piddly diddly department. She'll want her own tray.

Then Vati, Loonleader of the Universe, took over. "I'll deal with the bloody thing!" He dragged Angus into the laundry to put him on the cat tray. It took him about half an hour, even using the spade. Anyway, he got him in there at last. There was a lot of yowling and swearing and Vati came out two minutes later covered in kitty litter. Like the Abominable Ashtray! Even his beard was gray.

lo:3o p.m.

In the end, after Angus had laid waste to four loo rolls, I was made to take him out on his lead to see if it would calm him down. God, he's strong! I mean, normally I have very little control over him, but his love has given him the strength of ten mad cats. When we got out of the door he just took off with me on the end of the lead. Straight to Naomi's love parlor. At Mr. and Mrs. Across the Road's place there was a reinforced fence round the garden, but you could see the house and there was Naomi!! The sex kitten. Languishing in the kitchen window. On the windowsill. Looking all longing. She was like me. All puckered up and nowhere to go. Poor furry thing. Angus yowled and started doing this weird shivering thing. When Naomi saw Angus she immediately lay on her back with her girlie parts flowing free. She's a dreadful minx. No wonder Angus is a wreck, driven mad by her Burmese sex kitteny charms. Still, that is male and female for you. Sex God is probably at home even now thinking about me and shivering with excitement like Angus.

10:40 p.m.

But hopefully not rubbing his bottom against a dustbin.

10:50 p.m.

We would have been there all night, but fortunately Mr. Across the Road drew the curtains and I found a bit of old sausage and managed to get Angus to trail after it. He was so miserable that I didn't lock him in the kitchen. I let him sleep on my bed even though it is strictly verboten.

I said to him very seriously, "Angus, you are on best behavior. Just lie down and go to sleep." He was all purry and friendly and licky. You see, that's all he needs—a bit of understanding.

Aahhh. It's nice having a loyal furry pal. He's a lot more loyal than some I could name but won't.

Jas.

10:55 p.m.

And Rosie, Jools, Ellen.

11:00 p.m.

Night night, Sex God, wherever you are.

midnight

Vati just went ballisticisimus. Raving on and shouting, "That is IT, that is IT!!!"

Mutti was saying, "Bob, Bob . . . put the knife down."

Has he finally snapped and will have to go to a vatihome?

12:15 a.m.

Angus has pooed in Vati's tie drawer! Hilarious, really.

El Beardo as usual did not see the joke. He dragged Angus, who was spitting at him, into the kitchen and locked him in there. Then he shouted at me, "Right, that's IT! I'm going to the vet's."

I said, "Why? Are you feeling a bit peaky?" But he didn't get it.

thursday october 28th

10:00 a.m.

Vati said to me over our marvelous breakfast of . . . er . . . nothing, "He's going to the vet's and having his chimney swept as soon as I can make an appointment."

What in the name of Sir Julie Andrews is he talking about now?

11:00 a.m.
I've got much too much on my mind to worry about chimneys. I think I may have a lurker coming on. Emergency, emergency.

11:15 a.m.
Also the orangutan gene is rearing its ugly head again. My eyebrows are so hairy they are now approaching the "It's a mustache! It's a hedge-hog!!! No, no, it's GEORGIA'S EYEBROWS!!" stage.

It doesn't even stop at the head, this rogue hair business. I've just inspected my legs. I look like I have got hairy trousers on. Dad's razor is lying there calling to me, "Come on, use me. Just a few little strokes and you could look almost human." But no, no, I must resist after what happened last time. My eyebrows took a thousand years to grow back after I accidentally shaved them off.

Hmm, but maybe Mum's hair removing cream? Just a little dab here and there.

midday

Mutti asked me if I wanted to go tenpin bowling with them! Honestly! She and Vati went off with Libby skipping along. I think M and D were holding hands. Sweet really, I suppose. I just wish it didn't make me feel so sick.

12:30 p.m.

Jas came round AT LAST. I was a bit miffed with her about last night and not bothering to come round earlier. She didn't notice, of course. She just bent over to pick up my makeup bag. I could see her vast pantibus lurking under her skirt. I said, "Jas, do you mind? I'm not feeling very well. I think I might have jet lag from coming from Och Aye land."

"You haven't got a tan."

What is the point? I gave her my worst look but she just went on using my mascara. She CANNOT stop pouting every time she sees herself in a mirror. She said, "We had a great time at the pictures. Dave the Laugh is really . . . you know . . . (pouty pout) . . ."

"What?"

"Well, you know (pouty pout) . . . a laugh."

I tried not to be sarcastic or raise my eyebrows ironically, because I didn't want to draw any attention to them. I have not quite achieved the sophisticated look that I wanted with Mum's hair remover. In fact I have achieved the someone-has-just-stuck-a-firework-up-my-bottom look. But you can't really tell unless you pull my fringe back.

Anyway, you'd have to be on fire for Jas to notice anything. She was rambling on. "Do you think I should get my hair cut really short at the back and kind of longer at the front?"

I hadn't the remotest interest in Jas's head, but I know you have to let her rave on about herself a bit, otherwise you never get to talk about yourself. Then she said, "Ellen really likes Dave the Laugh."

I thought, Oh does she really? How patheticosimus. Ellen my so-called mate likes my castoff Red Herring. She is like a lurking piranha fish in a skirt.

But live and let live I say. OGs display pride and general sophisticosity at all times. Jas was unaware of my sophisticosity and went looning on. "She stayed round at my place for the night and we talked until about four A.M. That's why I am so tired."

"It's nice that you have got a new lezzie mate, Jas, but what has that got to do with me?"

"She didn't sleep in my bed."

"So you say."

"Well, she didn't."

"It's nothing to be ashamed of, Jas. If you swing both ways that is your personal choice. I'm sure Tom will understand if you tell him you are a bisexual."

"Oh shut up—you're being all moody and stressy because Robbie hasn't phoned you."

She was right actually, which is annoying. I feel all pent up, like in *Cell Block H*. I said, "Let's put some really loud CDs on and go dance crazy."

We did this fab dance routine. It was duo head shaking, kick turn, jump on bed, snog teddy, then back to the head shaking. I was feeling quite perked up. Then, of course, someone had to spoil it. I had forgotten about the Return of the Mad Bearded One. He came in the front door and it was stomp, stomp, "Bloody hell!", then crash, stomp, stomp, yell. "Georgia!!! Are you deaf?!!! Turn that racket down, I could hear it at the end of the bloody street!!"

I shouted back, "Pardon? Can you speak up, Dad, there's really loud music playing!!!"

Which made Jas and me laugh a lot. But not
El Beardo.

4:00 p.m.
Jas, my so-called best mate, had to go because
she was doing her homework. How sad is that?
Very, very sad. Also, she was doing it with her
boyfriend Hunky. Hell will freeze over and become
a skating rink for the mad before I will do my
homework with Robbie. Sex Gods and their girlfriends do not "do homework." Life is too short.

I tried to explain the tragedy of what she was
doing, but Jas just said, "I want to do well in my
German exam." I laughed. But she was serious.

I said, "It is so naff to do well in German, Jas."

Jas went all huffy. "You only say that because
you can't do it."

"Oh, that is so *nicht* true, Jas. *Ich bin ein guten*
German speaker."

But old swotty knickers went off anyway. Hmmm.

5:00 p.m.
Swiss Family Robinson have gone to the cinema
together now. It's just fun fun fun, all the way for
them.

All aloney. On my owney. It's bloody nippy noodles as well. What a life. I have been back a whole day and a night and he has not called me. Why oh why oh why?

I am so fed up.

5:10 p.m.
I might as well go to bed and grow my lurker.

5:20 p.m.
Phone rang. Probably Jas asking me something about her homework. I said, *"Jahwohl!"*

5:22 p.m.
The Sex God wants me to go round to his house!!! His parents are out.

I am so HAPPY!!!

5:30 p.m.
I changed into my jeans and quickly got made up. I went for the natural look (lip gloss, eyeliner, mascara and blusher) with a touch of panstick on the lurker. You could only see the lurking lurker if you looked up my nostril, and what fool was going to do that?

But as I was going out of my bedroom door I remembered my nungas. Perhaps I should take some precautions to keep them under strict control. Maybe bits of Sellotape on the ends of them to keep them from doing anything alarming? I'd like to trust them, but they are very unreliable. Sometimes they act like they have lives of their own. One day I will look down and they will have gone out to some nunga-nunga party by themselves. Oh, oh, I have early signs of absent brain coming on!!!

outside robbie's house
6:00 p.m.

I walked through the gate, breathing the atmosphere of Sex Goddiness, and knocked on the door. My heart was beating really loudly. The door opened.

The Sex God.

Himself.

In person.

In his gorgeous black jeans and thingy top. And his dreamy army things and gorgey leggy whatsits and mouthy thing and so on. He is SO dreamy. Every time I see him it's a shock. He smiled at me. "Georgia . . . how are you?"

Excellent question. Excellent. Good. I knew the answer as well. That was the marvelous thing. I knew the answer was "Great, how are you?" Unfortunately, all the blood in my brain had gone for a bit of a holiday into my cheeks. I had a very, very red face and a completely empty brain. I couldn't speak; all I could do was be very, very red.

He just looked at me, and he smiled this really beautiful smile, all curly round the teeth. Like he really liked me. Yuuummy scrumbos.

Then he pulled me into the house and shut the door behind me. I just stood there trying not to be red. He put his arms round me and gave me a little soft kiss on the mouth, no tongues (number three on the snogging scale). But my mouth had gone into pucker mode so when he stopped my mouth was a bit behind and still a bit open. I hoped I didn't look like a startled goldfish.

He kissed me again, this time harder and longer. His mouth was all warm and wet (not wet like whelk boy though). He put one of his hands on the back of my head, which was just as well as I thought my head might fall off. And then he started kissing my neck. Little sucky kisses right up to my ear. Fanbloodytastic. After a bit of that, and believe me I could have gone on doing that for years, he put his tongue ever so softly into my ear!! Really! Ear snogging!!! Fantastic.

I think I might have lost the use of my legs then because I fell over onto the sofa. However, I quickly leapt to my feet in a gazelle(ish) sort of way. I thought I would say something normal so that he would be fooled into thinking I was normal. I said, "Did you finish your demo-disc-type-thingymedendums?"

(Yes—very nearly English!! Good, good, keep it up!!)

He smiled at me and then went and put his demo disc on. It was very groovy, but I didn't know what to do with my face. Smile? Look dreamy? Hum? Nod along to the beat? In the end, I went for gazing out of the window and tapping my foot a bit. He came and stood behind me and put his hands on my waist.

So I turned around for more snogging.

bedroom

10:00 p.m.

I am in Love Heaven. What a mega fab day. He is the Sex God of the Universe and beyond.

I crept downstairs and phoned Jas. "Jas," I whispered.

"Why are you whispering?"

"Because M and D are in the front room, and I don't want them to know I am calling you."

"Oh."

"I have had the most amazing time, I—"

"Well, I haven't, I just can't decide whether to have my hair cut for the gig. . . . Do you think yes or no? I mean, it's nice to have it long but then it's nice to have it short, but then . . ."

"Jas, Jas . . . it is my turn to talk."

"How do you know?"

"I just do."

"Oh."

"Ask me what I have just done."

"Why? Don't you know?" And she started laughing.

I forgot I was supposed to be whispering and yelled down the phone, "Jas!!!" Then I told her. "I went round to Robbie's house to see him."

Jas said, "No!"

"Mais oui!"

"Sacré bleu."

"Aujourd'hui."

"Well, what happened?"

And I said, "Well, it was beyond marvy. We talked and snogged and then he made me a sandwich and we snogged and then he played me one of his tracks and then we snogged."

"So it was like . . ."

"Yeah . . . a snogging fest."

"Sacré bleu!" Jas sounded like she was thinking which is a) unusual and b) scary.

I went on, "Yes, and guess what?"

"What?"

"He put his tongue in my ear."

"Crikey. Did it . . . couldn't it . . . accidentally . . . like stick in your brain?"

Honestly, you would get more sense out of a potato. I ignored her obvious bonkerosity and went on, "But then this weird thing happened. He was playing me his demo CD and standing behind me with his hands on my waist."

"Ooer."

"D'accord. Anyway, I turned round and he sort of leapt out of the way like two short leaping things."

"Was he dancing?"

"No . . . I think he was frightened of being knocked out by my nunga-nungas."

Then we both laughed like loons on loon tablets
(i.e., a LOT).

bedroom
10:21 p.m.
Vati made me get off the phone and gave his famous
We-are-not-made-of-money speech, first given in
1846.

11:00 p.m.
Emergency snogging scale update:

- **(1)** holding hands
- **(2)** arm around
- **(3)** good-night kiss
- **(4)** kiss lasting over three minutes without a breath
- **(5)** open-mouth kissing
- **(6)** tongues
- **(6½)** ear snogging
- **(7)** upper body fondling—outdoors
- **(8)** upper body fondling—indoors (in bed)
- **(9)** below waist activity (b.w.a.)
- **(10)** the full monty

friday october 29th

9:58 a.m.

Dreamt of Robbie feeding me chocolate sandwiches. Which was really cool. But then he started nibbling my ears in a sort of peckish way, and he nibbled them both off. Then for some reason we were in the south of France at some big gig and it was really sunny and I got my shades out to put on and they just fell off because I had no ears to balance them on.

I don't know what this means. Probably it means I am feverish with love.

Very nippy noodles again. Brrrr. Oh, it snowed during the night, that's why. When I got out of bed and stood in the cold air my nipples did that sticking-out thing again. On the whole I seem to have very little control over my body.

Still, so what!!!

6:00 p.m.

Spent the day in a love haze punctuated by rescuing bits of my underwear from Angus's basket. He is in an awful mood. He climbed up the curtains like a Tyrolean mountaineer in a furry suit. If he

was a human he would go down to the gym and
work out his frustration by hitting something. Or
jogging. I know how he feels.

9:00 p.m.
I tried to encourage Angus to go cat jogging. He
didn't get it though. When I set off jogging he trot-
ted along quite nicely on his lead. For about a
minute. Then he got bored. He ran round and round
me like a mad loon until his lead was wrapped
round my ankles and all I could do was fall over
into a thorn bush.

9:30 p.m.
Phone rang. OhmyGod. I almost ripped it off
the wall.

It was Rosie checking arrangements for tomorrow. I could hardly hear her because there was
such loud music in the background. She said,
"Greetings, Earth creature . . . SVEN!!!!! You adorable Norwegian fool, turn the music down!!"

I heard laughing and stamping and then the
music went quieter. Rosie said, "Jas said you did
ear snogging yesterday."

Oh, thank you, Radio Jas.

saturday october 30th
9:30 a.m.

Phoned Jas for gang discussion. Where we should all meet today and so on. When she answered I came over a bit French. (Because I am in *Le* Luurve Heaven.) "*Bonjour*, Jas, it is *moi, ta grande amie*."

"*Ah, bonjour.*"

"*Ah, d'accord*, I have just *mang*ed my breakfast; I *mang*ed the *delicieusement* toast and *le coffee de* Monsieur Nescafé."

"*Magnifique.*"

"*De rigueur.*"

We are meeting at gang headquarters (Luigi's Cafe) at one o'clock and then going for a bit of heavy makeup trying-on in Boots, etc. I have only got a measly five pounds to spend. I hope Dad manages to persuade some poor fool to give him a job soon because I am running out of lip gloss.

11:00 a.m.

Bloody hell. You take your life in your hands going into the kitchen for a snack. Angus is in there and he is not pleased. I had to fend him off with a frying pan to get into the fridge.

Still, lalalalalala.

midday

Still in a European mood, I dressed French casual (same as sports casual—black Capri pants, black rollneck top, ankle boots—but with a lot more eyeliner). In fact, the combination of Frenchosity and my snogging extravaganza made me come over all forgiving and relaxed. I even waved to Mr. Next Door as I went down the road. Typically, he just tutted. But hey ho, tut on. Nothing can spoil my mood. Mr. Next Door was wearing an extraordinary pair of trousers; they seem to start under his armpits and be made out of elephant. He said, "I hope you are keeping that wild animal under lock and key. It's about time something was done with it."

Nobody can take a joke around here. Alright, Mr. Across the Road does have a point in that Angus did abscond with Naomi, but what does Old Elephant Trousers have to complain about?

What they both fail to see are Angus's very good qualities. He has many attractive cat qualities. For instance, he has EXCELLENT balance. Only last month he herded Snowy and Whitey, Mr. Next Door's Prat Poodles, into the manure heap and then leapt down from the wall and had a ride round on Snowy's back. Like Snowy was a little horsey.

How many cats can do that?

12:30 p.m.
While I was waiting at the bus stop for a bus to town, two blokes in cars hooted their horns at me (ooer). I really have become a boy magnet.

Then along came Mark Big Gob who I unfortunately made the mistake of going out with in my youth. Well, ten months ago, anyway. He was messing about with his rough mates waiting for the bus. No sign of his midget girlfriend. Perhaps he had mislaid her. His mouth is sooo big; how could I have snogged him? And he had rested his hand on my basooma. Still, let bygones be bygones. My basoomas are out of his hands now. I am, after all, the girlfriend of a Sex God and Mark is the boyfriend of some toddler. I smiled kindly at him, and that is when he said to me, "You want to be careful not to move too quickly, Georgia. You'll have someone's eye out with those."

And he meant my nunga-nungas! And all his mates laughed.

I stood there in a dignity-at-all-times sort of way until the bus came. I sat as far away from the BG and his rough mates as I could.

12:45 p.m.
It was a relief to get off the bus. As I got off I had to go past Mark and his mates. I made sure my nungas were not making a guest appearance by hunching my shoulders over.

12:50 p.m.
I've just seen a reflection of myself in a shop window looking like the hunchback of Notre Dame in Capri pants.

1:00 p.m.
In the cafe I met up with Rosie, Ellen, Mabs, Jools and Jas. Yesssssssss! The ace gang together again!! The girls are back in town, the girls are back in town!!! We had loads of really important things to talk about: makeup, snogging and, of course, berets. This term is not going so well on the beret front. Even the lunchpack beret has lost its charm.

Rosie said, "I walked by Miss Stamp with two oranges and a banana stuck under my beret and she just raised her eyes. Something must be done."

I had a flash of total whatsit . . . wisdomosity. "*Mes* huge *amies*, I have given this seconds of thought, and I know what the answer is."

They were all agog as two gogs. Jools said, "What?"

I brought out my gloves and beret from my rucky. *"Voilà."*

They looked at me. Honestly, it was like talking to the terminally deaf.

I said again, "*Voilà* . . . glove animal!!"

Rosie said, "What in the name of Slim's gigantic knickers are you talking about?"

Good grief. It is very tiring being the girlfriend of a Sex God and a genius at the same time. "Glove animal!!! A way of dressing sensibly and snugly using both beret and gloves. You pin a glove over each ear so that it hangs down like big dog ears and then you pop the beret over the top." I clipped my gloves over my ears and popped the beret over the top (risking my hair's bounceability factor).

"*Voilà,* glove animal!!!"
Magnifique, I think everyone will agree.

8:00 p.m.
Home again to my lovely delicious supper of . . .
er . . .

Mutti and Vati and Loonsister out AGAIN.
Still. In Love Heaven you are never really alone.

Angus is tied up to the kitchen table leg. I
gave him a hug to cheer him up, and he lashed out
at me. Also I notice that he has a pair of Vati's
Y-fronts in his basket. Good grief. He has gone
beyond sheer desperadoes. He is really sad without Naomi. I know how he feels. Every minute
without the Sex God seems about sixty seconds
long.

11:30 p.m.
Halloween tomorrow.

It's impossible to sleep in my bed with Libby's
pumpkin lantern in here. I suppose I should be
pleased she hasn't insisted on having her witch's
broom and . . .

"Libby, no, not the broom and . . ."

"Move over, bad boy."

sunday october 31st
halloween

I immediately annoyed Dad this morning by pretending that he was wearing a scary Halloween
costume. In fact, his leisure slacks and Marks and
Spencer's cardigan ARE very scary, but he didn't
get it.

Libby is in toddler heaven because some of her
little mates from kindy are coming across this afty
for apple bobbing and lanterns and stuff.

11:00 a.m.

In a rare moment of sanity Vati has been over to
see Mr. and Mrs. Across the Road and pleaded for
Angus's manhood. He was all pleased with himself when he came back.

"I thought I'd take a look at that garden fence,
Connie, see if we can keep Angus in a bit more. Then
he might not have to have his biscuits nibbled."

Biscuits nibbled? What planet does he live on?

He started rooting around in the toolbox. I wish
he would get a job and then he wouldn't be interested in DIY anymore. Mum said, "Bob, I beg you,
please get someone competent to do the fence.
You're only just back on your feet again."

Vati got all dadish. "Connie, I can fix a fence, you know."

We laughed. I helped Mum out. "Dad, there was the unfortunate leg-through-the-ceiling incident when you last went into the loft."

"There was a weakness in the roof."

"Yes, Dad, that was you."

"Don't be so bloody cheeky."

I am not wrong, though. The electrician who came to look at the fridge that blew up after Dad had "fixed it" accused Dad of being a madman. But grown-ups will never be told anything until it is too late. That is the sadnosity of grown-ups.

As Vati went into the cupboard under the stairs Mum looked at me, but what was I supposed to do? It's her husband; she should stop him. He came out of the cupboard with a hammer and a saw. I said, "Well, probably catch up with you later in Casualty then, Dad."

He swore in a very unpleasant way.

2:00 p.m.

Dad built a hilarious fence. It was sort of leany and falling-downy at the same time. It was supposed to keep Angus away from Naomi, but when

Dad was hammering in the final nail he said, "Yes, well, that should keep him safely in," and the whole fence fell over. And Angus just walked straight over the fence into Next Door's garden.

3:00 p.m.

Vati is having to pretend to be normal because Libby's kindy mates have arrived. Libby's an awfully rough hostess. When Millie and Oscar were bobbing for apples she "helped" them by banging them on the heads with her pumpkin lantern. Oscar couldn't walk straight for ages and Millie wanted to go home. Well, actually, all of the children wanted to go home.

5:30 p.m.

Angus is having a huge laugh. He keeps appearing on the top of fences and so on. He ate Snowy's play Bonio. Mr. Next Door said he will have to get a dog psychiatrist in.

Vati's been raving on and on. Outside I could see Mr. and Mrs. Next Door and Mr. and Mrs. Across the Road all muttering together and poking about with sticks. They are probably forming a lynch mob. For heaven's sake.

Vati said, "As soon as we find him, that is it—he has his trombone polished once and for all."

As Dad was grumping around, moaning on and on and banging things about in the kitchen, I said to Mum, "Will you tell Vati that I don't want to discuss things of a personal nature with him, but if he takes Angus to the vet and has his, you know, trouser snake addendums tampered with, he is no longer my vati. I will be vatiless."

Mutti just went tutting off into a world of her own.

Angus is a king amongst cats. He walks tall with his trouser snake addendums proudly dangling. Naomi is yowling all the time. Why don't they just let them be together?

NoVEMBER
AWAY LAUGHING oN A
FAST CAMEL

monday november 1st
at "breakfast"
7.50 a.m.

Back to school.

Sacré bleu, merde and double poo.

Angus is on his lead, yowling, tied to the kitchen table. It's like having a police car in the kitchen. He was brought back under armed guard this morning. The lynch mob only managed to get him because he tried to get in through Mr. Across the Road's catflap. To see his beloved sex kitten. No one seems to appreciate the romance of the situation. Angus had even taken Naomi a midnight snack of half-chewed haddock fillet. How romantic is that?

Vati has got a job interview this morning. With my luck he'll turn up serving hot dogs in a van outside school. With, as a *coup d'état*, Uncle Eddie as his assistant. Anyway, it means that Angus lives to polish his trombone another day.

Vati gave me a kiss on the head as he left!! Erlack!! I've asked him to respect my personal space. Well, I said, "Please don't touch me as I don't want to be sick down my school uniform."

I made for the door before anyone else could kiss me—I had seen the state of Libby's mouth after her cornflakes and Jammy Dodger. As I went through the door Angus made a desperate bid for freedom. He was fastened to the kitchen table leg, but that didn't stop him. He dragged the table along with him. It really made me laugh, because one minute Mum was eating her cornies on the table and the next minute the table and cornies were gone.

8:15 a.m.
Slouch slouch.

I saw Jas outside her gate. She was turning her skirt over at the top to make it short for the walk to school. We unroll as we approach Stalag 14 because of the ferret on guard there (Hawkeye). She lurks around the school gates like a lurking lurker. Hawkeye's life ambition is to give us bad conduct marks for breaking useless school rules. That's how fabulous her life is.

Anyway, I crept up behind Jas and yelled, *"Bonjour, sex bombe!!!"* and she nearly had a nervy spaz. Which was very funny.

I wasn't looking forward to facing *le* music. This was my first day back since I had been unjustly banned from school because Elvis Attwood had carelessly tripped over his wheelbarrow and injured himself. OK, he was chasing me at the time but . . .

When we reached the school gates I was so overcome with ennui and general pooiness that I forgot to do anything with my beret. Even Jas noticed. She said, "Gee, you've got your beret on properly."

"That is because for the time being the party is over, Jas. You may also notice that I am not wearing lip gloss."

"Crikey."

As I slinked through the gate to Nazi headquarters Hawkeye was there like an eagle in heat. She hates me. I don't know why. I am vicitimized by her. That is the sadness of my life.

As I went by her she said, "Walk properly!"

What does that mean, *Walk properly*? As an amusing example of my hilariosity, I did a bit of a limp. Hawkeye shouted after me, "Georgia, don't earn yourself a reprimand before you even get your coat off!! As soon as assembly is over report to Miss Simpson's office."

She is such a stiff! I said to Jas, "I bet she irons her knickers."

Jas started to say "What is so wrong with that . . . ?" but I had gone into the lavatory.

I sat down on the loo. Same old bat time, same old bat place. Good grief. In my despairosity I said out loud to myself, "What in the name of pantyhose is the point?" A voice from the next loo said, "Gee, is that you?"

It was Ellen. I grunted. But she was all chatty. Just because she has Dave the Laugh as a boyfriend. A dumpee of mine. She said through the wall, "Do you know what Dave says when he is leaving? Instead of saying good-bye?"

I wasn't remotely interested in what my cast-offs said instead of good-bye. They are quite literally yesterday's news. Also, Ellen is in my bad books. I was giving her my cold shoulder. However, she was so interested in her new so-called boyfriend, Dave the so-called Laugh, that she hadn't noticed my shoulder. I thought if I flushed the loo she might get the hint, but she didn't.

"He says, 'Well, I'm off then. I'm away laughing on a fast camel.'" And she absolutely pissed herself laughing.

What is the matter with her? *Away laughing on a fast camel?*

assembly
9:00 a.m.

Fab news! Slim told us that some complete nutcase (Miss Wilson) is going to give us a special talk next week. About "reproduction."

Lord save us.

Slim also said Miss Wilson would be answering any questions we might have about "growing up and so on." Hahahahahahahaha. Hell could freeze over before I would ask Miss Wilson about my girlie parts.

After Slim had bored us to death for half an hour everyone else went off to English and I lolloped off slowly to her office for a spot of mental torture. I wasn't the only one waiting for a duffing; Jackie and Alison, the Bummer Twins, were sitting round in her anteroom. They looked at me when I sat down. Jackie said, "Oohhhh, what have you been up to, Big Nose?" She must die. She must die.

Then we heard the sound of a distant elephant (Slim), and Jackie stubbed out her fag and popped in a mint.

Slim said, "Come through, Georgia." Then she sat down at her desk and started writing. I just stood there. How many times had I been in this room for no good reason? Millions. Slim looked up and said, "Well," and I said, "Yes, milady?"

She glared at me. "What did you say?"

"Oh, sorry. I was just thinking about my English homework assignment, Miss Simpson."

She trembled in her jelloid way. It was amazing the way each chin could shake at a different rhythm. She said, "Well, it makes a change for you to think of anything serious or useful, Georgia."

Oh, that is so UNFAIR. What about all the hours I had spent thinking up the glove animal?

Slim was raving on, "I hope for a great improvement in your attitude to school and work after your suspension. I hope it has given you pause for thought. But first of all, you will go to Mr. Attwood and apologize to him for causing his injuries."

Oh great. Now I had to go and speak to the most bonkers man in the history of bonkerdom.

When I left her torture chamber Jackie Bummer said, "Did the nasty teacher tell you off and make you scared?" But when Slim shouted, "You two articles in here now!!!" they leapt up like two salmons.

Jas told me later that the Bummer Twins had arrived this morning, had a fag and then stuck a first-year to a bench with superglue.

9:35 a.m.

I walked really, really slowly along to Elvis's hut. At least if I took ages to find Elvis I might miss most of English. Sadly, that is when I saw his flat hat bobbling around. Not on its own, unfortunately; he was underneath it. Pushing his wheelbarrow along. I walked up quietly behind him and said really enthusiastically, "MR. ATTWOOD. HELLO!!!"

He leapt up like a perv in overalls (which he is). "What do YOU want?"

"Mr. Attwood, it's me!!!"

"I know who you are all right. Why are you shouting?"

"I thought you might have gone deaf."

"Well, I haven't."

"Well you might have. You see, I know what it's like at your stage of life—my grandad is deaf. And he's got bandy legs."

"Well, I'm not deaf. What do you want? I'm still not right, you know. My knee gives me awful gyp."

"Slim . . . er . . . Miss Simpson said I had to come and apologize."

"Yes, well, quite right, too." He was SO annoying. And a bit pingy pongoes when you got downwind of him.

I said, "So then. See you around."

He said, "Just a minute—you haven't said you are sorry yet."

"I have. I just told you I had to come and apologize."

"I know, but you haven't."

I said patiently, "Well, why am I here then? Am I a mirage?"

"No, you're not a mirage; you're a bloody nuisance."

"Thank you."

"Clear off. And you should behave a bit more like a young lady. In my day you would have—"

I interrupted him politely. "Mr. Attwood, interesting though the Stone Age is, I really haven't got time to discuss your childhood. I'll just say *au revoir* and if I don't see you again in this life, best of luck in that great caretakers' home in the sky."

He was muttering and adjusting his trousers (erlack!), but he shambled off. He daren't say too much to me because he suspects I have seen his nuddy mags, which I have.

lunchtime

Hours and hours of boredom followed by a cheese sandwich. That is what my morning has been like. And I wish Nauseating P. Green would stop ogling me. Blinking at me through her thick glasses like a goldfish in a uniform. Since I saved her from being duffed up by the Bummers last term she follows me round like a Nauseating P. Green on a string.

Rosie said to me, "She loves you."

Good Lord.

1:30 p.m.

Nauseating P. Green even followed me into the loos. As I was drying my hands she said, "Georgia,

75

would you . . . would you . . . like to see some photos of my hamster? He's called Hammy."

Oh right, that's top of my list, photos of a hamster. I was going to say no, but she looked so blinky that I couldn't.

"P. Green."

"Yes?"

"Hammy has got about ten babies around him."

"I know; he's just had them."

Well, at least someone is going to be astonished by Miss Wilson's sex talk.

2:35 p.m.

Madame Slack was so overjoyed to see me that she made me sit right at the front next to Nauseating P. Green and Slack Alice, both of whom can only see the board if it's an inch away from their glasses. Jas and Ellen (Jas's bestest new lezzie mate) and the rest of the gang sat together at the back.

On the plus side, Madame Slack told us we are going to have a student teacher next week. That is usually *très amusant*. A bit of a light in a dark world.

4:00 p.m.

Bell rang.

At last escape from this hellhole. Jas and me were walking out of the gates when we saw Tom waiting for her. She went red as two short red things because she hadn't rolled her skirt over. She managed to pout though. Tom gave me a kiss on the cheek. *Mais oui!! Très* continental for someone who works part-time in a vegetable shop. He said, "Welcome back. You missed a cracking night at the cinema the other night. What did you get up to in Och Aye land?"

"I hung around a twenty-four-hour supermarket."

"Is that the groovy thing to do up there then?"

"No, it's the ONLY thing to do."

5:00 p.m.

Talk about being Queen of the Goosegogs. I had to walk along with Jas and Tom holding hands. (I don't mean we were all holding hands, although that would have been funnier.) I am giving Jas the cold shoulder as well as Ellen because of going to the cinema as a gang without the essential ingredient: me.

However, my shoulders are making little impression on anyone.

7:15 p.m.
Jas phoned.

"Gee."

"Yes, who is that?" (Even though I knew who it was.)

"It's me, Jas."

"Oh."

"Look, you could have come to the cinema with us, but you were in Och Aye land."

"Huh."

"And, well, it was just, you know, couples, and well, I don't think Robbie would have wanted to come. He doesn't really hang out with Tom much. You know Robbie's got his mates from The Stiff Dylans and because he's got the band and . . ."

She dribbled on for ages.

midnight
The nub and gist of Jas's pathetic apology is that I am going out with an older Sex God. We came to an understanding. The understanding is that she

has to show her remorse; she has to be my slavey girl for three days. And do everything I say.

tuesday november 2nd
lunchtime
I made slavey girl give me a piggyback to the loos. Hawkeye said we were "being ridiculous."

8:00 p.m.
The Sex God was waiting for me outside school!!! And he was in his cool car. Fortunately I had abstained from doing anything ridiculous with my beret. So I was able to get into his car only having to concentrate on not letting my nostrils flare too much . . . or knocking him out with my nunga-nungas. SHUT UP, BRAIN!!!

10:00 p.m.
I must stop being jelloid woman every time I see the Sex God. Why oh why did I say "I'm away laughing on a fast camel" instead of good-bye? What is the matter with me?

However, on the whole, taking things by and large . . . Yesssssssss!!!!!

I live at Snogging Headquarters. My address is:
Georgia Nicolson
Snogging Headquarters
Snog Lane
Snoggington

10:15 p.m.
Phoned Jas.

"Jas, I've done car snogging. Have you done that?"

"No. . . . I've done bike snogging."

"That's not the same."

"Oh. Why not?"

"It's just not the same."

"It is."

"No, it isn't."

"Well, there are still four wheels involved."

Good grief.

11:00 p.m.
In the car this afternoon Robbie put his head on my knee and sang me one of his songs. It was called "I'm Not There." I didn't tell Radio Jas that bit.

I never really know what to do with myself when he does his song singing. Maybe nod my head in time to the rhythm? How attractive is that from upside down? And also if you were passing the car as an innocent passerby you would just see my head bobbling round.

1:00 a.m.
Libby woke me up when she pattered and clanked into my room. When she had got everybody into my bed she said, in between little sobs, "Ohh, there was a big bad man, big uggy man."

She snuggled up really tightly and wrapped her legs round me. I gave her a big cuddle and said, "It's OK, Libbs, it was just a dream. Let's think about something nice. What shall we dream about?"

She said, "Porridge."

She can be so sweet. I gave her a little kiss on her cheek and she smiled at me (scary). Then she ripped the pillow from underneath my head so that Pantalitzer and scuba-diving Barbie could be comfy.

wednesday november 3rd
7:00 a.m.
Woke up with a crick in my neck and a sort of air-tank shape in my cheek where scuba-diving Barbie had been.

Dad came into the kitchen in a suit. Blimey. No one said anything. Apart from Libby, who growled at him. It turns out that it wasn't a nightmare she had last night. She just woke up and caught sight of Dad in his jimjams. Mum was in her usual morning dreamworld. As she came out of her bedroom getting ready for work, she was wearing her bra and skirt and nothing else. I said, "Mum, please, I'm trying to eat."

In the bathroom I checked the back of my head and profile. (There's a cabinet that has two mirrors on it. You can look through one and angle the other one so that you can look at the reflection of yourself sideways.) Then I put Mum's magnifying mirror underneath and looked down at myself, because say the Sex God had been lying on my knees sort of looking up at me adoringly and singing (which he had). Well, I wanted to know what that looked like.

I wish I hadn't bothered for two reasons: Firstly, when I looked down at the mirror I realized that my nose is GIGANTIC. It must have grown overnight. I look like Gerard Depardieu. Which is not a plus if you are not a forty-eight-year-old French bloke.

Secondly, you can definitely see my lurker from underneath.

8:18 a.m.

Jas was waiting for me at her gate. I was a bit aloof and full of maturiosity. Slavey girl said, "I've brought you a Jammy Dodger all to yourself."

"You can't treat me badly and then bribe me with a Jammy Dodger, Jas."

She can, though, because I was soon munching away.

On the way up the road I said to Jas, "Do you think my nose is larger than it was yesterday?"

She said, "Don't be silly. Noses don't grow."

"Well, everything else does—hair, legs, arms . . . nunga-nungas. Why should your nose be left out?"

She wasn't a bit interested. I went on, "And also can you see I have a lurker up my left nostril?"

She said, "No."

"But say you were sort of looking up my nose, from underneath."

She hadn't a clue what I was talking about. She has the imagination of a pea. Half a pea. We were just passing through the park and I tried to explain.

"Well, say I was singing. And you were the Sex God and you were lying with your head in my lap. Looking up adoringly. Marveling at my enormous talent. Waiting for the appropriate moment to leap on me and snog me to within an inch of my life."

She still didn't get it, so I dragged her over to a bench to illustrate my point. I made her put her head on my lap. I said, "So . . . what do you think?"

She looked up and said, "I can't hear you singing."

"That's because I'm not."

"But you said what if you were singing."

Oh for Goodness O'Reilly's trouser's sake!!! To placate her I sang a bit—the only thing that came into my head was "Goldfinger." It brought back horrible memories because Dad and Uncle Eddie had sung it the night Dad came home from Kiwi-a-gogo. They were both drunk and both wearing leather trousers, as Uncle Eddie said, "to impress the ladies." How sad and tragic is that?

Anyway, I was singing "Goldfinger" and Jas had her head on my lap looking up at my ever-expanding nostrils.

I said, "Can you see my lurker up there?"

Then we heard someone behind us having a fit. We leapt up. Well, I did. Jas crashed to the ground. It was Dave the Laugh, absolutely beside himself with laughing.

I said, "Er . . . I was just . . ."

Jas was going, "I was just looking up . . . Georgia's nose for . . . a . . . bit . . ."

Dave the L said, "Of course you were. Please don't explain. It will only spoil it for me." He walked along with us. I couldn't help remembering snogging him. And using him as a Red Herring. But he was funny. And he wasn't snidey. Just laughing a lot. In a Dave-the-Laugh way.

After he went off I said to Jas, "He seems to have forgiven me for being a callous minx, doesn't he? He is quite groovy-looking, isn't he?"

Uh-oh. I hope I am not becoming a nympho-whatsit. It is true though. I did think he looked quite cool. And a laugh. He's going to The Stiff Dylans gig this weekend. I said to Jas, "Do you think that he is going with Ellen?"

Why do I care? I am the girlfriend of a Sex God.

Still, I wonder if he is going with Ellen.

german
11:15 a.m.

To fill in the time whilst Herr Kamyer was writing something pointless on the blackboard about Helga and Helmut—Helga and Helmut are the HILARIOUS twins from our German language book called interestingly (NOT) *Helga and Helmut*. By the way, how many sausages can one person eat? Helmut is always stuffing one in his face. His lederhosen are probably as huge as Jas's pants. Anyway, as I say, to fill in the endless hours I gave Rosie a tattoo on her arm (in pen) of a lockjaw germ dancing. It was excellent. However, Jas (Mrs. Dense Knickers) said, "What is it?" My artistic talents are wasted on her. Also, and even more alarmingly, Jas seemed to be really interested in what happened to Helga and Helmut when they went shopping. I said to her, "They're not real, you know, Jas. They are German."

hockey
3:00 p.m.

Adolfa (Sports Oberführer and part-time lesbian) has been relatively quiet this term. She had extravagantly big shorts on today. As we got changed I

said to Jas, "It's you she wants, Jas. I know because imitation is the sincerest form of flattery.
Look at the size of her shorts. They are JUST like
your knickers."

Jas hit me. Slavey girl is getting a bit uppity.

6:00 p.m.

Doing homework (peanut butter sandwich–making
and hairstyling) with Ellen, Jas and Rosie. I casually found out that Ellen is meeting Dave the
Laugh at the gig.

I said, "Oh, are you a sort of item then?"

She went a bit girlish. "Well, you know, he said,
'Are you going to the gig?' and I said, 'Yeah,' and
he said, 'See you there then.'"

Rosie said, "Yes, but does he mean 'If you are
going, I'll see you there because you will be like
THERE to see'? Or does he mean 'See you there,'
like in see YOU there?"

Ellen didn't know. She was in a state of confusosity. Join the club, I say.

As I wandered home I was thinking, one thing
is true. He is not making the effort to meet her
before the gig. Hahahahaha.

7:00 p.m.

Hang on a minute, though. Robbie has not arranged to meet me before the gig either. Is he expecting me to just turn up because I am, like, his official girlfriend? Oh well, it's only Wednesday. He'll call me and sort it out. Probably.

7:30 p.m.

Uh oh. Angus went on a kamikaze mission (kattikaze mission) to his beloved sex kitten. When he was let into the garden for his constitutional poo parlor division he burrowed under the fence. Pausing only to eat the Prat Poodles' supper and trap some voles, he went over to Mr. and Mrs. Across the Road's house. On to their roof.

He must have lurked up there until Mr. Across the Road came out to mow his lawn, and then dropped his love gifts (two voles and a half-eaten ham sandwich) onto Mr. Across the Road's head. Taking advantage of Mr. Across the Road's momentary blindness, he leapt into the house to be reunited with his beloved. Unfortunately, he was an unwelcome houseguest and in the ensuing struggle there was some incident with the cockatiel.

From what I can gather from Mr. Across the Road's shouting, it may never speak again. Which would be a plus in my book, as it only ever said, "Who's a pretty boy?"

10:00 p.m.
No call from Robbie.

I started softening up Dad for Saturday. "Vati, you know how hard I have been working at school . . . ? Well . . ."

He interrupted me. "Georgia, if this is leading up to any suggestion of quids leaping out of my pocket into your purse . . . forget it."

What an old miser.

"Vati, it's not to do with money. It's just that my friends and I are going to a gig on Saturday night and—"

"What time do you want me to pick you up?"

"It's alright, Dad. I'll just, you know, come home with the rest of the gang and . . ."

He's going to pick me up at midnight. It's hardly worth going out. I made him promise me that he'd crouch down behind the wheel and not get out of the car.

midnight

SG hasn't called me. How often should he call me? How often would I call him? About every five minutes seems right.

Maybe that's too keen. It implies I haven't got any sort of life.

12:05 a.m.

I haven't.

1:00 a.m.

OK, every quarter of an hour.

1:15 a.m.

It says in my *Men Are from Mars* book that boys don't need to talk as much as girls. The bloke that wrote it has obviously never met my uncle Eddie. When he came round the other day he didn't shut up for about five million years. He ruffles my hair. I am fourteen years old. Full of maturiosity. And snoggosity. I would ruffle HIS hair to show him how crap it is. But he hasn't got any.

thursday november 4th
operation glove animal
8:30 a.m.

This is GA Day (Glove Animal Day). Everyone is going to turn up with ears in place today. Jas was grumbling and groaning about getting a reprimand. I said, "Jas, please put your ears on as a smack in the gob often offends."

Even she got into the swing of it once her ears were in place. It was, it has to be said, quite funny. Jas looked hilarious bobbing along with her glove ears. She even did a bit of improvising with her teeth, making them stick out and doing nibbly movements with them like a squirrel. We did a detour through the back alleyway near the Science block. Elvis was in his hut reading his newspaper. We just stood there in our glove animal way looking in at him through the window. He sensed we were there and looked up. We stared back at him. His glasses were a bit steamed up, so maybe he really thought we were some woodland creatures. Woodland creatures who had decided to go to school and get ourselves out of our woodland poverty trap . . . But then he started shouting and raving on, "Clear off and learn something instead of messing about. And make yourselves look normal!!!"

Oh, wise advice from the looniest-looking person in the universe.

Unfortunately, Hawkeye spotted us before we could scuttle into the cloakroom. She went ballistic, unusually enough. I tried to explain that it was a useful way not to lose your gloves but I only got as far as "It's a really sensible way of . . ." before she snatched them off my ears. She has very little sense of humor.

However, the last laugh was on her because she was so busy telling me and Jas that we were ridiculously childish and ripping our ears off that she didn't see the rest of the ace gang bob into school. It was very, very funny indeed seeing them bob through the gates and across the playground as if they were perfectly normal glove animals.

7:00 p.m.

No call from the SG.

Mrs. Across the Road came over. Mutti had gone to her aerobics class. Surely it can't be healthy for a woman of her size to hurl herself around a crowded room.

Mrs. Across the Road or "Call me Helen" is OK but a bit on the nimby girlie side. If you hit her with a hockey stick she would probably fall over. She's fluffy and blond (not natural I think).

Vati was acting very peculiarly. He was being almost nice. And laughing a lot. And he got out of his chair. Hmmm. After she'd gone he must have said at least two hundred and fifty times, "She seems very nice, doesn't she? Helen? Very . . . you know . . . feminine."

Oh no.

Also he said that they are going to get a pedigree sort of boyfriend for Naomi. I said, "She won't go out with anyone else. She loves Angus."

Dad laughed. "You wait, there will be little Naomis running about the place before you can blink. Women are very fickle."

I said with great dignity, "Vati, different women have different needs."

He laughed in a most unpleasant way. "No, Georgia, all women have the same needs. They all need locking up."

Oh, *très, très* grown-up, Portly One.

9:10 p.m.

Pre-gig nervosity. Not helped by the fact that when I went down on to the field to take Angus for his prison recreation period, Mark Big Gob threw a Thunderball firework at me. It exploded right in front of me. Angus didn't even notice, but it nearly blew my lip gloss off. I wonder if Mark is quite normal in the brain department.

Oh God, I've just remembered it's Bonfire Night tomorrow, an excuse for all the sad boys in the world to set fire to themselves with fireworks whilst showing off to their mates.

9:30 p.m.

Mum came in flushed as a loon. I said, "You are looking particularly feminine, Mum." But Vati didn't get it.

in my room

9:50 p.m.

Vati knocked on my door!!! I said, "I'm sorry, but sadly I'm not in."

He ignored that (*quelle* surprise!) and came in and sat on the edge of my bed. Oh God, he wasn't going to ask me if I was happy, was he? Or tell me about his "feelings."

He was all embarrassed. "Look, Georgia, I know how you feel about Angus. . . ."

"Yes. And?"

"It's just not fair on him, being all cooped up in the house."

"Well, that is not my idea."

"I know, but he won't leave that bloody Burmese alone."

"He loves her and wants to share his life and dreams with her, maybe buy a little holiday home in Spain for those cold—"

"He's a bloody cat!!!"

10:00 p.m.

Dad is going to take Angus to the vet's tomorrow to have his trouser snake addendums taken away. He said, "I know you will think about this and be grown-up about it."

I said, "Dad, as I have mentioned before, if you do this to Angus you are no longer my vati. You are an ex-vati."

I mean it.

lo:lo p.m.

Phone rang. Vati answered it, still all grumpy. I was in my room shaping the cuticles in my nails for Saturday. If I don't start my beauty routine now I'll never be ready in time. I heard Dad say, "I'll see if she's still up, it's a bit late to call. Who shall I say it is?"

By that time I had thrown myself down the stairs and ripped the phone out of his hand. How could he be so deeply uncool?

I calmed my voice and said hello, in a sort of husky way. I don't know why, but at least I wasn't assuming a French accent. It was the Sex God!!! Yeahhh!!! I got jelloid knickers as soon as I heard his voice. It's so yummy scrumboes. . . .

He said, "Is that your dad?"

I said, "No, it's just some madman who hangs around our house."

Anyway, the short and long of it is that he'll see me Saturday at the gig. He's rehearsing so can't see me before. *C'est la vie*, I think you will find, when you go out with *le* gorgeous pop-star.

friday november 5th
bonfire night

4:00 p.m.

Some of the Foxwood lads sneaked into school today and put a banger down a loo and the loo exploded! You could hear the explosion even in the Science block. Slim was so furious that her chins practically waggled off.

6:30 p.m.

Vati has actually taken Angus to the vet. I cannot believe it. I am not speaking to him.

He said, "The vet said he would be fit as a flea on Monday, and we can pick him up then."

Libby and me might go on dirty protest, like they do in prison. Not bother going to the loo—as a protest, just poo on the floor. Mind you, Libby is almost permanently on dirty protest so they might not notice.

8:00 p.m.

Mutti and the bloke that she sadly lives with have gone to the street bonfire. Mr. and Mrs. Next Door and Mr. and Mrs. Across the Street and the saddos from number twenty-four are all going to be there and then they are off to a party at number twenty-six. Can you imagine the fun that will be? Vati was wearing a leather cowboy hat. How tragic is that? Very, very tragic. Mutti asked me if I was coming. I just looked at Dad's hat. Anyway, as I am not speaking to any of them I can't reply. Dad leapt over the garden wall instead of going through the gate. Sadly he didn't do himself a severe injury, and so he lives to embarrass me to death another day.

Angus normally loves Bonfire Night.

Does he know his bottom-sniffing days are over?

8:30 p.m.

Jools, Rosie and Jas came round. They're all off to a bonfire party at Kate Matthews's place. SG is rehearsing again, but we're going to meet up later. The girls managed to find something to eat in the kitchen, which is a bloody miracle.

We sat munching and crunching our cornflake sarnies. Jools said, "I must get a boyfriend. I quite fancy that mate of Dave the Laugh's. What is he called . . . is it Rollo? You know, the one that's got a nice smile."

He was quite cool-looking, now she mentioned it. I said, "I wonder why he hasn't got a girlfriend. Maybe there is something wrong with him."

Jools was all alert. "Like what?"

"Well, you know Spotty Norman who has acne of the head?"

"Rollo hasn't got any spots."

"He might have secret acne."

"Secret acne?"

"Yeah, it only starts at the top of his arms."

"Who gets acne like that?"

"Loads of people."

"Like who?"

"Loads of people."

Actually I noticed that Rosie had a bit of a lurker on her chin. She had been poking it about and I told her she shouldn't do that. She should try my special lurker eradicator. You squirt perfume on the lurker. Really loads and loads and that dries it up. In theory. I used it on my nostril lurker and it worked a treat. Mind you, in the process I practically choked to death on Paloma (Mum's).

my bedroom
10:00 p.m.

The sky is lit up with rockets from people's firework parties. And I am alone in my room. I'm very nearly a hermitess. SG's rehearsal has run on, so we can't meet up. Still, I'm not going to mope round. I'm going to do something creative with poster paints.

11:30 p.m.

When Mutti and Vati came in I didn't speak to them. I just unfurled the CAT MOLESTERS banner I had made.

saturday november 6th
11:00 a.m.

The cat molesters went off shopping.

1:00 p.m.

I'd better start my makeup soon. It's only seven hours till the gig. But as I fully expect to be snogged to within an inch of my life, what about snogproof makeup? As Billy Shakespeare said, "To lippy or not to lippy; that is the question."

Rang Jas. Her mum called her and she eventually shambled to the phone. I said, "Oh, glad you could make it, Jas. My eyebrows have grown to the floor in the time it took you to get here."

Jas, as usual, took offense. "I was in my bedroom just working something out on the computer with Tom."

I laughed sarcastically. "Jas, you only snog in your bedroom."

"We don't."

"You do. Anyway, lots of fun though this is, I want to ask you something of vital importance to the universe. Well, my universe, anyway. What do you think about lippy and snogging?"

"What?"

"Well, do you put lippy on and then do you wipe it off before lip contact, or do you let it go all over Tom's face and Devil take the hindmost?"

2:00 p.m.
Results of lippy/snogging poll:

Jas only wears lip gloss, which she says gets absorbed in the general snogosity. Rosie says she puts on lippy AND lip gloss, then just goes for full-frontal snogging with Sven. She also says that by the end of the night he is usually covered in lippy, but he doesn't mind and wipes it off with his T-shirt.

Good Lord.

We must remember, however, that he is not English.

The rest of the gang seemed pretty well to go along with the lip gloss absorbed into the general snogosity theory.

So lip gloss it is.

3:00 p.m.

Surrounded by hair products.

My hair will not go right. It has no bounce-ability. It just lies there. Annoying me with its lack of bounceability.

Sacré bloody *bleu*. I won't be able to go out unless it starts bouncing about a bit. I look like a Franciscan monk. Or Miss Wilson.

I'm going to stick some of Mum's hot rollers in it.

4:30 p.m.

On my bed in rollers. V. attractive.

Reading my book *Don't Sweat the Small Stuff for Teens* to cheer me up. And calm me down.

4:45 p.m.

Hey, there is a chapter about hair! Honestly! How freaky deaky is that?

It's called "Be OK with Your Bad Hair Day."

5:00 p.m.

The short and short of it is that we are obsessed with our looks and imagine that other people really care about what our hair looks like.

But they don't!!

So that is OK then. Took out my rollers.

5:10 p.m.

Vati bounced into my room (not knocking, of course) and said, "Tea is on the—what in the name of arse have you done to your head? You look like you have been electrocuted."

I hate my dad. Twice.

5:30 p.m.

Time for my pore-tightening mask. (Because there is nothing worse than loose pores.)

I lay there with my pores tightening. In the book it recommends yoga for inner harmony. I must start doing it again.

5:35 p.m.

Mind you, the author says he is "super glad" that he took up yoga at a young age.

5:37 p.m.

Perhaps he is a "super tosser."

5:39 p.m.

Or am I being "supercritical?"

Who knows.

Phoned Jools with my pore-tightening mask still on, trying not to crack it. Dad was pretending to be an orangutan (not much pretending needed) as a "laugh." I ignored him. I said to Jools, "Nyut nar nu naring?"

"Purple V-necked top. Purple hipsters."

Hmm.

Phoned Rosie, "Nut nar nu noing nid nor nair ?"

"Pigtails."

Crikey. We seem to be running the gamut of style from hippie to Little Bo Peep and beyond.

6:00 p.m.

I've tried on every single thing in my wardrobe. Oh buggery, I am in a state of confusosity. I wish I had a style counselor. I'm going to get one when I appear at record awards ceremonies with the Sex God. It won't be Elton John's style counselor. It will be someone normal. And stylish. And a good counselor.

6:30 p.m.

I've decided to go for the radically sophisticated look for the gig (i.e., all black). With, for special effect, black accessories (providing I can sneak out with Mum's Chanel bag without her noticing).

6:35 p.m.

I'm wearing a V-necked black leather vest, short skirt and boots. What does that say about me? Casual sophisticate? Inner vixen struggling to get out? Girlfriend of a Sex God?

Or twit?

6:38 p.m.

I wonder what SG will be wearing. What does it matter? We are all in the nuddy-pants under our clothes.

I LOVE his mouth. It's so yummy and sort of curly and sexy. And it's mine, all mine!!! Mind you, I love his hair, so black and gorgey. And his eyes . . . that deep deep blue . . . mmmmm . . . dreamsville. And his eyelashes. And his arms. And his tongue . . . In fact, there isn't one bit of him I don't like. Of all the bits I've seen, anyway.

I wonder what his favorite bit of me is? I should emphasize it.

My eyes are quite nice. My nose, yes, well, we'll just skip over that. Mouth . . . mmm, a bit on the generous side, but that can be a good thing.

6:45 p.m.

Phoned Jas. "Jas, what do you think is my best feature? Lips? Smile? Casual sophisticosity?"

"Well, I don't know what to say now, because I was going to say your cheeks."

Good grief.

6:50 p.m.

Phoned Jas again.

"What do you think on the basooma front? You know, emphasize them, do the 'Yes, I've got big nunga-nungas, but I'm proud of them!' or strap them down and don't breathe out much all night?"

That's when Vati went ballisticisimus about me

being on the phone. "Why the hell do you talk rubbish to Jas on the phone when she is coming
round here in a minute and you can talk rubbish to
her without it costing me a fortune?!!!!"

It's not me that talks rubbish. It's him. He just
shouts rubbish at me. He's like Hawkeye with a
beard.

I said to Mutti, "Why doesn't the man you live
with go for a job as a combination cat molester
and teacher?"

beautosity headquarters
7:00 p.m.

Jas came round to my house for us to walk to
the clock tower together. Also I needed her for a
cosmetic emergency. I had forgotten to paint my
toenails, and my skirt was so tight I couldn't bend
my leg up far enough to get to my toes. I suppose
I could have taken my skirt off, but what are
friends for?

I am too giddy and girlish with excitement to
paint straight anyway. We went into the front room,
which is warmer than my room. Mind you so is
Siberia.

Vati was watching the news. Huh. Jas started

on toenail duty. I thought a subtle metallic purple would be nice. Robbie would think that was cool if my tights fell off for some reason. Anyway, then it said on the news, "And tonight the Prime Minister has just got to Number Ten."

I looked down at Jas and said, "Ooer." Meaning he'd got to number ten on the snogging scale. And then we both laughed like loons.

Vati just looked at us like we were mad.

clock tower

8:00 p.m.

Met the rest of the ace gang and we ambled off to the gig. This was my first official outing as girlfriend of a Sex God. I wasn't going to let it go to my head though.

Lalalalalalalalala. Fabbity fab fab. Eat dirt, Earth creatures.

When we got to the Buddha Lounge the first "person" I saw was . . . Wet Lindsay. Robbie's ex. There is always a wet fish in every ointment. Every cloud has got a slimy lining. She has got the tiniest forehead known to humanity. She is quite literally fringe and then eyebrow. She was talking to her equally sad mates Dismal Sandra and Tragic Kate.

Every time I look at Wet Lindsay I am reminded that underneath her T-shirt lurk breast enhancers.

I said to Jas, "Do you think that Robbie knows about her false nunga-nungas?" but she was too busy waving at Tom with a soppy smile on her face.

The club was packed. I wondered if I should go find Robbie and say hello. Maybe that wasn't very cool. Better do a bit of makeup adjusting first. Because if the talent scout was there he might be looking for girls to form a band as well. I said that to Jas. "Maybe we could be discovered, as a new girl band."

"We can't sing or play any instruments, and we are not in a band."

She is so ludicrously picky.

It was mayhem in the loos. You couldn't get near the mirrors for love or money. The Bummers were in there, of course, larding on the foundation. Alison must use at least four pounds of it trying to conceal her huge lurkers. Or am I being a bit harsh?

No . . . I am being accurate. And factual.

I came out of the loos into the club. It was very dark; you needed to be half bat to find your way round. And then, shining like a shining Sex God in trousers, I saw him. Tuning his guitar. He looked up and saw me and smiled. I went over and he grabbed me and dragged me into a room. ("Oh stop it, stop it!" I yelled . . . not.) It was The Stiff Dylans' dressing room. I'd never been backstage before. I suppose I will have to get used to it.

We did some excellent snogging (six and a half) but then he had to go and tune up with the rest of the band. He said, "See you on my break."

When I went back to the loos my lip gloss had completely gone!!! Absorbed in the snoggosity.

9:00 p.m.
Yeah! What a dance fest! I was so shattered after being thrown around by Sven that I had to go and have a little sit down in an alcove with Rosie and Jas.

I could see Wet Lindsay and her wet mates dancing right in front of the stage. How desperate was that? In fact, it was all girls at the front, most of them dancing around in front of my Sex God. Smiling up at him and shaking their bums round. But he only had eyes for me. Well, he would have done, had he had a talking sniffer dog that could have come round and found me sitting in the dark behind a pillar, and gone back and told SG where I was. There was an older bloke in a suit standing by the side of the stage. I bet he was the talent scout.

I said to Jas, "Come and dance in front of the talent scout with me."

She said, "No."

"Jas."

"No, and what is more . . ."

"What?"

"No."

"It's no then, is it, Mrs. Huge Knickers? Well, when I am happily being a backup dancer I will think of you packing potatoes."

She ignored me, but as I say, *In vino veritas.* I don't know why because I am really crap at Latin (according to Slim, spokeswoman for the Latin people).

Well, as usual, I would have to step boldly where no woman had stepped before. I went over and gave my all in front of the talent scout in a triumph of dance casualosity. He seemed quite impressed, but then he went off to the dressing rooms. Probably phoning his record company.

Phew, it was hot and sweaty. I nipped off to the

loos to make sure my glaciosity was still in place and I didn't look like a red-faced loon. My waterproof eyeliner seemed to be holding its own. Rosie was readjusting her piggies next to me in the mirror so I asked her, "Does Sven ever make you jealous?"

"No, not really. He's sort of quite grown-up in his own way."

As we came out of the loos we could see Sven almost immediately. He was in the middle of a big group balancing a drink on his head and doing Russian dancing. It's a mystery to me how he manages to get down so low, his jeans are so tight.

The Bummers were talking to some really lardy-looking blokes in leather jackets. They all had fags. You could hardly see their heads for smoke. Which was a plus. I did make out that one of the lardheads had a mustache. I shouted to Jools, "Imagine snogging someone with a mustache."

And she said, "What, like Miss Stamp?"

9:30 p.m.
Jools had been looking at Rollo for about a million centuries and moaning and droning on about him. He was hanging out with a bunch of lads round the

bar. I was trying to concentrate on looking at the Sex God. He is sooooo cool. He's by far the coolest in the band. Dom, Chris and Ben are all quite groovy-looking but they don't have that certain *je ne sais quoi* that the Sex God has. That extra snogosity. That puckery gorgeosity combined with fabulosity. That sexgoderosity.

Jools didn't seem to know I was in Snog Heaven because she was rambling on. "He's quite fit, isn't he?"

"Yeah, he's gorgeous and he's all mine, mine, miney."

"Gee, I mean Rollo, you banana."

I was less than interested but she went on and on. "Should I go across?"

Pause.

"Or is that too pushy?"

Pause.

"I think it's always best to play a bit hard to get, don't you? Yes, that's how I'll play it. He'll have to beg to get my attention."

9:35 p.m.

Jools was sitting on Rollo's knee and snogging for England. Oh well. As I said to Ellen, "She's

113

obviously gone for the playing-hard-to-get-ticket."

9:39 p.m.
Tom told me that the "talent scout" was Dom's dad who helps with the band's equipment. He told Dom he thought I was trying to get off with him. OhmyGodohmyGod. I would now have to spend the rest of the night and probably the rest of my life not looking at Dom's dad.

I told Ellen, but she was too busy waiting for Dave the Laugh to show up. I must have been to the loos with her about a hundred times just in case she has missed him in the dark somewhere.

I am without doubt a great mate. You wouldn't get Jas trailing backwards and forwards to the loos. Mostly because she seems to be glued to Tom. She has very little pride.

Quite a few lads have asked me to dance. Well, their idea of asking me to dance, which means they hang round showing off when I'm dancing with my mates. I must have that thing that you can get. You know, like baboons. When female baboons are in the mood they get a big red bottom and then the male baboons know they are in the mood and gather round. Yes, that must be it—I must have the metaphorical red bottom because of the Sex God.

10:00 p.m.

On his break Robbie came offstage and he looked over at me. This was it, this was the moment that everyone would know I was his girlfriend!! At last all my dreams were beginning to come true. I was going to be the official girlfriend (OG)!! No more hiding our love from the world. Just snogging-a-gogo and Devil take the hindmost. I couldn't wait to see Wet Lindsay's face when Robbie came over to me. Tee hee. Yessss!!!!

In the meantime I lived in Cool City. I was sipping my drink and pretending to talk to Jas and Tom, although every time Jas said anything it really annoyed me. I'd say, "OhmyGodohmyGod, I think he's coming over. . . . Oh, that absolutely useless tart Sammy Mason is thrusting herself at him now."

And Jas would say, "She's actually quite a nice person, really good at blodge."

Ludicrous, stupid, pointless things she was saying. In the end I said, "Jas, can you just pretend to talk to me, but don't say anything in case I have to hit you."

Now there was a whole group of girls round Robbie, giggling and jiggling about in front of him! Then Wet Lindsay slimed up. And actually touched his cheek. My boyfriend's cheek she touched. With her slimy hand. Tom said, "Leave it, Gee, just be cool. Honestly, he'll like it better if you don't make a fuss."

Huh. What did Hunky know about it? Then he said, "Besides which, you're not long off your stick, and she will definitely kill you."

Fair point. She had deliberately and viciously whacked me round the ankles in a hockey match last month and I didn't want to be hobbling round for another two weeks.

I couldn't bear the tension of waiting for Robbie to come over; it made me really need to go to the piddly diddly department. I nipped off to the loos. A minute or two later Rosie came in, and she wasn't alone; she had Sven with her. He said, "Oh *ja*, here ve is in the girlie piddly diddlys."

He scared four girls, who went screeching out.

He is a very odd Norwegian-type person. Perhaps they have whatsits in Norwayland? You know, bisexual lavatories. Do I mean that or unicycle lavatories? No . . . unisex lavs, I mean. Rosie was completely unfazed by him being there, but as we all know she is not entirely normal herself. She said, "Robbie says he will see you in the dressing room."

Oh hell's biscuits. Pucker alert, pucker alert!! After an emergency reapplication of lip gloss I made my way to the dressing room. I just got near when I saw Lindsay was there again! This time fiddling around with his shirt collar.

Unbelievable.

Robbie caught my eye and raised his eyebrows to me and then behind her back gave me like a "wait five minutes" sign with his hand.

10:02 p.m.

I was livid as an earwig on livid pills.

Wait five minutes because of her . . . ?

Unbelievable.

10:05 p.m.

Back on the dance floor all my so-called mates were too busy snogging their boyfriends to listen to me complain. OK, I would have to take action on my own. I said to Jas over Tom's shoulder because they were slow dancing, "I will not, definitely not, play second fiddle to a stick insect."

She said, "What are you going to do then?"

I had to sort of dance along with them in order to keep up with where her head was. "I'm going to be absent. Upstairs. Don't tell him where I am if he asks you." Then I hid upstairs in the club. I got a few funny looks from the snoggers up there as I crouched down by the stairs, but I didn't care.

I could look down and see Robbie looking for me. He even sent Jas into the loos to see if I was in there. She did a ludicrous comedy wink up at me as she went. What is she thinking? If she had been a spy in the war, German high command would have only had to get on the blower to her and say, "Vat haf you been told never to divulge?" and she would tell them everything, probably including the Queen's bra size (sixty-four double-D cup).

Anyway, I could see Robbie getting more and more worked up about not finding me. Ha and triple ha. Hahahahaha, in fact. So, Mr. Sex God, the worm is for once on the other foot.

On the downside I had managed to make myself a snog-free zone.

10:20 p.m.

After the SG had gone back onstage to play another set, I went into the loos. Ellen was in there looking all mournful. She said, "I'm going to go. Dave the L hasn't turned up. He said he would see me here, and he hasn't come."

I tried wisdomosity about elastic bands and when a boy says "see you" who knows what that means, etc., etc. but she wasn't interested.

She went off home all miserable.

Honestly, you try to help people even though you have troubles enough of your own. (And even though some people bring things on themselves because they get off with their best mate's red herrings.)

When I came out of the loos I made sure that Robbie could see how miffed I was. He tried his heartbreaking smile on me, but I ignored him with a firm hand and pretended to be laughing with my mates. I said to Rosie, "Wet Lindsay is a crap dancer, and her hair has no bounceability. Neither incidentally, despite all her efforts, have her basoomas. They just lie there. I think a bit of bounce in a basooma is a good thing."

I wondered what level of bounceability mine

had when I was dancing. I went to a dark corner at the back of the bar where no one was to inspect them whilst I danced. Well, they certainly did jiggle, not always in time to the music either. Perhaps if I kept my shoulders rigid they would keep still. As I was trying rigid shoulder dancing Dave the Laugh turned up. I was so shocked I went, "Where have you been?"

He grinned. He looked very cool in black. He said, "Why? Did you miss me? Mrs. Dumper." But he didn't seem bitter or anything. Perhaps he had forgiven me. He said, "God, it's hot in here. Do you fancy a cold drink?"

Well, no harm in a cold drink with an old dumpee is there?

Jas ogled me as I went off to the bar with him, but I just ogled back. Honestly, she acts like she's fifty. She'll start wearing head scarves soon and discussing the price of potatoes with anyone who will listen (i.e., no one). Anyway, if the Sex God could hang out with his exes, so could I.

Dave the L and I took our drinks outside for a breath of fresh air. I sort of said awkwardly, "Dave, I'm really sorry for, you know, using you like a Red Herring."

He said, "Yes, well . . . I was pretty upset at the time."

He seemed unnaturally serious. Oh God's pajamas. I was meant to be having a laugh. Why was he called Dave the Laugh if he was not a laugh? He should have been called Dave the Unlaugh. Shut up, brain.

I said, "Well, you know I just—"

He interrupted me, "Georgia, there is something you should know—I . . ."

Oh God. OhGoddyGodGod. He sounded like he was going to cry. What should I do? I hadn't been to boy-crying classes; I only went to snogging ones. I looked down at my drink and I could sort of sense him putting his head in his hands. I was just staring at my drink and avoiding looking at him. Then he said in a low sort of broken voice, "I haven't been able to get over you. . . . I think—I think . . . I'm in love with you."

Oh *sacré* bloody *bleu* and triple *merde*. I mumbled, "Dave, I don't know what to say. I, well . . . I . . ."

He said, "Perhaps if you could give me just one last kiss."

I looked round at him. And he looked at me.

And he was wearing a big red false clown's nose.

Actually it was really, really funny, even though the joke was on me. He just looked hilarious!! Both of us were falling about.

But then this awful thing happened. I accidentally found myself attached to his mouth. (He took the red nose off first though.)

midnight

I was in such a tizz of a spaz that I was on time outside for when Vati turned up. Is it really necessary for him to wear a balaclava? And also it's like being on a quiz show; he kept asking me things. "So did you have fun then? Did any lads ask you to dance?"

Why does he want to know everything? I'm not interested in him; why is he so interested in me? I would tell him what a complete fiasco he is making of himself, but I'm not speaking to him so I can't.

Anyway, if he did know that I had been snogging he would probably tie me to the kitchen table like Angus. Or take me to the vet's.

1:00 a.m.

I didn't say good night or anything to Robbie. I just couldn't. I didn't say anything to Dave the Laugh either. After the accidental snog I was in a sort of a daze. Dave the Laugh seemed a bit surprised, too. He said, "Er . . . right . . . well . . . I think I'll just, like . . . er . . . at . . . go to the . . ."

And I said, "Yes, er. I think . . . I'll like, you know . . . just er . . . you know, go and . . . er . . . go . . ."

But neither of us knew what we were talking about.

This time my big red bottom has taken things too far.

2:00 a.m.

Am I a scarlet-bottomed vixen?

What will I say to Robbie?

2:30 a.m.

For heaven's sake. It was just a little kiss! I am a teenager, I've got whatsit . . . lust for life. Also it was probably my hormones that made me do it (Officer).

3:00 a.m.

What's a little kiss between exes?

3:01 a.m.

And a tiny bit of tongues.

3:03 a.m.

And nip libbling.

3:05 a.m.

NIP LIBBLING??? What in the name of Jas's commodious panties am I talking about? You see. I am so upset I have got internal dyslexia. I mean lip nibbling, not nip libbling.

Anyway, I am not alone on the Guilt Train because Dave the Laugh is also on it. He is a two-timer with Ellen.

3:10 a.m.

Oh God, she is my mate. I am bad bad baddy bad bad. Jesus would never snog his mate's boyfriend.

3:15 a.m.

I will probably never be able to sleep again.

Zzzzzzzzzzzzz.

sunday november 7th

The phone rang. Libby answered it. "Heggo? Yes yes yes yes yes yes yes yes, listen."

I could hear her singing her version of "Dancing Queen," and there was a sort of banging noise as well—she would be doing the accompanying dance. God help the poor sod who was on the other end of the phone.

"Dancing bean . . . dancing bean . . . feel the touch of my tangerine . . . ine . . ."

It was so loud that even Mutti was forced to get up to try to shut her up. She said, "Libby, let Mummy talk." There was the sound of a struggle and spitting and then I heard Mum say, "Hello? Oh yes, well hang on. I'll see if she's up." She shouted up the stairs, "Georgia, it's Robbie for you."

I shot out of bed and downstairs. Checking in the mirror to make sure I didn't have idiot hair. Although that meant the Sex God would have X-ray vision if he could see down the telephone. Perhaps he did have extrasensory whatsit and he would sense my red-bottomosity. Oh God. The Sex God!!! As she handed over the phone Mum winked at me. Shutupshutup winking.

I tried not to sound like a scarlet minx. I wanted to achieve casualosity with a hint of maturiosity. With no suggestion of red-bottomosity.

"Hi." (How cool is that? V. cool, that's how.)

"Georgia? What happened last night? Where were you? Jas said that you got in trouble with your dad and had to leave."

Phew. For once in her life Jas had actually done something right.

I said, "Er . . . yes, he got the mega hump like he always does and, er . . . well, actually if I hadn't have gone he would have come in and danced and no one wants to see him doing the Twist." What in the name of Beelzebub was I talking about?

Robbie seemed to relax then. He said, "Listen, I'm really sorry about last night. I really wanted to be round you and then there was the Lindsay thing . . . and the bloke from the record company being there. He wanted to speak to us after the gig."

Anyway, it was really dreamy talking to him. The record bloke wants to sign up The Stiff Dylans.

Wow!!

Robbie said he would meet me at the bottom of the hill at lunchtime.

10:30 a.m.
Mutti followed me into my bedroom. She said, "So, Robbie . . . hmmm. Who is he then? Which school does he go to? He sounds quite sexy on the phone." (Erlack, my parents are OBSESSED with sex.) I went on applying my natural-looking makeup (just a hint of daytime glitter). I am not officially speaking to her either (as she is the cat molester's handmaiden). Except to ask her for my pocket money.

Mum went raving on. "Look, come on, love, stop sulking. It was the only thing to do. It's cruel to keep a wild animal cooped up all the time."

I said, "Well, let Vati go and have a sniff round in the garden then."

She went all parenty. "It's not funny to be so rude. We are only trying to do our best." She looked like she was going to cry as she went out.

Oh poo. Poo and *merde*.

10:00 p.m.
It was fab!!! Being with my BOYFRIEND. And what is fabbier is that we bumped into a couple of

Robbie's mates and went round to their house. Dom was there from The Stiff Dylans. He looked at me a bit funny. I wonder if he thinks I really want to get off with his dad. Oh *sacré bleu*. No one else was there that I knew; they were mostly much older than me. How cool is that? And Robbie was holding my hand!!! In front of them!!!

One of them asked me what I was going to do at university. Er. I said, "Backup dancing." I don't know why.

I didn't say anything else after that. I just smiled like an imbecile a lot.

Dom and Robbie talked about their record deal. They're all really nice. Then John asked me if I smoked and I said only if my hair is on fire, and they just looked at me.

11:30 p.m.
SG said he really rates me. He did the neck-kissing stuff and ear snogging. It was so dreamy. My only slight worry is Rosie's theory of things growing if they get snogged (like your lips). If he goes on snogging my ears, will I get elephant ears?

midnight

Lalalalalalalalalalala.

12:30 a.m.

I closed my eyes and started doing dreamy dreamy about snogging the SG. Doing a sort of rerun of the highlights. Mmmm. But then as Robbie stuck his tongue in one ear Dave the Laugh appeared out of nowhere. And stuck his tongue in my other ear.

12:45 a.m.

Like an ear kabob.

1:15 a.m.

That is it. I have put my red bottom to bed. It will not be rearing its ugly head again.

My nip libbling days are over.

I am and always will be the girlfriend of a Sex God.

The End.

1:30 a.m.

Still, it's a bit weird being with people older than me.

monday november 8th
7:45 a.m.

Woken at the crack of dawn by Vati yelling and carrying on downstairs. He was singing, "The boys are back in town, the boys are back in town. Yesssssss! Owzat!!!!!!!! The boy's a genius!!!!!!"

It turns out some fool has offered him a job. He is going to be in charge of waterworks or something. I said, "We'd better dig a well then."

But M and V were too busy snogging each other to hear me. Erlack a pongoes. Also they seem to be failing to notice that they do not exist for me.

Vati was UNBEARABLE at breakfast, wearing his dressing gown slung round his shoulders like a sort of prizefighter and lifting Libby above his head with one hand. Actually, that bit was quite funny because she clung on to the overhead lamp and wouldn't let go, and he very nearly lost his rag. I think he must be in some sort of hormonal middle-age thing because his moods are very unpredictable. One minute it's all jokes; the next minute you ask him for a measly fiver and he goes ballistic. He is alarmingly bonkers. And chubby. And a cat molester.

Met Jas. She said, "I told Robbie what you told me to, but I still don't understand why you had to rush off."

"Dad had got his balaclava on."

"Oh right, I see. Yes."

And alarmingly she seemed quite satisfied. That is the trouble with telling people porkies— it is so easy. Should I confess about Dave the Laugh? Jas is my best friend. We know everything about each other. I, for instance, have seen her knickers. But on the other hand, she can be a terrible pain about morals and stuff. She might say it wasn't very nice of me as Ellen is my friend, etc., etc.

Hmmm. I'll think about it later. In the next life.

assembly

9:00 a.m.

Ellen said, "Sorry I was a bit moody and stressy with you on Saturday; I know you were just trying to cheer me up. Dave the Laugh turned up just after I'd gone. Typical!"

OhmyGod. I am a facsimile of a sham of a friend.

131

french

1:30 p.m.

The whole school has gone bonkers!!! Our new
student French teacher turns out to be a David
Ginola look-alike!!! Honestly. He's bloody gorgeous. When he walked in even Rosie stopped
plucking her eyebrows. Monsieur "Pliss Call Me
Henri" has got sort of longish hair and really tight
blue jeans. We are keen as *la moutarde* on French
now. Any time he asks anything everyone puts
their hands up. I can't remember the last time I
saw anyone put their hand up in French. Usually
we put our heads on our desks for a little snooze
and just let our arms flop over if we are supposed
to be answering anything. It's our little way of letting Madame Slack know how interested we are in
Patapouf and Clicquot. Or whatever sad French
people she is talking about.

break

2:30 p.m.

And it isn't just us—you should see the teachers.
I even saw Hawkeye giggling when she was talking
to Pliss Call Me Henri!

The saddest of all is Herr Kamyer, who has

gone completely giddy at having another man in the building. Unfortunately, his idea of bonding involves a lot of spasmodic dithering about and saying "Oh, *ja*. Oh, *ja sehr* interestink, Henri."

When Monsieur Henri opened the staff room door for Miss Wilson, her tragic seventies bob nearly fell off. They are all being pathetic, pretending to be interested in garlic and Edith Piaf and so on. Sad.

I, of course, as anyone who knows me will tell you, have always loved *la belle* France.

4:40 p.m.

On the way home I said to Jas, "I have always *aim*ed *la belle* France."

"You said you didn't like it because it was full of French people."

"Well, there is that, but apart from that I *aime* it very much."

dinnertime
6:00 p.m.

I said to Mutti, "Can we have wine with our fish fingers like they do in *la belle* France?"

She just said, "Don't be ridiculous."

6:20 p.m.

Vati is bringing Angus home from the vet's tonight. Libby and me have made a hospital bed sort of thing out of his cat basket and some old blankets. Libby put one-eyed Teddy in it as well.

He'll be so sad and probably in agony. He will be a facsimile of a sham of his former cathood. He will just be like other cats now. Not the magnificent half cat–half Labrador that he used to be.

I said to Mutti, "I hope it will not put you off your beauty regime, having Angus's trouser snake addendums on your conscience."

7:30 p.m.

Hahahahahaha. Angus leapt out of his cat cage and immediately attacked Vati's trousers. When Dad went to put the car in the garage Angus shot out into the garden and over the wall. I heard Snowy and Whitey yapping and Mr. Next Door yelling.

Happy days!

my bedroom
7:50 p.m.

Although it's a laugh having the French heart-throb around, it hasn't quite taken my mind off my unfaithfulness with Dave the L. I don't know what to do. Am I the only person who has a secret red bottom? Oh, I have such guiltosity.

8:00 p.m.

How can I concentrate on my French homework? Even if I had remembered to bring it home from school with me.

In my book about not sweating the small stuff it says, "Don't keep your pain a secret."

Rang Jas. Even she is quite swoony about Henri. "He's quite, you know . . . handsome, isn't he? In a French way."

I said, "*Mais oui. Très sportif.* Er . . . but lots of *les garçons* are, aren't they? It's natural at our age to be attracted to good-looking guys."

Jas was raving on, unaware of my secret pain. "No, I don't think so. It's only Tom for me. He is my one and only Hunky."

Good Lord. I said. "Yes, but you said Henri was quite handsome."

"I know, but that is just fantasy, isn't it? I wouldn't dream of doing anything about it."

"Yes, but what if, for instance, it was hot and you thought he was going to say he loved you and then you noticed he was wearing a red false nose. What then?"

She pretended not to know what I was talking about. I must bear my secret burden of pain alone. *Quel dommage.*

One thing is for sure, I must never speak to Dave the Laugh again. I must eschew him with a firm hand.

9:00 p.m.
Dave the Laugh rang!

Uh-oh. He said, "Georgia. I just rang to say don't worry about anything. I know how weird you can get. But it's OK. We just had a laugh. No one needs to know anything about it. We can be mates. Don't worry, Mrs. Mad."

Crikey. How grown-up is that? Scarily grown-up.

He's right though. I am just too sensitive for my own good. I should relax. It was just a little kiss.

9:05 p.m.
And lip nibble. With a hint of tongues.

But that is all.

11:05 p.m.

I wonder what number on the snogging scale nip libbling should be.

11:10 p.m.

Emergency snogging scale update:

(1) holding hands

(2) arm around

(3) good-night kiss

(4) kiss lasting over three minutes without a breath

(5) open-mouth kissing

(6) tongues

(6¼) nip libbling

(6½) ear snogging

(7) upper body fondling—outdoors

(8) upper body fondling—indoors (in bed)

(9) below waist activity (b.w.a.) and

(10) the full monty

midnight

I wonder if it is possible to have two boyfriends. I mean, times are changing. Relationships are more complicated. In France men always have mistresses and wives and so on. Henri probably has two girlfriends. He would laugh if you told him you just had the one. He would say, *"C'est très, très tragique."*

So if he can have two I could have two. What is good for *le* gander must be *bon* for *la* goose *aussi*. *Je pense.* Oh, *merde.*

But would I want Robbie to have another girl-friend? No!!!!!

tuesday november 9th
7:50 a.m.

Angus is amusing himself by ambushing the post-man. Och aye, they may have taken his trouser snake addendums, but they cannae tak his freedom!!

walking to school with jas
8:30 a.m.

Jas was having a bit of fringe trouble (i.e., she had cut it herself and made herself look like Richard II), so she was even more vague than normal. She just went fringe fiddle, fringe fiddle. I was going to have to kill her. In a caring way. Oh, the burden of guilt. I wanted to shout out, "OK!! I have nip libbled with Dave the Laugh. Kill me now."

But I didn't.

german

10:20 a.m.

In the spirit of European whatsit and also because I had finished painting my nails, I asked Herr Kamyer what was German for snogging. He went amazingly dithery and red. At first he pretended not to know what snogging meant, but when Rosie and Jools started puckering up and blowing kisses at him he got the message. Anyway, it's called *frontal knutschen*.

As we left class I said to Rosie, "I rest my case vis-à-vis the German people. I will never *knutsch* any of them."

french

1:30 p.m.

When Jackie Bummer went up to collect her homework(!) she stood so close to Henri that she was practically resting her nunga-nungas on his head. If he had had the misfortune to have seen her in her sports knickers as I have, he would have been away laughing on a fast camel. (Or as Henri would say, "away laughing on *le vite* camel.")

Uh-oh, I am thinking about Dave the Laugh again. *Merde.*

6:00 p.m.

Robbie phoned to say he really likes me. (Yeah!!!) He is going down to London (Booo!) for his meeting vis-à-vis becoming a HUGE star. (Hurrah!)

A HUGE star with a really great girlfriend.

6:10 p.m.

I went into the kitchen to have a cheesy snack to celebrate. Angus was having a zizz in his basket. Even though he is no longer fully intact trouser snake–wise he is very cheerful. He was purring like a bulldozer. When I gave him one of his kitty treats he almost decapitated my hand. Libby wanted a kitty treat as well. I said, "They are not for human beings, Libby."

"I like human beans."

"Yes but—"

"Give me human beans as well!!!!"

I had to give her one. Then the Loonleader came in and said, "Who are all these mystery boys then that keep phoning you?"

I went "Hnyunk" which in anybody's except an absolute fool's language means, "It is none of your business, and I will be sick on your slippers if you go on."

Vati, of course, didn't get it. He raved on. "Why don't you bring them round here for us to meet?" On and on and ON about it.

I said, "As I have said many, many times, I have to be going now."

my bedroom
8:00 p.m.

Everyone has gone out. I've got so much homework and so on it will be a relief to really get down to it.

8:05 p.m.

Oh Blimey O'Reilly's pantyhose . . . what is the point of Shakespeare? I know he is a genius and so on, but he does rave on. *What light doth through yonder window break?*

It's the bloody moon, for God's sake, Will, get a grip!!

Phoned Rosie. "The Sex God has to go to London to see the record company people and discuss making an album. I don't mean to boast but I have to. . . . Not only am I the girlfriend of a Sex God, I am now going to be fantastically rich."

"Fab. Groovesville, Arizona. Are you going to be living in an all-white penthouse with parrots?"

Sometimes I really worry about my friends. Parrots?

Then I could hear in the background, "Parrots? Parrots? Oh *ja*." Sven seemed really interested in these bloody parrots, my new flatmates.

Rosie said, "Hang on a minute."

Her massive Norwegian boyfriend always seems to be round her house: that is because she has very, very nice parents who go out a lot. I could hear kissing noises and giggling and a sort of Norwegian parrot thing.

When she came back Rosie said, "Sven says, Can we come and live with you in your groovy London pad?"

"No."

"Fair enough."

11:00 p.m.

I won't let my newfound happiness with a famous popstar spoil me though, and I definitely want my own career. Using one of my many talents. Hmmm . . . What career combines being able to apply makeup with innovative trouser snake dancing?

I could be a heavily made-up girl backup dancer!

wednesday november 10th
biology
1:30 p.m.

I can do a magnificent impression of a bolus of food being passed along the alimentary canal. Mrs. Hawkins said it was "terrifyingly realistic." So I'll probably get top marks in blodge and become, erm, what is it you become when you do biology? . . . A bloke with a beard ferretting round in swamps. Maybe I'll stick with the backup dancer idea.

10:00 p.m.

I had to go to bed because Vati was singing "I Will Always Love Youuuuuuuuuuuuuuuuuuuuuuuuuuuuu-uuuuuuuuuuuuuuuuuuuu" by Whitney Useless.

11:00 p.m.

Just nodding off when I heard this noise at my window like pebbles being thrown against it. Angus has made a startling recovery, but surely even he hadn't learnt how to throw pebbles. I opened the window and looked out, and there below me was the Sex God!! Aahhhhh. He blew me a kiss when I opened the window, and he said, "Come down."

I put on my coat over my jimjams and had just a second to remember my emergency Sex God drill—lip gloss, comb idiot hair, suck in nostrils—before I crept downstairs and opened the door. The olds were all still up in the front room, singing the national anthem, only to a reggae beat. . . . I suspect a few barrels of Vino Tinto had been drunk.

Robbie gave me a really dreamy long kiss when I came out. I whispered, "Brrr, it's very nippy noodles, isn't it?"

Robbie looked at me like I was half insane (and half bonkers). Which I am so sure he is not wrong there. SHUT UP, BRAIN!!!!

in bed
midnight
He has gone.

To London.

Without me.

thursday november 11th
8:30 a.m.
Still, life carries on. Exams to be examined. Serious things to be thingied.

Today we have decided on Operation La Belle France.

The whole gang went to school wearing our berets like *les françaises* and also with our collars on our coats turned up. Rosie even brought a bunch of onions for Henri, which in my personal opinion is taking things just that little bit too far. He was all groovy and smiley and said, *"Merci, mademoiselle*, I will make the *delicieusement soupe a l'oignon ce soir* and I will think of you when I eat it."

Which is a plus and a minus in my book. *Très bon* to be thought of by Henri but not so *bon* to be associated with onions. He said it all in *la française* and I knew what he meant. I smiled at him to let him know that I knew what it meant.

11:OO a.m.
The French test didn't seem all that difficult.

We have got Henri fever. Badly. All this morning we wandered round going "Haw he haw he haw" in a French accent.

p.e.
1:30 p.m.
I think even Miss Stamp might be on the turn because of Henri. I could have sworn she has had a shave.

break
2:30 p.m.
Ellen and me were sitting on the radiator near the vending machine. In these cold autumn days it's quite pleasant having toastie knickers. I said to Ellen with great casualosity, "How's it going with you and Dave the Laugh?"

She said, "Quite cool."

What does that mean? I tell you what it means: it means that he hasn't told her about our accidental snog.

I may live to snog another day.

saturday november 13th
11:00 a.m.
Very, very bad Sex God withdrawal.

midday
Even though I am not in the mood for shopping

because I am so sad and aloney I forced myself to ask Mum for a fiver and made an effort to go out. Rosie, Jools, Ellen and Jas and me met at Luigi's as normal and then went off to Miss Selfridge. On the way there we had to go through the town center and we were just walking along all linked up when we saw Dave the Laugh with Rollo and a couple of other mates. Uh-oh.

Dave the Laugh said, "Hi, dream chicks."

He is a very fit-looking boy. It's funny that even though, of course, I am really sorry (honestly, Jesus) about the red-bottom business, it is always nice to see him. I never feel like such a stupid loon round him as I do with the Sex God. We were close to Jennings the greengrocer's, where Tom works, so Jas HAD to pop in to see her so-called boyfriend.

I said, "Ask him if he has got any firm legumes." But she didn't pay any attention to me.

Ellen was being really girlie round Dave and flicking her hair about. They were chatting and I was pretending to be looking at things with Rosie. But really I wanted to know what Dave the L was saying to Ellen. I still didn't know if they were official snogging partners.

The lads went off and Dave gave Ellen a little kiss on her cheek.

It made me feel a bit funny, actually. I don't know why.

3:00 p.m.

Ellen was all stupid for the rest of the afternoon. She is going to the flicks tonight, so she said she had to go home to get ready. I said to Rosie, "So are they an item then?"

Rosie said, "I know that she thinks he's really cool, but she won't tell me what number they have got up to. She says it's private."

I said, "That's pathetic."

And Rosie said, "I know, but I'll keep my beadies on them tonight at the cinema and see if I can tell."

It turns out that everyone—Jas and Tom, Rosie and Sven, Ellen and Dave, Jools and Rollo and a few more couples—are all going out together tonight. Everyone, that is, besides me.

Merde.

I am a goosegog in my own country.

3:30 p.m.
Phoned Jas.

"I am a goosegog in my own country."

"Well, come along tonight then."

"I can't. You'll all be having a snogging fest. Don't worry. I'll just stay in whilst my best mates all go out together."

She said, "Oh, OK then. See you later."

Charming. And typico.

8:00 p.m.
SG phoned. Oooohhhhh. The record company wants to sign them up!!! They are going along to this big music industry party tonight at some trendy club.

midnight
I am a pop widow.

sunday november 14th
lunchtime
1:10 p.m.
Phoned Rosie. She said, *"Bonjour, ma petite* pal."

"What are you doing?"

"Having an Abba afternoon. I am wearing my

mum's old crochet bikini and . . . Sven! Careful of that glass chandelier!!"

In the background I could hear all this clattering and, "Oh *ja*, oh *ja*, oh *ja*!"

I said, "What is Sven doing?"

"He's juggling."

Of course he was. Why do I ask?

2:00 p.m.

Jas is swotting with her boyfriend AGAIN.

No one will play with me. They are all doing their homework. Huh.

8:00 p.m

Alarmingly, I found myself in my room doing some French homework!!! Even Dad came to the door to look. This is a new sign of my maturiosity. Also, I must make sure I can order things in Paris when I am traveling over there with the band. I would feel like a fool if I didn't even know how to order mascara.

9:00 p.m.

The evening did end on a high note though. When I was in the kitchen making myself milky pops for my restless urges, Vati was hanging round in there. Talking to me and asking me stuff. I told him all about the SG and Dave the L (not). Then he said, "I think that Angus has definitely calmed down."

At that moment Angus came in through the cat flap in what can only be described as a bird's nest hat.

I love him, I love him!!!

monday november 15th
french
1:30 p.m.

Hmmm. Henri gave us back our test papers and I had come top!!! All the ace crew looked at me in amazement.

Jools said, "*Sacré* bloody *bleu*."

But Henri gave me a really dishy smile. He said, "This is vair, vair well done, m'mselle."

Blimey O'Reilly's trousers. He is quite literally GORGEOUS! If I wasn't the girlfriend of a Sex God and also dying to go to the piddly diddly department I would have snogged him on the spot.

break

2:30 p.m.

As we left French and went to the canteen Henri was ahead of us. He has got excellent bottomosity. Herr Kamyer came bounding and dithering along the corridor. He looked delighted to see Henri.

"*Guten tag*, Henri. Vould you like a cup of coffee?" And they went off to the staff room.

I said, "Herr Kamyer is making an absolute arse of himself, isn't he? Drooling around after Henri. Like a homosexualist."

Jas went all politically correct. "Well, there is nothing wrong with that. He might be gay, you know. He might be looking for happiness with the right man."

"Jas, don't be ridiculous. He wears tartan socks."

at home

4:30 p.m.

Yesss!!! I came top in French! That will teach Madame Slack. In fact, I will tell her when she gets back, possibly in French, that instead of the stick she should have used *le* carrot. Like Henri. Ooer.

7:00 p.m.

To celebrate Vati's fabulous new job at the water-works (!), I was forced to go out to a family meal at Pizza Express. Libby brought scuba-diving Barbie, Pantalitzer, Charlie Horse and a Pingu comic, so we had to have a table for eight because she wanted them all to have seats of their own. (Yes, even the comic). She tried to order them their own pizzas as well but Vati put his foot down with a firm hand. Even when she cried real tears. He said, "There are children starving in Africa."

I nearly said, Well, why don't you send your bottom off to them? That should keep them going through the winter."

But I didn't want to spoil a beautiful evening.

10:00 p.m.

Sex God phoned. Yummmmmm!

He is relanding on Sunday. Actually he is coming back on Saturday and going to a family party: it's his mum's birthday. Jas is going with Tom. I sort of waited for him to ask me.

He said, "It would be great if you could come, Georgia, but maybe we should wait and introduce you to them first before you just turn up? What do you think?"

"Er . . ."

midnight

What do I think? What does he mean, what do I think? How should I know? If anyone knows what I think it won't be me. I, of course, will be the last to know. Hmmm, I wish me and the Sex God could see more of each other and you know, do normal things like . . . Abba afternoons . . . and . . . snogging. And trouser snake dancing. And so on.

Maybe when we live in our penthouse flat in London.

1:00 a.m.

How many hours is it till the Sex God returns?

Twenty-four times five plus the difference between . . . oh God. I don't know. I can't do figures in my head very well. There are too many other really important things in there taking up the space. Fashion tips and so on.

tuesday november 16th

maths

2:45 p.m.

Didn't those Greek-type people have anything to do but loll round in baths going "Eureka"!!? And also I'll just say this about Pythagoras: didn't he have any mates? Mates that would say, "Hey, Pythy baby . . . SHUT UP!!!!"

4:01 p.m.

We were just pinning on our ears to do glove animal on the way home when we spotted Dave the Laugh and Rollo and Steve and a few others, hanging round . . . Ooer. Lad alert, lad alert!!! Damn, I didn't have any lippy on, but at least I could quickly rip my ears off. Ellen was patheticisimus—she ran back into the cloakroom, going, "Oops, forgot my fags!"

Oh yeah!

She came out five minutes later with just the merest hint of makeup on—lip gloss, concealer, glossy eyeshadow, mascara . . . skirt rolled over, hair tousled . . . really natural.

I said, "Found your fags then?" But she didn't get it.

Dave is cool-looking. In a someone-else's-boyfriend sort of a way. He gave Ellen a kiss on the cheek. Then he looked at me. I hadn't noticed how long his eyelashes are before. Probably because he had been a Red Herring and then he had been wearing a big red false nose. He said, "Hi, Georgia. Still grooving?"

I said, "Yeah, grooving like two grooving . . . er . . . groovers."

And he laughed.

Ellen said, "Are you walking home?" And we all set off together.

Dave has been banned from school for a week. Hmm . . . my kind of guy. I asked him why.

"Well, you know that methylated spirit just burns and doesn't burn anything else?"

Ellen (space rocket scientist—not) said, "Oh yeah. It's to do with its low combustion point, isn't it?"

And she was being all girlie and sort of hanging on his arm. I wondered what number they had got up to. Rosie said she thought number five (open-mouth kissing). She couldn't really tell in the dark at the cinema. Also, had he done that nip libbling thing? Shut up. Shut up. Remember I am the girlfriend of a Sex God.

Dave said, "Anyway, in science I put some meths on my hand and set fire to it. Then when Mr. Martin asked a question I put up my hand. On fire. It was hilarious in the extreme, even if I do say so myself. Which I just did, because I heard myself."

It really made me laugh.

Rosie has asked them all to come over to her house on Saturday because her parents are out for the night. After we split up at the bottom of the hill, I said, "It was a laugh about the hand-on-fire thing, wasn't it?"

And Ellen said, "Don't you think it was a bit dangerous?"

I have my doubts whether she is quite laugh enough for Dave the Laugh.

teatime

Vati was grumbling and raving on for England because the milkman won't deliver milk to us anymore. He says that Angus stalks him. Oh honestly, people are so weedy. I had more important things to think about than the milkman's trousers, believe me.

When Dad had gone off to visit the permanently

insane (Uncle Eddie), I said to Mum, "Mum, you know I don't really like talking about this sort of thing, but, well . . . did you ever, you know, when you were a teenager, did you ever two-time anyone?"

"Oh yes."

"How did you feel?"

"Great."

"Great?!"

"Yes."

"You didn't feel guilty then?"

"No."

"Well, you should have."

"Well, I didn't."

You see what I am up against.

thursday november 18th
physics
10:20 a.m.

The Bummer Twins cut off half Nauseating P. Green's tie. I tried to cheer her up. I had to even pretend that I was glad she had named one of Hammy's children after me. That is what I am like. I may have red bottomosity, but I also have wis-domosity and self-sacrificiosity. Which is not easy to say.

lunchtime

Nippy noodles. I'm sure Elvis Attwood turns the heating down when it gets cold. We all huddled on the radiator in the Science block. We were safe because it was Tragic Kate and Melanie Griffiths on prefect duty and neither of them are in peak physical condition (due to extreme breastiness in Melanie's case and general fatness in Kate's). They can never be arsed to check beyond the second floor. If Wet Lindsay or Hawkeye is on duty there is quite literally no hiding place. Once I had the unfortunate experience of hiding in the loo with my legs up against the door, pretending there was no one in there (as you do). Then, when I thought it was all clear, I looked down to see Hawkeye's beady eyes looking up at me from underneath the door. Scary bananas.

It's the dreaded sex and relationship lecture from Miss Wilson tomorrow. I said, "I will be wearing my earplugs. I cannot bear to have grown-ups discuss sex. It's unnatural."

Jas said, "Haven't your mum and dad told you the facts of life thing?"

I looked at her. "Erlack."

Actually, Mutti did once ramble on about eggs

and ovaries when my period started. I didn't happen to have my earplugs with me so I had to hum a little tune in my head.

I said to the gang, "All we can hope for is that we get some free sanitary towels."

Jas (the sanitary wear expert) said, "Don't you use tampons? They're so much more convenient. Why don't you use them?"

Resisting my natural urge to shove her off the radiator I explained, "Because if I use them, Libby finds them, takes them out of their little holder and calls them 'Georgia's mice.' She trails them around for Angus to hunt. You have no idea what it is like in my house."

special assembly
3:40 p.m.

Slim was beyond the Valley of the Jelloid. Mr. Attwood caught the Bummer Twins in his hut snogging with the two window cleaners who came to do the Science block windows!!!

Slim said it was "disgraceful behavior."

I don't know why she has got her gigantic knickers in such a twist. She is the one, after all, who is encouraging us to be interested in sex by making us go to lectures on it. But you cannot reason with multiple chin personalities.

Anyway, on the plus side, the Bummers are banned for two weeks and may actually be expelled. Oh dear. How sad. Never mind.

friday november 19th
11:00 a.m.
Another reprimand! Just because Hawkeye heard me say *"Schiessenhausen"* when I tripped over Jas's haversack strap. *Gott in Himmel*, you can't even say lavatory in German without some fascist taking offense.

r.e.
1:30 p.m.
Sex and relationship talk. We all tried to get as far to the back of the classroom as we possibly could.

It was EXCRUCIATING! First of all, we were shown a film about ovaries and sperm and so on, which was enough to put you off sex for life. Additionally the woman in the film looked like Meat Loaf. It was really giving me the mega droop.

To pass the idle hours Rosie sent round a note:

To whom it may concern.
You have to choose one of these.
Which would you rather?
1. Elvis Attwood gets to number seven with
you. Heavy tongues are involved. He is in
the nuddy-pants.
or
2. No snogging ever again.
Pass it on.

And we all had to put 1 or 2. Everyone put 2. The thought of Elvis getting to number seven (upper body fondling—outdoors) has made my nunga-nungas quiver.

The next note was:

Which would you rather?
1. Miss Stamp rubs you down with a towel
in the showers.
or
2. No snogging ever again.

I was very alarmed to see that Jas put number 1.

break

I said to Jas, "What kind of snacks have you got, lezzie?"

I can't bear to think about the second half of the sex and relationship lecture given by the saddest, most unlikely person ever to have sex or a relationship, Miss Wilson. I personally think that if you can't even put your tights on properly you are not likely to be tiptop in the snogging department. She raved and stuttered on about the "beauty of a fulfilling and caring relationship with someone you love."

Heavens to Betsy. Rosie colored all her teeth black with her fibertip pen which was very funny. (And much funnier later when she couldn't get it off.)

In the end Miss Wilson gave us each an egg. Cheers. Just what I've always wanted. What in the name of Lucifer is she on about? We have to take care of the egg and look after it and treat it like a baby. It is supposed to teach us about caring and nurturing.

It is totally sad and useless and *merde*.

8:30 p.m.

I annoyed Vati by telling him that the program he was watching on TV was unsuitable for my egg. Which by the way I have dressed in an old bootie of Libby's.

I think I may very well be an unusually good mother.

*Egg*cellent, in fact.

saturday november 20th
2:45 p.m.

Saturday night is party night.

I've asked Mum to baby-sit my egg. It will make a change for her to nurture her caring skills.

The ace gang is going to be there. (Well, apart from Jas, who is going to her so-called boyfriend's house to celebrate with her so-called boyfriend's parents.) Robbie said he would come round to Rosie's if he could after the family do. I feel sheer desperadoes to see him again. It's been ages since I saw him. Oh well. I wonder who will turn up tonight? Rosie and Sven, of course; Mabs and Steve, Jools and Rollo, Ellen and Dave the Laugh . . . Sara, Patty and me . . . and maybe some of Dave the Laugh's mates.

I'm sort of looking forward to it. It will take my mind off my jelloidness about the SG. Even though I will be, as per usual, the goosegog in the manger.

rosie's house
8:20 p.m.

Sven opened the door wearing a Durex on his head like a hat . . . er . . .

"'Ello, welcome to the fish party!"

What was he going on about?

When we went into the living room it was all full of netting and paper fish hanging up.

Rosie was wearing a really crap mermaid's outfit (her legs down one leg of her blue trousers and hobbling around). She said, "Cod evening."

Good grief.

Actually it was quite funny. There were fish-fingers as snacks. Dave the Laugh arrived with his mates. Ellen was really giddy, but I was cool as a mackerel. Sven said, "Let's dance," and we had to dance to fish-type music. Like the music from *Jaws*. And *Titanic*. Like fish. Which is not as easy as you would think because fish aren't big dancers. Dave was making me laugh because he really did look like a fish dancing! He even said,

"This dancing is playing haddock with my jeans."

Then we played sardines—well, we played Sven's version of it, which meant that essentially we all got into the wardrobe and some people snogged. Although I am not naming names. But it was Rollo and Jools, and Sven and Rosie. I was a bit too close to Dave the Laugh for my liking. He had to put his arm round me to stop falling over. It almost made me pucker up in the dark. . . .

Oh, stop it, stop it. I can feel my bottom getting redder and redder and bigger. I must not, MUST NOT get the big red bottom.

9:20 p.m.

Back in the living room the gang were playing True, Dare, Kiss or Promise. Then the doorbell rang. It was Mrs. Big Knickers herself and Tom. No Sex God though. I said to Jas confidentially, "Where is Robbie?"

"Who?"

God, she is annoying. She went off to help herself to snacks. I followed her and said, "Jas, what did he say?"

Then in front of the whole room she said, "You know when you did ear snogging with him? Well, what number is that officially?"

What is the matter with her?!! If anyone wants to know anything about my life all they have to do is to tune into Radio Jas.

9:30 p.m.

Hahahaha. Jas got "Dare" from me and I dared her to fill her knickers up with all the legumes in the vegetable basket. She was grumbling but in the end she had to do it and she went off to the kitchen.

I almost died with laughing when she came back. She had two pounds of potatoes, four carrots and a Swede down her knicknacks. And they were not full!!!

Rosie had to tell the truth about what number she and Sven had got up to. It was . . . eight!!!! They had got up to upper body fondling—indoors. Honestly!!! It gave me quite a turn. Rosie wasn't a bit embarrassed or anything. Then Steve got "Dare" and had to eat a raw onion.

Uh-oh, my turn.

Jas got her own back for the vegetable knicker extravaganza in a really horrible way. I got "True," and she said, "Do you fancy anyone besides the Sex God?"

Dave the Laugh looked at me. Everyone looked at me. What was I? A looking-at thing?

I said, "Er . . . well, I quite fancy . . . er, Henri." Phew.

That got them talking about Henri and his trousers. The game went on and then . . . Dave the Laugh got "Kiss." Jools said, "OK, Dave, you have to kiss . . ."

Ellen went all pink and incredibly girlish. But then Jools said, "You have to kiss . . . Georgia. . . ."

Why did she say that? What did she know? Was my big red bottom showing under my skirt????

Whilst everyone went "Snog, snog, snog!", I went into the kitchen to get myself a drink.

I was in a state of confusiosity. I wish I knew what I wanted. I wanted everything.

I wanted the Sex God and Dave the Laugh, and also possibly Henri.

Good Lord. I really was a nymphowhatsit.

That is when Dave the Laugh came out.

"Georgia."

"What?"

"You owe me a snog."

Oh God's pajamas!!! He was my best pal's

boyfriend. I was the girlfriend of a Sex God.

I would just have to say "No, Dave, the game is over."

And that is when I accidentally snogged him. AGAIN!!!

Oh, my lips had no discipline!! They were bad, bad lips!!! Then he stopped, mid–nip libbling, and said, "Georgia, we shouldn't be doing this."

That was what I was going to say!

He said, "Look, I really, really like you. I always have, you know that. But I am not an idiot, and, you know, other girls like me. They are only human; you have seen my dancing. . . ."

That made me laugh even amidst the drama-tosity.

He went on, because I seemed to be paralyzed from the nose downwards. Well, from the neck upwards and the nose downwards: "You have to choose. You go for a Sex God or you go for me, who really likes you and who you could have a great time with."

Then he gave me a little soft kiss on the mouth and went back into the living room.

midnight

In my bed. With my egg child tucked up next to me.

I am beyond the Valley of the Confused and treading lightly in the Universe of the Severely Deranged. *Sacré* bloody *bleu*. I am supposed to be thinking about makeup and my nunga-nungas. Not life-changing decisions. And egg babies. Why can't I just be left alone, why do I have to care about everything? I'm only fourteen. I only just snogged someone a few months ago and now I am practically married and have an egg child.

Jas hasn't got red-bottomosity, so it's all very well for her to be boring.

But my bottom demands to be heard.

1:00 a.m.

Oh *sacré* bloody *bleu*. I can't sleep.

Sex God or the Laugh?

Or both.

1:15 a.m.

Jelloid knickers or strange dancing?

Ear snogging or nip libbling?

It is a stark choice.

1:20 a.m.

I wonder what sort of snogging Henri does. Perhaps *les français* do other things that are not on
the English snogging scale. Nose libbling, *peut-
être*. That might be quite nice.

1:30 a.m

Nose libbling???!!!!

What am I talking about???!!!!

sunday november 21st
at breakfast

10:45 a.m.

I think I'm going mad. I feel so bonkers that at this
rate I might be driven to ask advice from my mutti.
I went into the kitchen and I began to say "Mutti, I
have a . . ." but then I was so astonished I forgot what I was going to say. For once in her life,
Mum had actually made breakfast for me and
Libbs. Boiled eggs and soldiers. Amazing. And
she was practically fully dressed. It was almost
like being in a real family. Possibly. I tapped the
top of my egg and scooped a bit out, and Mum
said, "Georgia, don't let Libby take eggs in your
bed. I found that one on your pillow."

I was eating my child.

That is the kind of person I have become.

A red-bottomed child eater.

What could be worse than that?

Then Vati came bursting through the door and said, "Christ on a bike . . . Naomi is pregnant!!!"

in my room
midday

In my bed of pain.

I can still see the little indent in the pillow where my egg child spent so many happy hours.

Who is Naomi pregnant by?

Have Angus's missing addendums made a surprise reappearance? Or has he been cuckolded by the little minx? Perhaps Vati is right that all women are fickle. My own mutti said she liked being a double dater. She thrust her nungas at Dr. Clooney. And now Naomi has allowed her girlie parts to flow free and wild. She has displayed appalling red-bottomosity.

But how can I point the fingers of shame? I am just the same.

No, I am worse.

Much, much worse.

I am a red-bottomed child eater.

Oh *merde*.

The End

4:00 p.m.

However, on the bright side—God wouldn't have made me have a red bottom in the first place unless he was trying to tell me something. He is, as we all know, impotent. (Or do I mean omnipotent? I don't know, but anyway he is some kind of potent.) Perhaps he is saying, "Go forth, Georgia, and use your red bottom wisely."

Hmmmm. So maybe I could have the Sex God AND Dave the Laugh?

And perhaps for diplomatic world relationship type stuff Henri as well?

Cor, it's all a go!!!

Georgia's Glossary

articles • (as in "You two articles get in here now!") A term of disdain used by so-called grown-ups. Because of their disdain of you they no longer see you as a human being but merely as a thing, an article.

backup dancer • This is like a backup singer, only it is dancing. At the back. Do you get it?

balaclava • This is from the Crimean War when our great-great-grannies spent all their time knitting hats to keep the English soldiers warm in the very, very cold Baltic. A balaclava covers everything apart from your eyes. It is like a big sock with a hole in it. Which just goes to show what really crap knitters our great-great-grannies were.

bangers • Firecrackers. Fireworks that just explode with a big bang. That's it. No pretty whooshing or stars or rocketing up into the sky. Bangers just bang. Boy fireworks. Boys are truly weird.

Blimey O'Reilly • (as in "Blimey O'Reilly's trousers") This is an Irish expression of disbelief and shock. Maybe Blimey O'Reilly was a famous Irish bloke who had extravagantly big trousers. We may never know the truth. The fact is, whoever he is, what you need to know is that a) it's Irish and b) it is Irish. I rest my case.

blodge • Biology. Like geoggers—geography—or Froggie—French.

Boots • A large drugstore chain selling mostly cosmetics.

David Ginola • A spectacularly good-looking French football player who plays in England. He has very long hair that he conditions and swishes round. He also carries a handbag. In any other circumstances he would definitely be a homosexualist. However, we must remember he is French.

DIY • Quite literally "Do It Yourself!" Rude when you think about it. Instead of getting someone competent to do things around the house (you know, like a trained electrician or a builder or a plumber), some vatis choose to DIY. Always with disastrous results. (For example, my bedroom ceiling has footprints in it because my vati decided he would go up on the roof and replace a few tiles. Hopeless.)

duffing up • Duffing up is the female equivalent of beating up. It is not so violent and usually involves a lot of pushing with the occasional pinch.

Durex • Oh do I really have to go into this? Honestly, everyone is OBSESSED with sex. A Durex is a . . . oh, you know. Yes, you do. It's a thingy. A boy thingy. Now do you get it? Oh very well, you asked me . . . a Durex is a condom. See. I knew you wouldn't like it if I told you.

fringe • Goofy short bit of hair that comes down to your eyebrows. Someone told me that American-type people call them "bangs" but this is so ridiculously strange that it's not worth thinking about. Some people can look very stylish with a fringe (i.e., me) while others look goofy (Jas). The Beatles started it apparently. One of them had a German girlfriend, and she cut their hair with a pudding bowl and the rest is history.

ginger nob • Someone with red hair. Red hair in England is a sign of lunacy. This stems from Henry VIII, who had red hair and also cut people's heads off. A lot. For a laugh.

goosegog • Gooseberry. I know you are looking all quizzical now. OK. If there are two people and they want to snog and you keep hanging about saying "Do you fancy some chewing gum?" or "Have you seen my interesting new socks?" you are a gooseberry. Or for short a goosegog, i.e., someone who nobody wants around.

goss • Gossip. Not to be confused with guss (gusset).

gyp • Who knows what this means? It's just something you say, like "Gadzooks!" Essentially *gyp* means "a pain." Elvis Attwood says I give him gyp. He also says his old war wound gives him gyp as well.

haggis • Something else that the Jock McThicks have made up to horrify the civilized world. It is a pudding made out of stuffed sheep's stomach.

Irn-Bru • Pronounced "iron broo." A disgusting drink made from sugar and old socks. Probably. People in Och Aye land think it is yummy scrumbos.

Jammy Dodger • Biscuit with jam in it. Very nutritious (ish).

Jock McThick • Is a generic term for anyone from Scotland that you can't be bothered to find out the name of. Can also be called Jock McTavish. Ditto French people (Jacques Lefrog) or German (Hans Lederhosen).

Kiwi-a-gogo land • New Zealand. "A-gogo land" can be used to liven up the otherwise really boring names of other countries. America, for instance, is Hamburger-a-gogo land. Mexico is Mariachi-a-gogo land and France is Frogs'-legs-a-gogo land. This is from that very famous joke told every Christmas by the elderly mad (Grandad). Oh, very well, I'll tell you it.

A man goes into a French restaurant and says to the French waiter, "Have you got frogs' legs?"

The waiter says, *"Oui, monsieur."*

And the man says, "Well, hop off and get me a sandwich then."

This should give you some idea of what our Christmases are like.

la mouche • Or possibly *le mouche*. This, as everyone who is *très bon* at *le français* (i.e., *moi*) knows, means "the fly."

loo • Lavatory. In America they say "rest room," which is funny, as I never feel like having a rest when I go to the lavatory.

lurgy • Is when you feel icky-poo. Please tell me that you know what *icky-poo* means. Oh good Lord. It means "poorly." Lurgy is like a bug. An illness bug. Ergo, tummy lurgy = stomach bug.

milky pops • A hot milk drink usually drunk by children to calm them down at night. You'd have to give it intravenously to Libby to calm her down. Or alternatively make the hot drink, put it in Libby's cup and then hit her over the head with it.

Miss Selfridge • A store where teenage girls go and buy clothes.

naff • Unbearably and embarrassingly out of fashion and nerdy. Naff things are: Parents dancing to "modern" music, blue eyeshadow, blokes who wear socks with sandals, pigtails. You know what I mean.

nervy spaz • Nervous spasm. Nearly the same as a nervy b. (nervous breakdown) or an F.T. (funny turn), only more spectacular on the physical side.

nippy noodles • Instead of saying "Good heavens, it's quite cold this morning," you say "Cor—nippy noodles!!" English is an exciting and growing language. It is. Believe me. Just leave it at that. Accept it.

nuddy-pants • Quite literally nude-colored pants, and you know what nude-colored pants are? They are no pants. So if you are in your nuddy-pants you are in your no pants, i.e., you are naked.

Number 10 • Number 10 Downing Street in London, where the Prime Minister lolls around.

nunga-nungas • Basoomas. Girl's breasty business. Ellen's brother calls them nunga-nungas because he says that if you get hold of a girl's breast and pull it out and then let it go—it goes *nunga-nunga-nunga*. As I have said many, many times with great wisdomosity, there is something really wrong with boys.

Och Aye land • Scotland. Land of the Braves. Or is that Indiana? I don't know, and I know I should because we are, after all, all human beings under our skins. But I still don't care.

Pantalitzer • A terrifying Czech-made doll that sadistic parents (my vati) buy for their children, presumably to teach them early on about the horror of life. Essentially the Pantalitzer doll has a weird plastic face with a horrible fixed smile. The rest of Pantalitzer is a sort of cloth bag with hard plastic hands on each side like steel forks. I don't know if I have mentioned this before, but I am not reassured that Eastern Europeans really know how to have a laugh.

pantibus • Latin for pants. Possibly. Who cares? It is a dead language. Who is going to complain if it isn't Latin for pants—Romulus and Remus?

pensioner • In England we give very old people some money so that they can buy thick spectacles and snug incontinent pants and biscuits. This is called their pension money.

piggies • Pigtails. Or "bunches," I think you call them. Like two little side ponytails in your hair. Only we think they look like pigtails. English people are obsessed with pigs; that is our strange beauty.

pingy pongoes • A very bad smell. Usually to do with farting.

porkies • Amusing (ish) Cockney rhyming slang. Pork pies = lies. Which is of course shortened to porkies. Oh, that isn't shorter, is it? Well, you can't have everything.

prat • A prat is a gormless oik. You make a prat of yourself by mistakenly putting both legs down one knicker leg or by playing air guitar at pop concerts.

pushbike • A pedal cycle, bicycle. Nothing will make me go on a bicycle again since my skirt got caught in the spokes of the back wheel and my panties were exposed.

rate • To fancy someone. Like I fancy (or rate) the Sex God. And I certainly *do* fancy the SG as anyone with the brains of an earwig (i.e., not Jas) would know by now. Phew—even writing about him in the glossary has made me go all jelloid. And stupidoid.

R.E. • Religious education.

Sellotape • Sellotape is a clear sticky tape. Usually used for sticking bits of paper to other bits of paper but can be used for sticking hair down to make it flat. (Once I used it for sticking Jas's mouth shut when she had hiccups. I thought it might cure them. It didn't, but it was quite funny, anyway.)

snogging • Kissing.

soldiers • Toast cut into narrow strips and then dipped into your boiled egg. It's an Olde-English-nursery-rhyme thing. Before you ask, no, toast dipped in egg does not look like a soldier. Obviously. Soldiers are not generally an inch high and covered in butter. As I have told you, we English are a mystery even to ourselves.

sporrans • Ah, I'm glad you asked me about this because it lets me illustrate my huge knowledgosity about Och Aye land. Sporrans are bits of old sheep that Scotsmen wear over their kilts, at the front, like little furry aprons. Please don't ask me why. I feel a nervy spaz coming on.

swot • A person who has no life and as a substitute has to read books and learn things for school. Also anyone who does their homework on time.

tart • A girl who is a bit on the common side. This is a tricky one, actually, because if I wear a very short skirt I am cool and sexy. However, if Jackie Bummer wears a short skirt it is a) a crime against humanity and b) tarty.

tosser • A special kind of prat. The other way of putting this is "wanker" or "monkey spanker."

weedy • Like a weed. You know like weeds in a garden. Those useless spindly annoying things that get in the way of flowers. A weedy person is like that, useless, spindly and annoying (although obviously not green).

whelk boy • A whelk is a horrible shellfish thing that only the truly mad eat. Slimy and mucuslike. Whelk boy is a boy who kisses like a whelk, i.e., a slimy mucus kisser. Erlack a pongoes.

DANCING IN MY
NUDDY-PANTS

Once again, this work of geniosity is dedicated to my lovely family
(whom I lobe very much) and my beyond marvy mates.
To Mutti, Vati, Soshie, John, Eduardo delfonso delgardo, Honor,
Libbs, Millie, Arrow and Jolly, Kimbo, the Kiwi-a-gogo branch,
Salty Dog, Jools and the Mogul, Big Fat Bob, Jimjams,
Elton, Jeddbox, Lozzer, Mrs. H, Geoff, Mizz Morgan,
Alan "it's not a perm" Davies, Jenks the Pen, Kim and Sandy,
Black Dog, Downietrousers and his lovely fiancée, Andy Pandy,
Phil and Ruth, Cock of the North and family,
Lukey and Sue, Tony the Frock, Ian the Computer,
the Ace Gang from Parklands, St Nicks.
Much love and thanks to the the fabulous
Clare (the Empress) and to Gillon, as always.
And with lots of love to my new family in Hamburger-a-gogo land
and the HarperCollins crew. Especial thanks to Alix Reid and
Tara and the very talented design and marketing types who have
made me the HUGE (but charmingly modest) person I am today.
And finally, *Dancing in My Nuddy-Pants* is dedicated to the
lovely people who have read my books and written to tell me
how much they *aime* them.
I love you all.
I do.
Honestly.

A NoTE FRoM GEoRGIA

Hello, my gorgey little chums,

It's me here writing to you once again from the seat of civilization (and no, I do not mean the lavatory . . . or rest room as you lot alarmingly call it). What I mean is I am writing to you from my bedroom to welcome you to another exciting(ish) diary of my fabulous life. Within these pages I run the gamut of emotions from A to—er—C, with just a dash of heavy snogging. You will laugh, you will cry, you will plead that you have a headache, but you know in the end you will have to read my book. And so you should, because as you know by now I am a naturally shy person and not one to dance around in the nuddy-pants for no good reason. Besides, it has taken me minutes . . . er . . . no, hours to write this diary for your enjoymentosity.

I do it only because I love you.

P.S.

I mean this with deepest sinceriosity.

P.P.S

Which is not an easy thing to say. You try it and see.

P.P.P.S.

Some complete fool (my vati) says that in Hamburger-a-gogo land "fanny" means bottom.

This can't possibly be true. Teeheeee heeee.

P.P.P.P.S.

It is true, isn't it?

P.P.P.P.P.S.

Do you know what "fanny" means in English?

P.P.P.P.P.P.S.

I do; however it is a secret I will take with me to the grave.

Possibly.

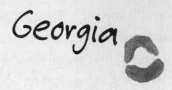

Georgia

SHE WHO LAUGHS LAST
LAUGHS THE LAUGHINGEST

sunday november 21st
my bedroom
4:05 p.m.

I've just seen a sparrow be quite literally washed off its perch on a tree. It should have had its umbrella up. But even if it had had its umbrella up it might have slipped on a bit of wet leaf and crashed into a passing squirrel. That is what life is like. Well, it's what my life is like.

Once more I am beyond the Valley of the Confused and treading lightly in the Universe of the Huge Red Bottom. What is the matter with me? I love the Sex God and he is my only one and only, but try telling that to my lips. Dave the Laugh only has to say, "You owe me a snog," and they start puckering up. Well, they can go out on their own in the future.

4:30 p.m.

I wonder why the Sex God hasn't phoned me? The Stiff Dylans got back yesterday from their recording shenanigan. Maybe he got van lag from traveling from London? Or maybe he has spoken to Tom and Tom has just happened to say, "Oh Robbie, we all went to a fish party last night and when we were playing Truth, Dare, Kiss or Promise your new girl-friend Georgia accidentally snogged Dave the Laugh. You should have been there, it was a brilliant display of red-bottomosity. You would have loved it!"

Oh God. Oh Goddy God God. I am a red-bottomed minx.

4:35 p.m.

On the other foot, no one saw me accidentally snog Dave the Laugh, so maybe it can be a secret that I will never tell. Even in my grave.

4:45 p.m.

But what if Jas has accidentally thought about something else besides her fringe and put two and two together *vis-à-vis* Dave the Laugh, and blabbed to her so-called boyfriend Tom.

She is, after all, Radio Jas.

4:50 p.m.

I would phone Jas but I am avoiding going downstairs because it's sheer bonkerosity down there. Mr. and Mrs. Across the Road have been over at least a trillion times saying, "Why? Oh why???" and, "How?" and occasionally, "I ask you, *why*? And *how*?"

At least I am not the only red-bottomed minx in the universe, or even in our street, actually. Naomi, the Across the Road's pedigreed sex kitten is pregnant, even though she has been under house arrest for ages. Well, as I have pointed out to anyone who can understand the simplest thing (i.e., me and . . . er . . . that's it), Angus cannot be blamed this time. He is merely an innocent stander-by in furry trousers.

5:05 p.m.

I was forced to go downstairs in the end to see if I could find a bit of old Weetabix to eat. Fortunately Mr. and Mrs. Across the Road had gone home. However, the Loonleader (Dad) was huffing and puffing about trying to be grown-up, twirling his ridiculous beard and adjusting his trousers and so on.

I said, "Vati, people might take you more seriously if you didn't have a tiny badger living on the
end of your chin."

I said it in a light-hearted and *très amusant*
way, but as usual he went sensationally ballistic.
He shouted, "If you can't be sensible, BE QUIET!"

Honestly, the amount of times I am told to be
quiet I might as well have not wasted my time
learning to speak.

I could have been a mime artist.

5:15 p.m.
I mimed wanting to borrow a fiver but Mutti pretended she didn't know what I wanted.

5:30 p.m.
Mr. and Mrs. Across the Road came around again
with the backup loons (Mr. and Mrs. Next Door). I
thought I had better sneak down and see what was
going on. No sign of Angus, thank the Lord. I don't
think this is his sort of party (*this* being a cat-
lynching party).

Mr. Across the Road is a bit like Vati, all shouty
and trousery and unreasonable. He said, "Look,
she's definitely, you know, in the . . . er, family way.

The question is, who is the father?"

Dad (the well-known cat molester) said, "Well, as you know, we took Angus to the vet and had him . . . er, seen to. So there is no question in that department."

Mr. Across the Road said, "And they were . . . dealt with, were they? His . . . well . . . I mean they were quite clearly . . . er, snipped?"

This was disgusting! They were talking about Angus's trouser snake addendums, which should have remained in the privacy of his trousers. They rambled on for ages, but as Gorgey Henri, our French student teacher, would say, it is *"le grand mystère de les pantaloons."*

Which reminds me, I should do some French homework so that I stay top girl in French.

5:35 p.m.

This is my froggy homework: "Unfortunately whilst staying in a *gîte*, you discover that your bicycle has been stolen. You decide to put an advert in the local paper. In French, write what your advert would say."

My advert reads, *"Merci beaucoup."*

5:45 p.m.

Still no call from SG. I am once more on the rack of love.

Phoned Jas.

"Jas."

"What?"

"Why did you say 'what' like that?"

"Like what?"

"You know, sort of . . . funny."

"I always say 'what' like that, unless I'm speaking French; then I say *'quoi?'* or if it's German I say—"

"Jas, be quiet."

"What?"

"Don't start again, let me get to my nub."

"Sorry, go on then, get to your nub."

"Well, you know when we were playing Truth, Dare, Kiss or Promise . . ."

She started laughing in an unusually annoying way, even for her—sort of snorting. Eventually she said, "It was a laugh, wasn't it? Well, apart from when you made me put all those vegetables down my knickers. There's still some soil in them."

"Jas, now or any other time is not the time to discuss your knickers. This is a situation of sheer desperadoes, possibly."

"Why?"

"Well, I haven't heard from the Sex God and I thought maybe . . ."

"Oh, didn't I tell you last night? He told me to tell you to meet him by the clock tower. He has to help his olds unpack some stuff for the shop this afternoon. Apparently they are going to sell an exciting new range of Mediterranean vine tomatoes that—"

"Jas, Jas. You are obsessed by tomatoes, that is the sadnosity of your life, but what I want to know is this: WHAT TIME did Robbie say to meet him at the clock tower?"

She was a bit huffy with me but said, "Seven thirty."

Oh, thank you, thank you. "Jas, you know I have always loved you."

She got a bit nervous then. "What do you want now? I've got my homework to do and—"

"My *petite amic*, do not *avez-vous une* spaz attack, I'm just saying that you are my number-one and tip-top pal of all time."

"Am I?"

"*Mais oui.*"

"Thanks."

"And what do you want to say to me?"

"Er . . . good-bye?"

"No, you want to say how much you love me *aussi*."

"Er . . . yes."

"Yes, what?"

"Er . . . I do."

"Say it, then."

There was a really long silence.

"Jas, are you there?"

"Hmm."

"Come on, ours is the love that dares speak its name."

"Do I have to say it?"

"Oui."

"I . . . love you."

"Thanks. See you later, lezzie." And I put down the phone. I am without a shadow of doubtosity VAIR *amusant*!

6:05 p.m.

Just enough time for a beauty mask to discourage any lurking lurkers from rearing their ugly heads, then in with the heated rollers for maximum bounceability hairwise. And finally, a body inspection for any sign of orangutanness.

6:20 p.m.

Now, a few soothing yoga postures to put me in the right frame of mind for snogging. (Although I bet Mr. Yoga says, "Avoid headstands whilst using hair rollers, as this causes pain and crashing into the wardrobe." Only he would say it in Yogese, obviously.)

Uh-oh, I feel a bit of stupid brain coming on. Think calmosity.

6:25 p.m.

Fat chance. I was just doing "down dog" when Libby burst in and started playing the drums on my bottom, singing her latest favorite, "Baa, Baa, Bag Sheet," that well-known nursery rhyme. About a bag sheet that baas. "Baa, Baa, Bag Sheet" has replaced "Mary Had a Little Lard, Its Teats Was White Azno," which she used to love best.

6:30 p.m.

No sign of Angus. The loons are still having a world summit cat meeting downstairs. I heard clinking from the kitchen, which means that the *vino tinto* is coming out.

Usual dithering attack about what to wear. It's officially dark so I need to go from day to evening wear. Also it's a bit nippy noodles.

6:40 p.m.

So I think black polo neck and leather boots . . . (and trousers of course). And for that essential hint of sophisticosity I might just have to borrow Mum's Paloma perfume. She won't mind. Unless she finds out, of course, in which case she will kill me.

6:45 p.m.

Mum has got a plastic rain hat in her bag! How sad it would be to see her in it.

Still, on the plus side it means that she is taking a more reasonable attitude towards her age. Hopefully it means that she will be throwing away her short skirts and getting sensible under-wear.

Oh, hang on, it's not a rain hat; it's a pair of emergency plastic knickknacks for Libbs. Fair enough, you can never be too careful *vis-à-vis* emergency botty trouble and my darling sister.

7:00 p.m.

Sex God, here I come!!!

   .I didn't bother to interrupt the loon party; I just left a note on the telephone table:

Dear M and V,
I hope the cat-lynching party is going well.
I have found a bit of old toast for my tea and a
Jammy Dodger to avert scurvy and gone out.
Remember me when you get a moment.
Your daughter,
Georgia
P.S. Gone to meet Jas. Be back about 9 P.M.

    Hahahaha, *très amusant*(ish).

7:30 p.m.

As I came into the main street I could see the Sex God was waiting for me by the clock tower. I ducked into a shop doorway for a bit of basooma adjusting and lip gloss application. Also, I thought I should practice saying something normal so that even if my brain fell out (as it normally does when I see him) my mouth could carry on regardless. I thought a simple approach was best. Something like, "Hi" (pause, and a bit of a sexy smile, lips parted, nostrils not flaring wildly), and then, "Long time no dig."

Cool—a bit on the eccentric side, but with no hint of brain gone on holiday to Cyprus.

I came out of my shop doorway and walked towards him. Then he saw me. Oh heavens to Betsy, Mr. Gorgeous has landed.

He said, "Hi, Georgia" in his Sex-Goddy voice and I said, "Hi, Dig."

Dig???

He laughed. "Always a bit of a tricky thing knowing what you are talking about at first, Georgia. This usually makes it better. . . ." And he got hold of my hand and pulled me towards him. Quick visit to number four on the snogging scale (kiss lasting three minutes without a breath). Yummy scrumboes and marveloso. If I could just stay attached to his mouth forever I would be happy. Dead, obviously, from starvation, but happy. Dead happy. Shut up, brain, shut up! Brain to mouth, brain to mouth: Do not under any circumstances mention being attached to his mouth forever.

The Sex God looked at me when he stopped his excellent snogging. "Did you miss me?"

"Is the Pope a vicar?" I laughed like a loon at a

loon party (i.e., A LOT).

He said, "Er no, he's not."

What are we talking about? I've lost my grip already.

Luckily SG wanted to tell me all about London and The Stiff Dylans. We went and had a cappuccino at Luigi's. As I have said many times, I don't really get cappuccinos. It's the Santa Claus mustache effect I particularly want to avoid. Actually, I have perfected a way of avoiding the foam mustache: what you do is drink the coffee like a hamster. You purse your lips really tightly and then only suck through the middle bit. Imagine you are a hamster having a cup of coffee at Hammy's, the famous hamster coffee shop. Shut up, brain, shut up!!!

The Sex God told me all about an agent-type person offering them a record deal and them staying in this groovy hotel with room service and looking around London.

I said, in between sips of hamster coffee, "Did you see the Changing of the Gourds?"

He said, "Changing of the Gourds?"

Oh no . . . I had forgotten to unpurse my hamster lips.

"Guards. The Changing of the *Guards*."

He really didn't seem to mind that he had a complete idiot for a girlfriend because he leaned over the table and kissed me. In public! In the café! Like in a French film. Everyone was looking. Of course then it meant that I had to nip off to the loos for emergency lip gloss application. It's very hard work being the girlfriend of a Sex God.

We left Luigi's and walked towards my house hand in hand. Thank goodness Robbie is tall enough for me. I don't have to do the orangutan lolloping along that I had to do with Mark Big Gob. I think that must mean that we are perfect partners, because our arms are the same length.

10:05 p.m.

When we reached the bottom of my street I said to the Sex God that it would be better if he wasn't exposed to my parents because of the Angus fandango.

He asked me what had happened and I said, "Well, in a nutshell, Naomi is pregnant and the finger of shame is pointing towards Angus, even though he is, well, you know . . . not as other men in the trouser snake addendum department."

* * *

When I eventually managed to tear myself away, SG gave me a really amazing number six with a dash of six and a quarter (tongues with lip nibbling). I managed to not fall over and I waved at him very nearly like a normal person when he went home. I like to think I handled the whole incident with sophisticosity.

That is what I like to think.

SG is meeting me on Tuesday after Stalag 14. Hurrah!

Everything is going to be fabbity fab fab and also possibly *bon*. Forevermore.

10:32 p.m.

Wrong. Vati had his usual outburst of insanity when I let myself in.

"You treat this house like a bloody hotel!"

As if. The sanitary inspectors would close the place down if they saw the state of my room. What decent hotel has a toddler pooing in its closets?

kitchen

Mutti was wearing what I think she imagines is a sexy negligee. I tried to ignore it and said, "What happened at the cat-lynching party?"

"Well, even though Mr. and Mrs. Across the Road think in principle Angus should be made into a fur handbag, they had to admit that he must be innocent of Naomi's pregnancy."

She seems to think it is all quite funny. But then this is the same woman who, when I asked if she had ever two-timed anyone, said, "Yes, it was great."

Poor Angus is an innocent victim of Naomi's red-bottomosity. This is a lesson for me about where blatant and rampant red-bottomosity can lead. I have had a lucky escape.

10:45 p.m.
I'm so exhausted by the tension of life that I barely have the energy to cleanse, tone and moisturize, let alone tape down my fringe. I am so looking forward to lying down to rest in my boudoir of love.

11:00 p.m.
Libby has got all her toys in my bed AGAIN! All their heads are lined up on my pillow. And some of her toys are quite literally just heads. I don't know exactly how beheading is going to be useful

in her future career, but she is bloody good at it.

Libbs popped out from my wardrobe in the nuddy-pants, but wearing A LOT of Mum's eye shadow, and not on her eyes.

"Heggo, Ginger, it's me!"

"I know it's you, Libbs—look, sweetheart, wouldn't you like to go in your own snuggly, cozy bed and—"

"Shut up, bad boy. Snuggle."

"Libby, I can't snuggle; you've got too many things in my bed."

"No."

"Yes."

"Get in."

"Look, let me just take something out to make a bit of room. . . . Look, I'll just take this old potato . . ."

"Grrr . . ."

"Don't bite!"

midnight
If I have to sing "Winnie Bag Pool" to Mr. Potato one more time I may have to kill myself.

Knocked on my so-called parents' bedroom door and talked to them from outside in the hall.

I've seen Dad in his pajamas before and it's not a sight for someone as artistic and sensitive as *moi*.

"Hello . . . it's me. Georgia. Remember me? Your daughter. And your other daughter, Libby, do you remember her? Two-foot-six, blond, senselessly violent? Ring any bells?"

Vati yelled, "Georgia, what is it now? Why aren't you in bed? You've got school tomorrow."

"Hello, Father, how marvelous to speak with you once again."

"Georgia, if I have to get out of bed and listen to more rubbish from you . . . well, you're not too old to smack, you know!"

Smack? Has he finally snapped? He's never smacked anyone in his life.

Mutti opened the bedroom door unexpectedly as I was leaning against it and I nearly fell into her basoomas.

She finally persuaded Libby to go into her and Dad's bed. So thankfully Libbs clanked off with Mr. Potato, Pantalitzer, Charlie Horse, scuba-diving Barbie and the rest of her "fwends."

I was just snuggling down to go off into Boboland when I heard her pitter-pattering back into my room. Oh dear God, she hadn't left something disgusting lurking in the bottom of my bed, had she?

She came right up to me and whispered in my ear, "I lobe you, Ginger. You are my very own big sister."

Awww. I put my hand on her little head. Sometimes I love her so much I feel like I would plunge into a vat of eels to save her. If she fell in one, which in her case is not as unlikely as you might think.

As a lovely good-night treat, she sucked my ear, which was not pleasant, especially as she was breathing very heavily. It was like a big slug snoring in your ear. Still, very sweet.

Ish.

12:10 a.m.
I've accidentally got to six and a half on the snogging scale with my little sister.

12:12 a.m.
The Sex God does varying pressure, like Rosie says foreign boys do. Soft, then hard, then soft. Yummy scrumboes.

Oh Robbie, how could I ever have doubted our love?

12:15 a.m.

Dave the Laugh is a bit full of himself, anyway. At the fish party he said, "You have to choose: a Sex God or me, who you can really have a laugh with."

Yes, well, I have chosen. And I have not chosen you, Mr. Dave the Laughylaugh. She who laughs last laughs the laughingest.

12:20 a.m.

He *has* got fantastic lip nibbling technique, though.

12:25 a.m.

I have gone all feverish now. I wonder where Angus is? I've not heard any wildlife being slaughtered for ages. Or the Next Doors' poodles Snowy and Whitey (also known as the Prat Poodles) yapping. He must be feeling really depressed. In a cat way.

Haunted by his lost love.

Half the cat he was, and only fading memories of his trouser snake days.

12:29 a.m.

What is it with my bed? Angus has got a perfectly

cozy cat basket, but *oh* no, he has to come in with me.

12:37 a.m.
And why does he like my head so much? It's like having a huge fur hat on.

monday november 22nd
8:25 a.m.
Everyone late for everything. When Mutti took Libby to kindy, both had hair sticking on end as if they'd been electrocuted. They should try the cat hat method—it keeps your hair very flat.

Run, run, pant, pant.

Jas and I panted up the hill to Stalag 14, past the usual assortment of Foxwood lads. They are so weird. Two passed us and started doing impressions of gorillas. Why? Then another group went by, and the biggest one, no stranger to all-overhead acne, said, "Have you got a light?"

Jas said, "No, I don't smoke," and he said, "No chance of a shag, then, I suppose?" And he and his mates went off slapping and shoving each other.

I said to Jas, "They show a distinct lack of maturiosity, but never fear, that is where I come in.

I have thought of something *très très amusant* to do with glove animal if it snows this winter."

Jas didn't say anything.

"Jas."

"What?"

"I said something *très amusant* and you *ignorez-vous*ed me. You do remember good old glove animal, don't you?"

"I know I got three bad conduct marks because you made me wear my gloves pinned over my ears like a big doggy with a beret on top."

"*Voilà*, glove animal. Anyway, I think he should make a comeback this term and liven up the stiffs."

She was pretending not to listen to me, but I knew she wanted to really. She was doing fringe fiddling. However, I resisted the temptation to slap her hand, and said, slowly so that she could understand me, "Glove animals have to wear sunglasses when it snows."

"What?"

"Is that all you can say?"

"What?"

"You are doing it to annoy me, *mon petit* pal, but I love you."

"Don't start."

"Anyway, we will have to wear sunglasses with glove animal if it snows, to prevent . . . snow blindness!!"

She didn't get it, though. I have to keep the comedy levels up at school all by myself.

assembly
9:20 a.m.

I told the rest of the ace gang about the glove animal and snow blindness hilariosity and they gave me the special Klingon salute. Then I got the ferret-eye from Hawkeye and had to pretend to listen to our large and glorious leader, Slim. Her feet are so fat that you can't actually see any shoe at all. It is only a question of time before she explodes.

Slim was rambling on about the splendor of Shakespeare's *Hamlet* as an allegory for modern times.

For once she is right. Shakespeare is not just some really old boring bloke in tights, because after all it was he who said, "To snog or not to snog, that is the question."

How true, Bill.

break

Our new pastime to fill in the long hours before we are allowed to go home is called "Let's go down the disco." Anytime any one of the ace gang says it, we all have to do manic disco dancing from the seventies (excess head shaking and arm waggling). Even if I do say it myself, it is a piece of resistance.

german

We disco danced at our desks pretty much all the way through German whilst Herr Kamyer wrote ludicrous things on the board about Herr Koch. I said to him when we were leaving class, "*Vas is der point?*"

lunchtime

Very nippy noodles shivering around outside.

I said to the gang, "What harm have we ever done to anyone that we are made to go outside in Antarctic conditions?"

Rosie, Ellen, Jools and Mabs all said, "None, we have never done anything."

But Jas, who seems to have turned into the Wise Woman of the Forest, said, "Well, there was the locust thing, and the dropping of the blodge lab skeleton onto Mr. Attwood's head and . . ."

Honestly, if I wasn't the girlfriend of a Sex God I would have had to duff Jas up, she is so ludicrously "thoughtful" these days. I think I liked her better when she was all depressed and didn't have a boyfriend. Regular snogging has brought out the worst in her.

The Bummers came by all tarted up. Jackie wears even more makeup than those scary circus people. You know, when you go to the circus and you accidentally see a trapeze artist close-up and they are orange.

Alison Bummer, unusually spot free, with just the one gigantic boil on her neck, shouted over to us as they headed for the back fields and town. "Bye-bye, little girls, have a nice time doing your lessons."

I said, "Honestly, I don't know how they get away with it. They turn up for register, hang around torturing P. Green for a bit, have fifty fags in the loos and then bog off to town at lunchtime, to see their lardy boyfriends."

We had a tutting outbreak as we shared our last snacks.

Rosie was shivering. "It is vair vair nippy noodles. I think I have got frostbite of the bum-oley."

Eventually, in between Nazi patrols led by Wet Lindsay—who may be head girl, but is still: a) wet and b) boyfriendless—we managed to sneak into the Science block.

science block
on our usual radiator

Ellen said, "It was a groovy fish party, wasn't it?"

Rosie said, "*Magnifique*. I found bits of fishfinger everywhere, though. Sven got a bit carried away."

I said, "He should be."

Jas said to Ellen, "What happened at the end? With you and Dave the Laugh, you know, when he walked you home?"

Ellen went all red and girlish. "Oh, you know."

I was prepared to leave it at that, but not old Nosey Knickers. She rambled on. "Did you and Dave the Laugh . . . do anything?"

Ellen shifted around on the knicker toasting-rack (radiator) and said, "Well . . ."

I said, "Look, if Ellen wants to have some personal space, well . . ."

But Ellen was keen as *le moutarde* (keener) to talk about my dumpee. "He did, er, walk me home and . . ."

The ace gang were all agog as two gogs, apart from me. I was ungogged. In fact, I was doing my impression of a cucumber (and no, I do not mean I was lying on some salad . . . I mean I was being cool).

They all said, "Yes . . . AND???"

"Well, he, you know, well, he, well . . ."

God's shortie pajamas, I was going to be a hundred and fifty years old at this rate.

Ellen went red and started playing with her piggies (very annoying) and went on. "It was cool, actually. We got, well, we sort of got to number three and a bit."

What is "sort of number three and a bit" on the snogging scale? Perhaps I should "sort of" give her a good slapping to make her talk some sense. But no, no, no, why did I care? I was a mirage of glaciosity.

As the bell went for resumption of abnormal cruelty (Maths), Ellen said to me, "Dave does this really groovy thing, it's like, er . . . lip nibbling."

He had nip libbled with her!! The bloody snake

in the tight blue jeans had nip libbled her. How dare he??

Ellen was rambling on. "We should add lip nibbling to our snogging scale."

Jas said, "We already have, it's six and a quarter."

Ellen said to Jas, "Oh, have you done lip nibbling, then? With Tom?"

Jas went off into the dreamworld that she calls her brain. "No, because Tom really respects me, and knows that I want to be a prefect, but Georgia has done it. And she's done ear snogging."

Then they all started. "Is that what the Sex God does?" "Does it make you go deaf?" and so on. Triple *merde*.

As we went into Maths, Ellen said, "You know when we played that game and you were supposed to snog Dave, well . . . did you?"

I went, "Hahahahahahahahahahaha." Like a hyena in a skirt. And that seemed to satisfy her.

Once again I am in a state of confusiosity. In fact, I can feel my bottom throbbing again when I get a picture of Dave the Laugh nibbling my lips.

And now Ellen's.

He is a serial nip libbler. I am better off without him.

french

Mon Dieu. Fabulosity all round. We are going on a school trip to *le* gay Paree next term. We were yelling, *"Zut alors!"* and *"Mon Dieu!"* and *"Magnifique!"* until Madame Slack threw a complete nervy strop. The fabby news is that Gorgey Henri is going to take us. The unfabby news is that Madame Slack and Herr Kamyer, dithering champion for the German nation, are also going. Still, that will be a bit of light relief. Herr Kamyer is almost bound to fall in the Seine at some time over the weekend.

I wrote a note to Rosie: "How much do you bet we can do the famous 'Taking a souvenir photograph' of Herr Kamyer on the banks of the Seine and he falls in when we say, 'Just step back a bit, Herr Kamyer, I haven't quite got your *lederhosen* in yet'?"

4:20 p.m.

Walking home with Jas. I was trying to use her as a windbreak, but she kept dodging away from me.

She is unusually full of selfishosity for someone who loves me.

I said, "Thank Cliff Richard's Y-fronts that nobody knows about my accidental snogging incident."

"What snogging incident?"

"I can't tell you. It's a secret I'm taking to my grave."

Oh *sacré bleu*. What is the matter with Jas (besides the obvious)?

When I accidentally told her my secret that I will never tell, even in my grave, she went on and on about how I should be ashamed. She is so annoyingly good, like Mother Teresa with a crap fringe.

home

Mutti in an unusually good mood. She had even bought a pie for us on the way home. Scarily like a real mum—apart from the ludicrously short skirt. She's not going to tell me that I'm going to have another little brother or sister, is she?

Still, I can't think of everyone else. I am not God. I have enough to worry about thinking about myself.

8:00 p.m.

I am so worried about school tomorrow. I have so much to do.

8:10 p.m.

I can do my nails and foundation and eye stuff during R.E.—Miss Wilson won't notice, as she will be sadly rambling on about the Dalai Lama or yaks or whatever it is she does talk about. But I suppose even she might notice if I took my curling tongs into class. I'll have to do my hair at lunchtime and hope the Bummers don't decide to put their chewing gum in it for a laugh.

looking out of my bedroom window

I'm amazed to see Naomi the sex kitten lounging around on the roof of our shed, showing off her fat tummy. She has got very little shame for an illegitimate bride. Angus is in the garden below her, blinded by his love. Well, actually he's mostly blinded by the dirt he's digging up. He's got a huge bone from somewhere and he's burying it. Maybe for a midnight snack. He doesn't really seem to understand that he is not a dog. I may have to do some diagrams of mice for him to explain it.

221

I went downstairs to the kitchen to find M and V absolutely all over each other. It's like living in a porn movie to be in our house. Honestly, isn't she sick of him yet? (I am.) He's been back about a month; surely by now they must be discussing divorce.

I said, "Erlack," in a caring way to let them know I was there. But my finer feelings make no difference to the elderly snoggers. They just started giggling, like . . . giggling elderly snoggers.

I said, "Vati, I don't want to be the person responsible for one of your unreasonable outbursts of rage, but—"

He said, "OK, as I am in a good mood you can have a fiver, because you did so well on your French test."

I was quite literally gobsmacked. For a second. Then I grabbed the fiver.

"Er, thanks . . . but, erm, I feel, in all fairness to you, I should let you know that Naomi is on our shed roof and that Angus is not a million miles away from her. In fact, as I left my room, he was licking her bottom."

No one went ballisticisimus, because apparently Mr. and Mrs. Across the Road have worked out that the pedigreed boy cat they had over to visit with Naomi must have had more than a few fishy snacks with her.

Vati said, "Either that or she is having a virgin birth."

Hey, she might be! She might be having a little furry Baby Jesus (lots of them, in fact). She is due to give birth at Christmas, after all. And God works in mysterious ways, as everyone knows.

I said to Jas on the phone, "It makes you think, doesn't it?"

She was all weird and huffy. "No, what makes me think is this: How come some people, naming no names, but you, Georgia, can tell such porkies to their so-called friends?"

She was rambling on about Ellen and Dave the Laugh, of course.

I said with deep meaningosity, "Jas, she who casts the first stone has to cast the logs out of her own knickers first."

That made her think. Then she said, "What in the name of frankincense are you talking about?"

I had to admit she had me there.

Her trouble is that she has never done anything adventurous, her bottom has never glowed with the red light of ... er ... red-bottomosity.

I said to her, "Jas, Jas, my little nincompoop, I didn't MEAN to snog Dave the Laugh. It was an accident. I am a teenager and I can't always control my bits and pieces."

"What bits and pieces?"

"Well, you know, I have very little control over my nunga-nungas, for instance ... and at the fish party with Dave my lips just sort of puckered up."

"I'm a teenager and I can control my bits and pieces."

"What about your fringe?"

"That is not the same as snogging someone else's boyfriend."

"You are getting very set in your ways, Jas."

"I am not."

"Well, name an interesting thing that you and Tom have done lately."

"We've done loads of really interesting, crazy things."

"Like what? And don't tell me about collecting frog spawn."

"Well, Tom is going to do ecology and so on. . . . Do you know we found some badger footprints in the park near—"

"Jas, I said name an interesting thing that you and Tom have done lately, not something about badgers."

But she had gone off into the twilight world of her brain. "Tom gave me a love bite."

"Non."

"Oui."

"I've never seen it."

"I know."

"Where is it?"

"On my big toe."

9:00 p.m.

I am worried that in my capacity as the Sex God's girlfriend I may have to give a celebrity interview about my life and Jas will have to come on it. And she will talk rubbish. And perhaps show her love bite. Or knickers.

9:15 p.m.

Still, it has taken her mind off the Dave the Laugh fiasco.

I will have an early night to prepare myself for heavy snogging duties. I want to look all gorgey and marvy for SG and not have those weird little piggy eyes that I get sometimes when I have been kept awake all night by loons (Angus and Libby). Mutti has let Libbs sleep in the cat basket with Angus tonight, so I am safe.

9:35 p.m.
Ah . . . very nice and cozy in bed, although I am having to sleep sitting up because I have rollers in my hair for optimum bounceability.

9:40 p.m.
Phone rang. Vati yelled, "Georgia, another one of your little mates on the phone. You'd better hurry, I think it's an emergency. She might have run out of lip gloss."

Vair vair vair *amusant*, Vati.

As I came down the stairs, he said, "We mean no harm, take us to your leader," because of my hair rollers. He really is in an alarmingly good mood.

It was Ellen. Uh-oh. I hoped she couldn't detect my red minxiness.

"Georgia, can I ask you something?"

"Er, like what?"

"Well, you know Dave the Laugh?"

DID I KNOW DAVE THE LAUGH???!!!

I sounded a bit vague. "I know Dave the woman, but Dave the Laugh . . . ? Oh er, Dave the Laugh . . . yes, what about him?"

"Well, you know I really think he's groovy and so on and he did the lip nibbling thing, and that was, you know, quite groovy and not, you know, ungroovy . . . and how I have thought he is quite groovy for a long time and lip nibbling would, like, mean he thought I was groovy as well . . ."

(It was going to be the twenty-second century at this rate by the time she got round to telling me what she was on about.)

"Well, anyway, it's nearly Tuesday."

"Yes, and . . . ?"

"Well, he hasn't çalled me yet," she went on. "Well, what should I do?"

"Did he say he'd call?" (Not that I am remotely interested in what my ex-snoggees say. I am just being a great pal.)

"Not exactly."

"What did he say exactly?"

"He said, 'I'm away laughing on a fast camel—see you later.'"

"Oh."

"What?"

"It's the old 'see you later' thing, isn't it?"

"You mean it might be see you later, as in see you later not *see* you later?"

"Exactamondo."

She went on and on about Dave the L and about how surely he wouldn't nip libble her if he didn't like her, etc., etc. . . . I was so tired I tried to lie down on the floor, but couldn't because of my rollers. Good Lord, what am I? The Oracle of Delphinium?

Eventually she rang off.

10:00 p.m.

What if Ellen finds out about me and Dave the Laugh? Will she still like me and realize that it is just one of those things? Or will she beat me to within an inch of my life?

How would I feel if the boot was on the other cheek?

I wish I wasn't so caring and empathetic. As Hawkeye said in English, I have a very vivid imagination.

10:15 p.m.

Actually what she said was that I had a "hideous"

imagination. But she is just jealous because she has no life to speak of (apart from torturing us).

10:40 p.m.
My nose feels very heavy. I'd better have a look at it in case there is a lurking lurker situation.

10:47 p.m.
Hmm. I can't see anything. It doesn't get any smaller, though. I must make sure I always suck it in when I see the Sex God full on.

10:55 p.m.
On the plus side, my nungas don't seem any more sticky-out than they are normally. Perhaps they have stopped growing. Or maybe they are on Christmas vacation, before they burst (quite literally) into life in spring.

11:00 p.m.
I'll just give them a quick measure.

11:05 p.m.
Sacré bloody *bleu* and also *mon Dieu*!! They measure thirty-eight inches!! That is more than a yard. There

must be something wrong with the tape measure.

11:10 p.m.
I've done it again and it's still the same. It amazes me that I can lumber around at all. It's like carrying two small people around with me.

I'm really worried now. I wish there was someone I could talk to about this sort of thing. I know there is an unseen power at work of which we have little comprehension, but I don't really feel I can consult with Jesus about my basoomas.

Or Buddha.

Anyway, I don't want to offend Buddha and so on, just in case He exists, which I am sure He does . . . but . . . I have seen some statues of Buddha, and frankly his nunga-nungas are not small either.

midnight
When I was in M&S the other Saturday, I saw a sign that said they had a breast measuring service (top job . . . not). Maybe I should get properly measured by a basooma professional and learn the truth about my condition(s).

1:00 a.m.

Angus is on the road to recovery. I can hear him serenading the Prat Poodles with a medley of his latest hits: "Yowl!" and "Yowl 2: The Remix."

I got up to look. He is so brave in the face of his pain. I really love him, even if he has destroyed half my tights. He could have just given in, but no, there he was, biffing the Prat Poodles like normal. Naomi was parading up and down on the Across the Roads' windowsill, sticking her bottom in the air and so on. She is an awful minx. She is making a mockery of a sham of her so-called love for Angus. It's like in that old crap song where the bloke is wounded in the Vietnam War and his wife goes off with other men because he can't get out of his wheelchair. He sings, "Ru-beeee, don't take your love to town."

That is what Angus would sing. "Naom-eeeee, don't take your love to town." If he could sing. Or speak. And had a wheelchair.

SCHOOL PANTO FIASCO
(A.K.A. COMPLETE PRATS IN TIGHTS)

tuesday november 23rd
breakfast

Dad was singing, "Sex bomb, sex bomb, I'm a sex bomb," and doing hip thrusts round the kitchen. He'll end up in casualty again if he's not careful. He was being all interested in me as well. Red alert, red alert!

He gave me a hug (!) and said, "I thought we'd all go to the cinema tonight. My treat."

I said, "Fantastic!" He thought I meant it and went off happily to flood people's homes or whatever it is he does at the Water Board.

I said to Mum, who was trying to get all the porridge out of Libby's hair before she went off to kindergarten, "Mum, I can't go to the cinema tonight, I . . . I've got to stay behind and help with . . . the school panto."

She didn't even look up. "I didn't know you were in it."

"I'm not, I'm just, er, helping backstage. 'Bye, Mutti. 'Byeeee, Bibbet."

"'Bye-bye, Gingey, kiss Mr. Cheese bye-bye."

It was disgusting kissing Mr. Cheese. (Mr. Cheese is a bit of old Edam in a hat.) Not as disgusting as it will be at the end of the day when Libby brings him home again from playschool. With a bit of luck Mr. Cheese will be eaten by one of Libby's little pals.

I had a look at my pocket mirror as I walked round to Jas's place. Eight out of ten on the hair bounceability front. I am sooo excited. I love the Sex God and it will be beyond fabulosity and into the Valley of Marv when we go on tour to America. I think I could easily write song lyrics myself.

I said that to Jas as we walked to school. "Thank you, ladies and gentlemen, this one is called 'Sex God' and it goes like this: 'Oh, Robbie, you're the one for me, with your dark blue eyes and your . . .'"

I had a bit of writer's block then and I said to Jas, "What rhymes with 'me'?"

"What about 'two-timer'? Or 'crap mate'?"

"Jas, don't start again . . . oh hang on, I know: 'You're the one for me, with your dark blue eyes and your . . . snogability!!!' I am clearly a genius."

I put my arm round Jas in my happinosity and said, "You can show me your love bite when we get to Stalag 14."

She went a bit red and said, "OK, but don't tell anyone else about it." Which is ironic coming from Radio Jas.

assembly
Slim really on tip-top boring form this morning.

She bored us beyond the Valley of the Dim and into the twilight world of the Elderly Mad.

Speaking of which, we saw Elvis Attwood tapping at pipes with his hammer as we went out.

I said to him, "I think you should receive a knighthood, Mr. Attwood, for your services to caretaking. Surely you of all people deserve to be hit over the shoulders with an old sword."

10:00 a.m.
What IS it with this place???!!! Rosie and I have got bad conduct marks AND have to stay behind and help with *Peter Pan* every night this week after school. I cannot believe it! Just because we have

naturally high spirits and *joie de vivre*. (And also got caught doing our "Let's go down the disco" dance to "There Is a Green Hill Far Away" in Assembly.)

It is so obviously hilarious. And not at all "indicative of stupendous childishness," as Hawkeye said.

10:30 a.m.

Perhaps I am Spawn of the Devil in a skirt and have the third eye. No, I mean the second whatsit . . . sight. Because I told Mum that I was staying behind to help with *Peter Pan*, even though I wasn't, and now I am. I may have special powers.

11:00 a.m.

No, I haven't got special powers. I tried for about a million years to make the wall clock fall onto Hawkeye's head, but it just gave me a very bad headache.

in the loos

I said to Jas, "For once in the entire existence of humankind my hair has got bounceability and whatsit and I am on detention."

She said, "Well, you shouldn't be so silly."

What is silly about disco dancing?

She wanted to show me her love bite, but I couldn't summon up any interest.

r.e.

Miss Wilson has written on the board: "Relationships—what are the ingredients?"

Good Lord, she would be the last to know, and also I don't think I have ever seen anyone over the age of six months wearing a pink smock, apart from her. Has she really not got one single mate who would have said to her, "Put the smock in the bin and we will never mention it again"?

I wonder if I should make Naomi a little pregnancy smock. In the spirit of Christmas?

Rosie has made some dreadlocks for her pencil and stuck them on to the end of it. She wrote me a note: "As a Rastafarian he has strong views on religious freedom."

I wrote back: "It's a pencil, you fool."

And she wrote: "That is what makes it even more remarkable."

But we are only trying to cheer ourselves up because of the *Peter Pan* fiasco.

What am I going to do about the Sex God? He is supposed to meet me after school. I wrote to Jas: "If I tell SG I have been given detention duties helping complete prats into tights he will think I am a silly little schoolgirl."

She wrote back: "You ARE a silly little schoolgirl."

Cheers, thanks a lot. Good night.

last bell
3:50 p.m.

I ran down the corridor to the cloakrooms and threw myself in front of the mirror. This was my plan: emergency makeup, dash to the school gates, quick snog, explain to Robbie about my unfair incarceration by the Nazis (but not exactly mention the "Let's go down the disco" incident, in case it was construed as a bit on the childish side), another quick snog, possibly number four, then quick as a bunny back to the main hall before ten past four.

Pant, pant. *Alors, alors.* Mascara, lippy, lip gloss, rolly-over skirt, bouncey hair, bouncey hair.

Right. Ready for the Sex God in five minutes and thirty seconds. A new world record.

When I stepped out into the corridor, I walked straight into Hawkeye lurking like a piranha. Oh, *Scheissenhausen*.

She loomed over me. "Georgia, you are helping with the Christmas entertainment. Why does that require mascara? Remove it and go along to the main hall NOW!"

I slunk back in the loos. This called for the famous getting-out-through-the-loo-window-and-jumping-onto-the-back-field routine. I almost decapitated two First Years getting out of the window, but I made it. I ran along the back field and then down fag-ash alleyway (so called because it is where the Bummers hang out) that runs between the Science block and . . . there he was, waiting for me. Sex God unleashed. He looked amazingly groovy. All the girls streaming out of the gates were eyeballing him as they went by. He said hi to Ali King and she practically evaporated on the spot.

After a quick suck in of the nostrils I sauntered out with an attractive air of casualosity and said, "Hi."

Blimey, I'd managed to say something normal to him. That was a turn up for *les livres*. He smiled his smile and said, "Hi."

He put his hand through my hair (feeling its incredible bounceability, probably) and leaned down and kissed me. Wow. I knew that everyone walking past us was looking, but I had my eyes closed. I did try slightly opening my eyes, but I could only see a big sort of blurry pink thing, which gave me a bit of a turn, until I realized it was my nose really close up.

4:15 p.m.

Probably because I am such a kind and caring person, Jesus has decided to take me for His sunbeam by letting me off the hook. The Sex God told me that he had to go and have a conference call with some record people from Hamburger-a-gogo land and so he couldn't see me tonight.

I feel a mixture of sadnosity and reliefosity, with just a hint of peckishness.

4:30 p.m.

Rosie and I have the ridiculously sad task of helping the "cast" of *Peter Pan* into their costumes and sorting out the props. We are in charge of the "dressing room," or P.E. changing room, as the

239

normal might call it. We have to hang everything up in order and on different pegs, whilst Miss Stamp dashes about "supervising."

Wet Lindsay has got the leading part of Peter in *Peter Pan*, which I think is unfortunate casting, because she has to wear a green tunic and tights. She has got astonishingly sticklike legs. Also, for no good reason (other than I stole her boyfriend), she has taken against me. She wouldn't have me as her little helper, so Rosie has to help her into her tights and so on. (Erlack.) Tragic Kate is Wendy in the show and I have to help her into her duff wig with plaits.

Hours of boredom stretch ahead. Will I never be free of this hellhole?

5:10 p.m.
The SG will be talking to people in Hamburger-a-gogo land now.

6:00 p.m.
I said to Rosie, "Do you and Sven talk a lot?"

Rosie thought a bit. "Sven talks a lot."

"What about?"

"I haven't got the faintest idea. He's not, as you

know, English. Reindeer, possibly."

"Don't you mind that all you do is snog?"

"No."

8:00 p.m.

Home again, in the sanctity of my luurve boudoir.

Mon Dieu, how boring was the rehearsal? It was almost as boring as Dad's stories about Kiwi-a-gogo land. Still, home at last and my bedroom is a Libby-free zone!

I haven't listened to my dolphin CD for a bit. I think I will put it on and meditate on my inner me.

8:10 p.m.

I don't know who it is that thinks dolphins are soothing. It's just squeak squeaky squeak.

8:15 p.m.

I do feel a bit sorry for them, though, because they get all those depressed people insisting on swimming with them. It might cheer up the depressed people, but I bet it depresses the arse off the dolphins. They just want to go out with their mates for a laugh and no sooner do they start playing Chase the Cod or whatever, than all these miserable types come and hang around stroking their snouts and crying.

Or am I being a bit harsh?

8:35 p.m.
Everyone out as usual, round at Uncle Eddie's. God it's boring being by yourself. I may be forced to do my blodge homework.

9:00 p.m.
Rang Jas.

"Jas."

"Quoi?"

"What are you doing?"

"Blodge homework."

"Moi aussi. Are you drawing a hydra?"

"Oui."

"Have you drawn its wafting tentacles yet?"

"Non."

"I have. Also I have drawn in some cheesy whatsits being wafted in by its tentacles."

"Hydras don't eat cheesy whatsits. They are pond life."

"That's a bit rude, Jas."

"It isn't—it's a biological fact."

"OK, Jas, but have you considered this? Perhaps hydras don't eat cheesy whatsits because no one has had the GOOD MANNERS to go down to the pond and offer them round! Don't hydras deserve to be treated like human beings?"

9:15 p.m.
Oh, I am so bored!!

In my *Don't Sweat the Small Stuff for Teens* it says: "Do something interesting and useful for others."

9:30 p.m.
I can get forty-eight little plaits in my hair.

9:35 p.m.
It makes me look like a complete prat, though.

9:40 p.m.
Phone rang!!

"Georgia."

Yes and three times yes!!! It was Robbie.

The record company has done a deal with a big American company and they want The Stiff Dylans to go over there on tour. Wow.

Rang Jas and told her.

"What do you think I should wear to go on tour? You can never go wrong in black, can you?"

"Your dad will never in a million trillion years let you go to America on tour with a band."

"You will see, my little pal."

10:00 p.m.

I will miss my ace gang when I go off with the Sex God to America.

Mutti, Vati and Libbs all came home. Libbs said, "Heggo, Gingey," and put her little arms up for me to lift her up. There was the usual wrestling match trying to get her into her own bed but no spitting, thank goodness.

I will really miss her when I go on tour.

10:15 p.m.

I went into the living room to talk to my dear old vati. I feel quite fond of him now I won't be seeing him for much longer. He was lolling on the sofa watching TV, twirling his beard.

"Dad."

"Hmm."

"Er . . . you know . . . if I had a really good, life-changing experience offered to me, well . . . would you let me go?"

He said, "What fool has offered to adopt you?" And laughed like a bearded loon (which he is).

I went on with great dignosity. "Yes, very funny, Dad. Anyway, say I was invited to America—could I go?"

"No."

"Well, could I go to Paris on the school trip, then?"

"I thought you hated Edith Piaf."

"I do, but I *aime* very very much the other French people."

Anyway, the long and the long of it is that I can go on the Paris trip. I gave Dad a little kiss on his cheek when he said yes, and he looked like his head was going to fall off with surprise. But I can be a very kind and caring person, especially if I am about three thousand miles away in a different country.

midnight

But this is only one string in my mistress plan. First Paris, France, and then Paris, Texas!!!

Howdy Hamburger-a-gogo types!!

friday november 26th

french

We've all signed up to go on the French trip to *le gay Paree*, apart from the Bummers (hurrah) and Nauseating P. Green and ADM (Astonishingly Dim Monica). P. Green and ADM are not allowed to go because their mums are worried about the drinking water being polluted in France, and also that they might lose their glasses. Which I think would be a plus.

Gorgey Henri was talking about the trip and sitting on his desk. Phwoar. I know that I am putting my red bottom aside with a firm hand but he is very groovy-looking.

When Gorgey Henri said, "I will show you . . . how you say . . . my EVERYTHING in Paris," I said, "Ooer," which made Rosie laugh uncontrollably for about five minutes.

4:20 p.m.

Forced to stay behind again to help with the *Peter Pan* fiasco. I think it's a crime against humanity to have to look at Wet Lindsay's stick legs night after night. But can I explain that to lesbian of the modern world Miss Stamp? No. She is in a fever of excitement, adjusting costumes, and sending Nana the dog (a.k.a. Pamela Green) scampering around. P. Green is alarmingly good as a dog. I may teach her some amusing tricks.

backstage
6:00 p.m.
Backstage, rifling through the props box, because Tinker Bell (played by Melanie Andrews, 48DD in the basooma department) broke her wand when Nana leapt up at her by mistake.

I said to Rosie, as we rummaged around trying to find another one, "Do you think it's awfully wise to let Melanie Andrews loose on stage?"

Rosie said, "No, I don't. She's not small, is she? What if her enormous basoomas make her topple over and she kills a first former?"

I said, "I think in our capacity of backstage staff we should ban her on health and safety grounds."

tuesday november 30th
The Stiff Dylans are rehearsing every night. Robbie said I should come along and listen at the weekend when they are doing their new set. I think

I should take an interest in my new life. I could make some suggestions about lyrics and so on.

saturday december 4th

Sven and the lads have organized a nature ramble tomorrow afternoon. I asked Rosie, "What does that mean?"

"Well, you know, we ramble off to the park and then we snog."

I can't go, though, because I am going to go to rehearsal with The Stiff Dylans. They have a mini-tour of Scotland and Wales just after Chrimbo. Then they will be cutting their new album. Man. That is not what the album is called. That is just what pop-type people say.

I rang Jas to tell her. "The Stiff Dylans are cutting a new album, man."

"Why is it called *Man*?"

Sometimes when I talk to Jas I can feel the will to live ebbing away.

sunday december 5th

Remind me never to go to a band rehearsal again. It is soooooo boring watching other people do stuff. And talking about themselves. And me not being in it. I just sat at the back and nodded my head for about a million years.

Also, I believe the rest of the lads think I'm a bit weird. I don't know why. I have always been the height of sophisticosity around them. Well, apart from when Dom, the drummer, asked me what I was going to do at college and I said, "Backup dancing."

Oh and also when I danced around at a gig in front of Dom's dad because I thought he was an American talent spotter, but he wasn't. He was just Dom's dad waiting to help them pack up. And he thought that I was trying to get off with him.

But apart from those two minor hiccups I have been sophisticosity all round, I like to think.

Anyway, here is a brief resume of my glorious night:

a) nodded my head for a million years
b) sat on a drum kit in the van on the way home
c) lost my balance and put my foot through the bass drum
d) had to be dropped off first because I had to be in by ten o'clock on a school night

Double *merde*.

At least when I have to do the boring old panto stuff I can have a bit of artistic license with Rosie.

I wonder how the nature snog went. I suppose Dave the Laugh went with Ellen.

I don't think that The Stiff Dylans think I am full of maturiosity. I think they think I am the Yoko Ono of the band and that I will split them up.

monday december 6th

I can't believe the poo-osity of my life. Hawkeye said that as "a special treat" Rosie and I could help backstage at the panto every night until the final performance.

Hawkeye is without a doubt a sadist and ex–prison warden. And probably a man.

panto rehearsals

I taught Nauseating P. Green to catch a mini Mars in her mouth from four feet. She is taking this dog business alarmingly seriously. She even brought me a stick, but as I said to Rosie, "I draw the line at tickling her tummy."

Wet Lindsay was trying to take her tights off by herself when she lost her balance and nearly crashed into the sanitary towel dispenser. It really cheered me up. She got the mega-hump when I was laughing and doing my impression of her crashing about stuck in a pair of tights. Which was vair vair amusing but old Tiny Forehead didn't think so. After calling me "a pathetic little twit" she stomped off into a stall to get changed.

However, as any fool knows, I am the mistress of invention and with the aid of my compact mirror I was able to look under the door of the stall. I made Rosie come and have a look in the mirror because she didn't believe that Wet Lindsay wears a thong in real life. But she had to believe the evidence of her own peepers when she saw the thong nestling in Wet Lindsay's bum-oley. RoRo had to have a reviving chewy fruit before she could speak again. Then she said, "I am very sensitive, you know. That sort of thing may ruin my chances of becoming a vet."

So all is well that ends well.

10:00 p.m.

Our house had been a relatively loon-free zone, but it was too good to last. Uncle Eddie was round tonight. As usual, he came balding into my room with one of his hilarious "jokes." He said,

"Can a cross-eyed teacher control her pupils?" And looned off laughing like a bald loon.

10:15 p.m.
Robbie phoned and he didn't mention the bass drum incident, which is a plus. He said, "What have you been up to, sex kitty?"

Prrrrrrrrrrrrrrrr!!!!

midnight
I do feel like a bit of a French Resistance person, though, because I only see Robbie sort of in secret. There is no normal stuff with him. I said that to Rosie, and she said, "What do you call normal?"

"Well, you and Sven, you see each other all the time and you must do normal stuff."

She just looked at me. "Have you met Sven?"

Hmmm, she has a point. Jas and Tom do normal stuff, though. In fact, they act like they have been married for about a trillion years. I'm not saying I want to be as boring as Jas and Tom—collecting frog spawn and doing homework together is too tragic for words. But what do you do with Sex Gods? Besides snog and worship them, I mean.

thursday december 9th

Opening night of the panto. When the audience started clapping to prove they believed in fairies, Tinker Bell flew out of control and crashed against the back piece of scenery, which fell over to reveal Miss Stamp having a fag. Very funny indeed, I thought.

And much less boring than watching Peter Pan prancing around in green tights.

9:50 p.m.

Something quite alarming happened tonight. I was just sneaking off from the dressing room when Nauseating P. Green came bounding along, still with her dog ears on. And she had her mum, who is not unblessed in the huge glasses department, with her. They were both blinking at me and following me out of the door. Like two giant goldfish in skirts.

P. Green said, "I told Mum that you were the one who really helped me with my dog tricks."

Mrs. Nauseating P. Green said, "It's really nice that Pamela and you are such good friends. Would you like to come round to our house on Christmas Eve? We do round robin storytelling and dress up."

253

I said, "Hrrmmmmm . . . Oh, is that the time, I must dash!" And made a desperate bid for freedom.

As we walked home, Rosie said, "She loves you very very much. You are her bestest pal." Good grief.

friday december 10th

Christmas frenzy mounting. I put some tinsel around my sports knickers for that little festive touch in P.E. Miss Stamp for once did not have a nervy spaz, which was a bit scary. Things soon got back to normal in Latin, though, because Hawkeye made us take the false snow (cotton wool) off our heads.

wednesday december 15th

last day of term

Hurrah!!! Thank you, thank you, Baby Jesus!!! Free, free at last!

last german lesson

We were all a bit on the hysterical side. I think the teachers must have been out for a pre-Christmas beverage, if you know what I mean, because Herr Kamyer told us an incomprehensible joke about a Swiss cheese (please don't even ask) and then laughed for about forty years. AND as we were going down the corridor we bumped into Gorgey Henri.

"Merry *Noël*," I said to him and he kissed my cheek and said, "*Merci, au revoir.* I look forward to 'aving you all again in the New Year."

Which made us apopletic with laughter. I thought I might have to throw a bucket of cold water over Rosie and Jools.

Henri smiled at us and said, "You are so crazee." Then he walked off in his groovy gravy jeans.

"Gorgey Henri is quite literally . . . gorgey," I said. "He is yummy scrumboes and also . . ."

Rosie said, "Scrummy yumboes?"

"*Mais oui.*"

6:30 p.m.

Last night of the panto. *Mucho excitemondo* (not).

Miss Stamp bought Coca-Cola and cakes for the cast as an end-of-show party thing. Unfortunately the little cakes were saying, "Eat me, eat me, you know you want to," and so Rosie and I were enticed by them. We only ate a few, but

Hawkeye noticed and now we are banned from the party. *Quel dommage* (not).

8:00 p.m.
Peter and the rest of the ridiculous Lost Boys are poncing around on stage. I may have to eat myself soon, I am so bored. I wonder where the Sex God is now? And if he is thinking about me. I wonder if he thinks about me as many times a minute as I think about him.

I've had to pretend that I am in training for hockey every night this week. Somehow, even though I believe that the only good relationship is an open and honest one, I can't bring myself to tell him that I am helping people into tights.

8:10 p.m.
Rosie found something *très très magnifique* in a props basket at the back of the store cupboard— theatrical fur. Fake fur that you stick on with a special glue and you can make beards and sideburns and so on with it.

8:25 p.m.
Rosie and I have to be on duty at the side of the

stage, handing things over to Wendy and Peter and Captain Hook and so on when they come off. They are all sooo excited. And theatrical. Wet Lindsay just shouts orders like "Sword!" or "Panstick!" if she has to have her stupid shiny forehead touched up. It's VERY annoying, and boring beyond even the Valley of Boredom.

But now we have introduced the theatrical fur into the proceedings. Every time one of us has to go and get something from backstage we stick on a bit of theatrical fur, but just carry on doing our tasks as normal.

8:45 p.m.

At first we had a sort of six o'clock shadow effect, but by the final curtain we had entered properly into the spirit of hairiness. Rosie had big furry hands and sideburns and I had one huge eyebrow right across my forehead. And no one noticed!!! Too busy admiring themselves to notice that two teenage werewolves were handing them their props. Very very funny.

Rosie and I were nearly dead from laughing by the time the curtain came down. The cast went out front to talk to their parents, still in their ridiculous outfits, even Nana. In fact, if I was P. Green's mum I would be worried about ever getting her out of her dog costume.

Whilst they did that we sneaked off home. I have rarely seen anything as funny as Rosie in her school uniform and beret with HUGE sidies and furry hands.

Luckily I managed to skedaddle home without seeing anyone I knew.

bed

It took me about a year to get my eyebrow off. In the end I had to use nail polish remover. I've practically removed my forehead.

I must get plenty of beauty sleep and regrow my forehead because I am seeing my boyfriend this weekend. It's only one hundred and eighty hours until he leaves for the Isle of Man with his family for Christmas. And fifty-six of those will be spent sleeping. Unless Libby visits my bed.

saturday december 18th

churchill square

Out with the ace gang shopping for Chrimbo presents and lurking around hoping to bump into lads. We were just having a rest on a wall when the Bummers came sauntering past. Jackie Bummer was dressed completely in leather. Leather skirt, jacket, boots, coat . . . all of it nicked, I bet. She is like a walking crime wave. As a decent citizen I should turn her over to the Old Bill; however, I have my principles and I will never be a snitcher. Especially as snitchers can end up on the wrong end of a duffing incident.

Jackie looked at us like we were snot on legs and said, "Have to dash, little girls, only six shoplifting days till Christmas."

God, they are soooo common and tarty.

4:00 p.m.

At home with my thoughtful Chrimboli gift. I hope Dad appreciates the ENORMOUS lengths I went to to get him some new socks. I had to wander around very old people's shops for ages to find anything suitable.

5:00 p.m.

I wonder why I haven't heard from SG yet? I've got eight outfits on standby duty and have applied undercoat foundation but it's very tense-making not knowing what is going on.

living room

Mutti and Vati wrestling about tickling each other. Vati had a very alarming pair of jogging trousers on. I suppose it's nice that they are so affectionate, but I don't like to think of certain people snogging. The Queen, for instance. Imagine the Queen getting to number seven with Prince Philip . . . erlack. Or Herr Kamyer with Hawkeye . . . erlack, erlack! Or Mr. and Mrs. Next Door in the nuddy-pants.

I must stop this and think of something normal. I might have to go and rub myself with salt to get myself clean again.

Mutti said, "Oh, by the way, when you were in town that really good-looking boy came round. What's his name?"

My face had gone all rigid.

Mutti went on. "You know, the older Jennings boy . . . he's in that band you go to see . . . is it The Bob Wilsons or something?"

The Bob Wilsons!!! OhmyGod, ohmyGod. I must go to my room immediately.

As I left the room Mutti said, "I thought he was really tasty. He said would you ring him."

Then Vati got hold of her and he was sort of tickling her with his beard and growling like a lion in jogging trousers.

bedroom

The Sex God has seen my dad's beard and trousers. He has been exposed to my family. He might even have spoken to Libby. She may have mentioned poo. Will he ever forgive me?

Phoned the Sex God.

"Hi."

"Er, Robbie, I'm really, really, really sorry about my parents, they're just . . . you know . . . I'm really sorry."

He laughed. "Your dad is quite cool."

"Pardon?"

sunday december 19th

Went to band rehearsal again. I have perfected the art of head-nodding and doing my nails at the same time. Dom was looking at me a bit funny, especially as he caught me nodding along to the music when they weren't actually playing any. But at least he has been able to mend his drum. You can still see a slight foot shape in it, though, which in my opinion adds a hint of *je ne sais quoi* to an otherwise ordinary drum kit. At the end the other lads' girlfriends turned up. Mia said hi to me and then, "We're going to the Phoenix bar, are you coming?"

Robbie said, "Well, I'm a bit shattered so we won't." But I knew he really meant that I was officially too young to go.

It's a shame that my internal maturiosity is not recognized by the constabulary.

monday december 20th

I haven't had much time to see the ace gang as I have been hanging out with Robbie. How cool is that? Double cool with knobs, that is how cool. Sometimes we talk in between snogging. Well, mostly he talks because I think it is safer that way, and besides I have lots of other things to worry about whilst he is chatting on about The Stiff Dylans and world peace and so on. Things like avoiding nostril flair, or nip nip eruption, or even, as happened the other night, uncontrollable desires to start "Let's go down the disco" dancing when he put some classical music on.

Rang Jas to catch up. "Hey. What has the ace gang been up to?"

"We only saw you yesterday, Georgia."

9:35 p.m.

But I know the ace gang had a group outing to the cinema last night because Ellen came round to show me her Instamatic photos. How keen is that? To take photos at the cinema. They got thrown out and I'm not surprised. No one would have been able to see the screen with Sven and Dave the Laugh wearing their Christmas antlers.

The gang have probably missed me A LOT, even though they haven't said so.

Ellen said it was "fun" and "a laugh." I didn't ask her about Dave the Laugh, but she told me anyway, about a zillion times . . . that they are "an item." Huh. Who cares?

midnight

I noticed in the photos that in addition to his

antlers, Dave the L was wearing the comedy red nose that he wore when he told me he loved me and I accidentally fell over and kissed him. But accidental snogging and red-bottomosity are yesterday's news.

wednesday december 22nd

11:00 a.m.

The Sex God has gone off to the Isle of Man with Tom and the rest of his family. Then he goes straight off on tour of Och Aye land and Prestan-a-gogogogogo land (Wales).

We spent our last night together at his house because his parents were away. It was really groovy with mucho ear nibbling and snogging *extraordinaire*. I'm getting the hang of hands now (mine, I mean). I don't just let them dangle about, I give them lots to do. Hair stroking and back stroking and so on. (His hair and his back, not mine.) I think that snogging keeps me in tip-top physical condition. I may suggest to Ms. Stamp that she put it into the training schedule for games. Hang on a minute, though. She might want to join in.

When the Sex God and I had to part (which

took about an hour and a half because I kept coming out of my door after he had said good-bye and we would do all the good-bye stuff again), he handed me a small package and said, "Don't do anything too loony while I am away, gorgeous. Here is something for you for Christmas. I'll get you something else from Scotland or Wales." Which is nice.

Unless he gets me a sporran. Or a tartan bikini. Shut up, shut up, brain. It's only because I am full of sadnosity, probably.

I told Jas and she said, "Tom gave me a locket that has a photo of me and him in it that we took at a booth in Seaworld. It's got a backdrop of sea creatures and so on."

I said, "I hope you didn't make any dolphins be in it, because they have hard enough lives as it is, without being made to get into photo booths with you and Tom."

I was quite tearful after SG left. I hope he will like the identity bracelet I got him with my name on it. Jas said I should have had *his* name engraved on it, which is what she did with Tom's.

* * *

Phoned Jas again. "Jas, why have you put Tom's name on his identity bracelet? Doesn't he already know who he is?"

She sighed like someone who is incredibly full of wisdomosity, which is ironic, and said, "What if he was unconscious or something and no one knew who he was?"

"And you think 'Tom' would do the trick, then?"

She said, "I have to go now." But I don't think she really did have to go.

I will put the little package that SG gave me for a Chrimboli gift under my bed.

12:30 p.m.

Poo. I suppose I will have to get used to being a pop widow. I have to develop my own interests. I must use the time he is away wisely. I hope it snows early next term and then I can try out the hilariosity of my new idea *vis-à-vis* glove animal and snow blindness.

1:00 p.m.

I wonder how much money I will need to go to America? I've got some money saved up, if I can find my bank book.

1:20 p.m.

Hmm. £15.50.

1:30 p.m.

If I am saving up for Hamburger-a-gogo I can't use money to buy any more Chrimboli prezzies. I will have to be creative.

Luckily I'm very artistic, as everyone knows. Miss Berry, the Art teacher, thinks I have a special talent. Not for art, though, sadly. She said I had a special talent for wasting everyone's time. Which is a bit harsh.

I am going to start making my Christmas gifts out of colorful materials and a needle and cotton.

10:00 p.m.

I made some carrot twins for Libby. Two nicely carved carrots with rather attractive gingham headscarves and cloaks on. And for Mutti, a pair of sleep glasses. I cut the spectacle shape out of some fun fur fabric and attached an elastic band. I think she will love and appreciate them, but you can never tell.

As a thoughtful and forgiving gift at this special time of year, I took Naomi's pregnancy smock, which I had spent many, many minutes making, over to Mr. and Mrs. Across the Road's house. It has got tiny bows on it and four leg holes, which is unusual in a pregnancy smock. I left it on the doorstep with a note saying, "Best wishes from one who only hopes there to be love and peace in the world."

saturday december 25th
christmas day

Woke up to quite a few prezzies. Libbs climbed in my bed and we opened things together. I am very nearly quite fond of my mutti and vati. Vati gave me some CDs I actually wanted! Libby LOBED her carrot twins and dumped Mr. Potato into the dustbin of life. (Which is just as well, as he was all crinkled and green.)

Mum, in a rare moment of sanity, has bought me a really good bra . . . which fits and is actually quite nice. Not too thrusting and not too baggy. Even when I jump up and down, there is very little ad hoc jiggling. Perhaps now I will be able to dance free and wild, with no danger of knocking anyone out with my nunga-nungas.

No sign of snow yet, although it is very very nippy noodles.

1:00 p.m.

M and D and Libbs have gone to visit miscellaneous loons, so I have a private moment to open SG's gift.

It's a compilation tape of songs that he has recorded solo, and it's got "For Georgia, with love, Robbie" written on the little cover thing. In years to come I will be on TV saying, "Yes, Robbie did write the track 'O Gorgeous One' for me. Likewise 'Cor, What a Smasher' and 'Phwoar.'"

1:30 p.m.

Hmm. There isn't a track called "O Gorgeous One" or "Cor, What a Smasher." There are tracks about endangered species and one about Vincent van Gogh. Not exactly dance extravaganza music; more, it has to be said, music for slitting your wrists to.

2:00 p.m.

I love him for his seriosity.

3:30 p.m.

Big, big news breaking. And no, it is not that Father Christmas is just Dad in a crap white beard (even though that bit is true too). After Christmas lunch, Mr. Across the Road dashed over and had a brandy with Dad because . . . Naomi is in labor!

I said, "Quickly, we must get her on a donkey and head for Bethlehem!" But they all looked at me in that looking-at way that adults have when they do not comprehend the enormity of my hilariosity.

I phoned Jas to let her know the joyful good news. "Naomi is having some furry Baby Jesuses."

"Non."

"Mais oui."

"What shall we do?"

I said, "You get the donkey and I'll sort out the snacks."

4:00 p.m.

Angus is in (even for him) a very bad mood. He's been doing slam dancing in the kitchen to Christmas carols playing on the radio (i.e., he just throws himself against things for no reason). When "Away in a Manger" came on he leapt out of the sink and up onto the plate rack, and then just sort of tap-danced his way along. Four plates and a soup tureen bit the dust.

4:30 p.m.

Decided to take Angus out for a Christmas walk to help him work off his frustration and also ensure that we have something to eat our dinner from. I'm under orders to keep him on his lead in case his inner cat pain drives him to beat up little dogs.

4:35 p.m.

As I was leaving Libby said, "I want to come."

Auntie Kath in Blackpool sent her an all-in-one leopard costume jumpsuit. It's got a tail and ears and whiskers and so on. Libby has had it on all day. Cute.

5:00 p.m.

We had to turn back and get Angus's spare lead because Libby is a cat as well. I hope I don't bump into anyone I know.

5:30 p.m.

It's taken over half an hour to get out of the garden. Libby goes so slowly on her hands and knees.

Once I got her to move on, Angus found something

disgusting to dig up. What sort of people bury manky old bits of clothing in other people's gardens?

5:45 p.m.

So that is where Dad's fishing socks went. I remember Dad saying to Mum, "Have you seen my fishing socks?" and Mum saying, "They've probably gone out for a bit of a walk." Because they were so pingy pongoes, even Angus has reburied them.

6:00 p.m.

Angus managed to shake me off the end of his lead by heading straight for a lamppost at eighty miles an hour and swerving at the last minute. Now he is prancing around on Mr. Next Door's wall. The Prat Poodles are going berserk trying to leap up at him. Now and again he lies down and dangles a paw near them.

Snowy and Whitey have gone completely loopy now. Whitey leapt up and missed Angus's paw and crashed into the wall, but Snowy kept leaping and leaping and Angus was raising his paw slightly higher and higher.

In the end, Angus biffed Snowy midleap, right over on to his back. You'd think that Angus would be a bit miserable, or quiet even, as his beloved sex kitten gives birth to another man's kittens. But no, he is an example to us all. I don't know what of.

6:05 p.m.
Sheer stupidity leaps to mind.

in my bedroom
7:00 p.m.
Uh-oh, Mr. Across the Road came and banged on our door. I looked down the stairs as Vati answered. It was weird, actually, because usually Mr. Across the Road can rave on for England but he didn't seem to be able to speak. He just gestured with his hand for us to follow him. Perhaps he has taken up mime as a Christmas hobby.

We all trailed over to his house. I don't know why I am supposed to be interested. In fact, I thought as a mark of solidarity with Angus I would refuse to go. But I quite wanted to see the kittens.

Angus was on the wall and tapped my

head with a paw as I went by. I said, "I'm sorry about this, Angus."

He just yawned and lay on his back chewing his lead.

7:10 p.m.

When we got into his kitchen, Mr. Across the Road took us to Naomi. He didn't say a word. And Mrs. Across the Road was just staring down at the cat basket as if there was something horrible in it.

Naomi was lying in the basket like the Queen of Sheba, surrounded by kittens. Seven of them . . .

All of them look like miniature Anguses!!!! Honestly! They all have his markings and everything. This is quite literally a bloody miracle!

10:00 p.m.

Another long, long night of Mr. and Mrs. Across the Road coming across and saying, "Why? Oh why??" and "How?" and occasionally, "*Why*? And *how*?"

In the end they worked out that Angus must have sneaked into Naomi's love parlor before his trouser snake addendums were, you know . . .

adjusted. Super-Cat!!! He is without doubt the 007 of the cat world.

sunday december 26th
boxing day

The tiny(ish) kittykats are so gorgey. Jas came over and Libby and Jas and I went to visit. Mr. and Mrs. Across the Road let us in but were very grumpy about it and were tutting and carrying on. Mr. Across the Road kept calling Angus "that thing." Which was a bit uncalled for.

And Mrs. Across the Road said, "Two hundred guineas, she cost us, and for this to happen with a . . . with a . . ."

"Proud, heroic Scottish wildcat?" I asked.

"No, with an out-of-control . . . *beast*!"

They're just a bit overcome with joy at the moment, but I am sure they will come round in a few thousand years.

Even though they are only a few hours old Angus and Naomi's kittykats are not what you would call the usual sort of kittykat. They haven't even opened their eyes yet, but they are already biting each other and spitting.

I used my womanly charms (which Jas rather

meanly said made me look like an ax murderer) and begged Mr. and Mrs. Across the Road to let Angus at least lick his offspring.

3:00 p.m.
Eventually they said he could if he was kept on his lead at all times.

He strutted around purring like a tank (two tanks), biffing the kittykats with his head and licking Naomi. Awww.

That is what I want me and the Sex God to be like. Not necessarily including the bottom-exposing thing that Angus and Naomi go in for A LOT.

tuesday december 28th
Robbie has phoned me eight times!!!

It's a bit weird because there is always someone around earwigging. Dad's got ears like a bat. (I'll surprise him one day by walking into the front room whilst he is hanging upside down from the light fixture.) When I was talking to Rosie about how to put your tongue behind your back teeth when you smile because it makes you look sexier he came bursting out of the kitchen and said, "Are you going to be talking rubbish on the phone for much longer? I want to make a call myself this century."

I said patiently, "Vati, as I have pointed out many, many times, if you would have the decency to buy me my own mobile phone in keeping with the rest of the universe, then I wouldn't have to use this prehistoric one in the hall." But he just ignored me as usual.

wednesday december 29th

I arranged with Robbie that he would call me at four o'clock today (as opposed to Isle of Man time, which is about 1948, according to Robbie. I think they still have steam trains). This is the cunning plan we made, in order to be able to say what we like to each other (for example, "You are the most Sex-Goddy thing on legs, I want to suck your shirt, etc., etc."). I told Robbie the telephone number of the phone box down the road and he is going to ring me there.

in the phone box
4:00 p.m.

Mark Big Gob went by with his midget girlfriend. Rosie didn't believe me when I told her how very very tiny Mark's girlfriend is, but she is. You could quite easily strap a bowl of peanuts to her tiny head and use her as a sort of snacks table at parties. That is how small she is.

Mark Big Gob gave me a hideous wink as he went by. It's hard to believe that he actually dumped me before I was going to dump him for being so thick. How annoying is that? Vair vair annoying, but . . . then the phone rang and my beloved Sex God of the Universe and Beyond spoke to me.

at jas's
5:00 p.m.
Jas's mutti and vati are out and we are practicing for our trip to Froggyland by eating a typico French peasant meal: *pomme de terre* and *les* baked beans *avec le* sauce *de* tomato. Oh, and of course, *de rigueur* . . . we wore our berets and stripey T-shirts.

I said, "I 'ope that Gorgey Henri can control his passion for me when we reach Paree."

Jas was also wearing what she imagines are sexy shades. She's wrong, though—they don't make her look French, they make her look blind.

She said, "Gorgey Henri does not have *la*

passion for you, he thinks you are *la* stupid school-girl."

"Oh, *mais non*, *ma* idiot, *au contraire* he thinks I am *la* genius."

We both had a lot of frustrated snogging energy so we had to do "Let's go down the disco" dancing on Jas's bed for about an hour. We were pretending we were in a French disco inferno, which means we yelled, *"Mon Dieu!" "Zut alors!"* and *"Merde!"* A LOT.

midnight
I think I may actually have broken my neck from doing too much head banging.

thursday december 30th
Woke up this morning and there was a sort of weird light in the bedroom. When I opened the curtains I discovered that it had snowed overnight!!!

Mr. Next Door was already up wearing ludicrous snow wear—bobble hat, duffle coat and rubber trousers, clearing his path with a shovel. He got to the end of the path near the gate and then had a breather to survey his handiwork. He probably imagines he is like Nanook of the North.

It's a shame if he does, because as he walked back up his newly cleared path, he went flying on a slippy bit and ended up skidding along on his rubber trousers.

Happy days!

11:45 a.m.

Oh, *très sportif.* We are going to have the Winter Olympics! All the gang are going to meet up on the back fields for snow fun and frolics.

"What are you going to wear?" I asked Rosie.

"Short black leather skirt, new knee boots and a LOT of lip gloss."

"That is not exactly sensible winter wear."

"I know," she said. "I may freeze to death, but I will look fabbity fab fab."

She is not wrong. I may have to rifle through my wardrobe for glamorous *après-ski* wear.

I don't know why I am bothering, really, as the Sex God is not here, but you have to keep up appearances for good humorosity and fashionos-ability's sake.

Phoned Jas. "Jas, what are you wearing for the sledging and snow sports extravaganza?"

"Well, I was thinking snug and warm."

"Well, you can't just wear your huge winter knickers, Jas."

"Hahahaha-di-haha. What are you wearing?"

"Hmmm . . . ski pants, ankle boots and I think roll-neck top and leather jacket. Oh, and waterproof eye makeup in case of a sudden snowstorm."

12:00 p.m.

I think snow wear quite suits me. My hat deemphasizes on the conk front which is always a good thing. Lashings and lashings of mascara and lip gloss for extra warmth and I am just about ready.

I managed to sneak out of the house without Libby hearing me. I love her, but she is being a pain about this cat costume thing—she won't take it off and it is beginning to be a bit on the pingy pongo side.

1:00 p.m.

I was a bit late because Angus kept following me and I had to chuck snowballs at him to dodge him.

Dave the Laugh, Ellen, Jools, Rollo, Mabs, Sam, Rosie, Sven, Jas and some lads I didn't know were sledging down a hill on the back fields. Well, apart from Ellen, who was in a ditherama at the top of the hill. She was not exactly dressed for downhill sledging (her skirt was about half an inch long and she was wearing false eyelashes). But neither was anybody else exactly dressed for downhill sledging, and that wasn't stopping *them*. As the rest of them whizzed down the hill in a sledge sandwich—boy-girl-boy-girl sledge—Ellen was fiddling with her hair and gazing down the hillside.

She said, "I've been going out with him for nearly three weeks now. In hours, that is . . . er . . . a lot."

I didn't say anything.

"Do you think he likes me as much as I like him?"

I didn't say anything. I am keeping my wisdomosity to myself.

"Do you think I should ask him?"

"What?"

"Ask him how much he likes me?"

"Er . . . I don't know . . . I mean, boys are, you know, not girls with trousers on, are they?" I astonished even myself with my outburst of extreme wisdomosity. Ellen looked at me all blinky and expectant, like I was a fortune-teller or something. I felt a bit like that bloke in *Julius Caesar*, the one who says, "Beware the idle of March."

Ellen asked me why she shouldn't ask him. Good question. Good. "Er . . . because Dave might feel like you are putting pressure on his individualosity."

"His individualosity?"

"Yes."

"What, by asking him if he likes me as much as I like him?"

"That's the one."

"Well, what should I do instead, then?"

"Be cool, and, you know . . . er, funny and relaxed . . . and fun and happening and . . . er . . . so on." What am I talking about? Alarmingly, Ellen seemed to think I made sense.

By this time, Dave and the gang had struggled back up the hill with the sledge. Dave said, "Nippy noodles, isn't it?" He was smiling at me. He's got a really cool, sort of naughty, smile. It makes you think of lip nibbling. "Look, girls, I couldn't put my hands down the front of your jumpers, could I? To warm them up? There would be nothing rudey-dudey in it, you understand. To me your nunga-

nungas are just a pair of giant mittens."

Ellen looked a bit puzzled. As I have said many times, I wonder if Ellen is quite a good enough laugh for Dave the Laugh.

friday december 31st
new year's eve
2:00 p.m.

The ace gang are going to SEVEN parties, but as a mark of respect Jas and I have decided not to go with them. We are having our own widows' celebration.

Actually, I would rather go out than be cooped up with Jas, but I know that Dave the Laugh will be there and I don't want to entice my bottom into another display of redness. Especially as I have got snogging withdrawal VERY badly.

11:00 p.m.

This is the glorious start to my New Year . . .

Jas and I stayed in and watched people on television kissing each other and waving their kilts around. Jas is staying over and my so-called parents and Libby have gone out to some sad party. They actually asked if I would like to go with them.

When I indicated that I would rather set fire to myself they left me alone. However, as a special treat Mum got us some food. I said to Dad, "Jas is more of a champagne girl, really, so if you could just get a few bottles. I think that would make our fabulous evening go with a swing."

He didn't even bother to reply.

On the stroke of midnight, Jas said, "Shall we?"

And I said, "Jas, don't even think about asking me to snog you."

She got all huffy. "No, I wasn't going to. I was going to say, shall we have a celebratory disco inferno dancing experience with the aid of soft toys?"

12:30 a.m.

And a happy New Year to one and all!!!

Our New Year "Let's go down the disco" experience, with the aid of Charlie Horse and Teddy as partners, was actually quite good fun on the funosity scale. Although I was slightly worried about Jas because she did actually snog Teddy.

She said, "I'm pretending it's Tom."

I said, "Teddy is very very like Tom in many

ways—his furry ears, for instance."

We were just biffing each other with Charlie and Teddy when the phone rang.

It was SG and Tom phoning from the Isle of Man. Yeahhhhhhh!!!

The Sex God said, "Happy New Year, gorgeous, see you soon." Then he had to go and toss dwarfs or whatever it is they do in the Isle of Man to celebrate. I read that they still beat criminals with bits of old twigs there, so anything could happen.

Jas was Mrs. Moony Knickers after talking to Hunky, and we just went back to watching people snogging and singing on TV.

1:15 a.m.
Ho hum pig's bum.

When my "family" got home, as a hilarious treat, Dad had brought home a bit of coal. He said, "It's called 'first footing.'" It should be called "first loon in." He burst in like the original red-faced loon and said, "Happy New Year." Then he tried to hug me and Jas. We beat him off with Teddy and Charlie Horse and then Libby joined in and hung on to his beard, as Jas and I made a bid for freedom to my room.

sunday january 2nd
11:30 a.m.

To keep our spirits up, Jas and I made a list of things to take to Froggyland with us.

"We are going to have to hire an extra ferry to take our hair products over," I told her.

monday january 3rd
2:00 p.m.

Moped around at Jas's. We are united in widow sadness. We listened to sad songs and practiced being interviewed on *Michael Parkinson*. Jas is hopeless at it. When I (as Parky) asked her what her hopes for the future were, she said, "World peace and more freely available organic vegetables." How interesting is that?

Not, is the correct answer.

Ooooh, I am soooo bored and lonely. NOTHING happens around here.

I lolloped home up our street. At least Angus is happy, though. He is lolling around on the wall overlooking Mr. and Mrs. Across the Road. He is a very proud dad. I wonder how long it will be before we are allowed to name the kittykats? Mr. and Mrs. Across the Road are being very unreasonable about it all and won't discuss it.

When I got back to the house Mum said, "Robbie rang you. The number's beside the phone."

I got the usual jelloid knickers (and added leg tremblers and a quick spasm of quivering-a-gogo).

Should I phone him back or just wait for him to phone again? I must think.

Perhaps if I ate some chocolate orange egg it would calm me down. There was one left under the tree.

The front room was a nightmare of beardosity. Vati had some of his mates from work and Uncle Eddie round watching the football. He was slurping beer and being all jolly. "Georgia, this is Mike, Nick, Paul and Bingo . . . the lads!"

Lads? Since when were lads eighty-five? And a half.

The great tragedy is that the "lads" are going to be forming a football team. I was about to say, "Should men in your physical condition hurl themselves around a football pitch?" But then Dad dropped his bombshell.

"Georgia, what is this with Robbie? Why is he phoning you all the time and coming round? How old is he?"

I said with great dignosity, "Father, I am afraid I can't discuss my private life with you as I have a date with *Lord of the Flies*."

He said, "Who's he, then?" And the "lads" all laughed.

I said, again with great dignosity, "It is a book by William Golding that I have to study for my homework."

10:30 p.m.
I can't phone Robbie because then Dad will know that I am phoning him and that will make him even more full of suspiciosity.

11:00 p.m.
Lord of the Flies is so boring . . . and so weird. I always thought boys were very very strange, but I didn't think they would start eating each other. Bloody hell, I must make sure I never end up on an island with a bunch of boys!

wednesday january 5th

Tom arrived back from the family Chrimboli. Jas was ridiculously excited. She is a fair-weather pal, because I know I will be dumped now that her so-called boyfriend is back. And SG isn't back until next Tuesday.

friday january 7th

Snowed like billio overnight. Angus leapt out of the front door like he normally does and completely disappeared from view, the snow was so deep. He loves it and is leaping and sneezing about in the back garden.

Rosie and the gang are going sledging down the back fields. But I am not in the mood for winter sports until my beloved returns. I explained this to Rosie and she said, "Make love, not war." What is she talking about?

Besides, I saw Ellen and Dave the Laugh holding hands down at Churchill Square yesterday and it made me feel a bit funny. I don't know why.

saturday january 8th

10:00 a.m.

Robbie phoned from East Jesus (or Prestan-agogogogoch . . . anyway, somewhere in Welsh country). The gigs are going really well, but he is shattered and can't talk much because his throat is sore from singing. He said, "I miss you, gorgeous."

Boo hoo, this is so sad.

Still, he is back on Tuesday. I may distract myself by doing snogging exercises to limber up.

sunday january 9th
3:00 p.m.

My exercise regime: doing my yoga sun salute ten times and then pucker-ups (like Mick Jagger) forty times.

6:00 p.m.

Stalag 14 starts again tomorrow. Shall we never be free? On the bright side, the snow gives a very good comedy opportunity for an outing of glove animal.

8:00 p.m.

Rang around the ace gang.

"Rosie."

"*D'accord.* It's me."

"Is it you?"

"Yes."

"Good-bye."

"Good-bye."

Rang back. "I'll just say this: Operation Glove Animal and Snow Blindness."

"Pip, pip."

Phoned Jools and Mabs and Ellen, who are all prepared. Then I phoned Mrs. Useless Knickers. "Jas, it's snowing. Prepare glove animal."

"Oh no, we'll only get bad conduct marks immediately."

"Yes, but think of the hilariosity of it."

"But . . ."

"Jas, if you can't think of the hilariosity, think of the severe duffing you will get if you don't do it."

monday january 10th

8:30 a.m.

*Rendez-vous*ed at the bottom of the hill, where we all clipped on our glove ears under our berets and put on sunglasses. As we bobbled up the hill, Rosie was nearly going to the piddly-diddly department on the spot as she was laughing so much.

Mabs did actually walk into a tree because she couldn't see through her sunglasses. Oh, how we laughed.

As we approached the school gate, we could see Hawkeye lurking. We tucked our ears up under our berets but kept our sunglasses on.

Hawkeye tutted and ferreted at us as we walked by. She said, "What is this nonsense?"

I said, "It's to prevent snow blindness, Mrs. Heaton."

She said, "It's a pity there's no way to prevent stupidity." Which I think is quite bad manners for someone who is teaching the youth of today, but I didn't say so.

tuesday january 11th
8:25 a.m.

Sex God back today AND the kittykats have opened their eyes!!! They are soooooo sweet and, as I explained to Jas, "Now they can see to fight properly."

9:00 p.m.

Robbie came round to see me as soon as he got

back. How cool is that?

When he arrived at the door, Dad called me and then he and Mum spent about a million years raising their eyebrows and looking "wise." And trying to be modern and to get on with the youth, which is ludicrous.

Vati started to talk about Kiwi-a-gogo land. I said, "Fancy going for a walk, Robbie? I'm a bit . . . er . . . hot."

And Dad said, "It's pitch-black and about minus seven outside." He was going to go on and on, but then I saw Mutti give him a look, a "modern, understanding mum look," that said, Come on, Bob, remember when you were that age? Which is a physical impossibility for my dad. How very very embarrassing. Shut up, stop looking, shut up, shut up.

Vati said, "Be back by eleven."

Oh, how sad and embarrassing.

Robbie took my hand and once we got away from our house into the dark street he snogged me. Yipppppeeeee!

midnight
Cor, bloody nippy noodles out there. But I have

my love to keep me warm (that and the extra pair of knickers I put on).

I must say, I think my puckering exercises have paid off, because I haven't got any aches or pains. Robbie told me about being on tour. He said he wasn't sure that he really liked it. But I'm sure that is just a phase he is going through. Once we are squillionaires he will change his mind.

1:00 a.m.

I wonder why he asked me if I liked the countryside? Maybe he wants us to go and snog in the great outdoors?

wednesday january 12th
8:15 a.m.

Dad brought me a cup of tea in bed this morning! I said, "Vati, why are you waking me up in the middle of the night? Are you on fire?"

I had to pull the sheets up really quickly in case he could see any bits of my body. He hung around after he had put the cup down. He was sort of all red and beardy.

"Georgia, I'm not trying to . . . well, I know you

have your own mind . . . and Robbie seems like a really, you know, great bloke . . . but he's, you know, a big lad and well . . . well, it's just that . . . well, don't get too serious too soon."

What in the name of Buddha's bra is he going on about now?

Then he ruffled my hair (very very annoying) and went out. Robbie's a "big lad." What does that mean?

I really will have to break the news soon that I am going off on tour to Hamburger-a-gogo land with The Stiff Dylans. Vati obviously doesn't think I am capable of maturiosity. But he is wrong.

Wrongy wrong wrong.

I wonder how much money I will need for *le* gay Paree weekend, for essentials and so on? I might test the water *vis-à-vis* spondulicks for my trip to Hamburger-a-gogo land with a simple enquiry about available finance for Froggyland.

front room
7:30 p.m.
Vati was actually doing a push-up when I came in. I hope he is insured.

"Vati."

"Urgh."

"Can I have two hundred and twenty pounds for my weekend in Paris, please?"

I thought I was going to have to use my first-aid skills on Vati. Which would have been a shame as I only know how to force a boiled sweet out of someone if they are choking to death.

saturday january 15th
11:00 a.m.

The snow has melted, thank the Lord. It is so hard on the elderly. However, they can be quite suspicious, the elderly. I offered to go shopping for Mr. and Mrs. Next Door yesterday in case they were frightened of going out. And they were quite surly about it. I said to Mr. Next Door, "I couldn't help noticing that you are even more unsteady than usual on your feet in this kind of weather." And he told me to go annoy someone else, which is a bit rude, I think.

2:00 p.m.

As everyone is out, SG came round. We snogged for thirty-five minutes without stopping (I timed it because I could see the clock over Robbie's shoulder). Rosie rang whilst he was here and said they were having an indoor(!) barbecue at her house tonight. The theme is "sausages." Robbie couldn't make it, though, because he is rehearsing.

Bye-bye, dreamboat.

8:30 p.m.
I didn't go to the sausage extravaganza. Heaven only knows what sausages would bring out in me; I was bad enough at the fish party. I will concentrate on my French vocabulary instead so that I can ask for things in Paris.

9:00 p.m.
Sausage is *saucisson* in French. Shut up, brain.

9:05 p.m.
I am a bit worried because Robbie turned up this afternoon not in his groovy mini, but on a second-hand bike.

11:30 p.m.
I hope he doesn't suggest we go for bike rides

together. It is minus a hundred and eighty degrees, and the last time I rode a bike my skirt got caught in the back wheel and I had to walk home in my knickers.

FROGLAND
EXTRAVAGANZA

monday january 17th
stalag 14
quatre days to our frogland extravaganza
french
M'sieur "Call Me Henri" really is sooo cool and
gorgey. He told us what we are going to do on our
school trip to *la belle* France and what we should
bring. We're going to stay in Hôtel Gare du Nord
and visit the Champs Elysées and the Pompidou
Centre. Loads of *très bon* stuff. Madame Slack
came in and took all our forms that we had to take
home for signing—the forms saying that even if
we were set fire to by raving French people, the
staff are not responsible, etc. She also said,
"Girls, on Saturday there will be a choice of excursion in the morning. You can go on a grand
tour of the sewage system of Paris with me, go up
the Eiffel Tower with M'sieur Hilbert or to the

Louvre with Herr Kamyer. Please come and sign up for your choice."

As we queued up we argued about which trip to go on as a gang. Jas was the only one who wanted to go down into the sewers. I said to Jas, "What is the point of going down the sewers?"

"Because it is historical and we might learn a lot of stuff we don't know."

I said, "*Au contraire*, we will learn a lot of things we DO know. We will learn that French sewers are like English sewers, only French."

Jas looked like a goggle-eyed ferret.

I explained. "It is just tunnels full of French poo—how different can French poo be from English poo?"

So we are all going up the Eiffel Tower with Gorgey Henri.

Ellen said, "I'm looking forward to going and everything, but I will really miss Dave the Laugh. . . . He's such a . . ."

I said, "Laugh?"

"Yes," she said, and went all red. Good Lord.

I am, of course, used to being away from the Sex God. He's only been back a week and I'm off to Frogland.

I sometimes wish he was more of a laugh, though. There is a slight danger that underneath his Sex God exterior there lurks a sensible person. He has just bought a bike to save the environment. And it might not stop there . . . he might possibly buy some waterproofs.

thursday january 20th

Slim gave us her world famous (not) "Representatives of Great Britain abroad" speech. Apparently we have the weight of the reputation of the British Isles on our shoulders.

I said to Jools, "I'm already tired, and we haven't even got on the coach yet."

midnight

I've managed to whittle down my necessities to one haversack full. Jas and I are doing sharesies on some things to save space. For instance, I am supplying our hair gel for the weekend and she is supplying moisturizer. I will not be sharing knickers with her, though.

I said *au revoir* to *mon amour*. He came round on his bike AGAIN, and also (this is the worst bit), he talked to my dad about Kiwi-a-gogo land . . . and he didn't shoot himself with boredom. In fact, he even asked questions, which proved he had been listening to Vati raving on about Maoris. *Très* weird.

friday january 21st
aboard l'esprit
midday
On our way to *la belle* France at last. If we ever get there it will be *le* miracle, because: a) it is a French ferry and b) we have a madman at the helm. When we set off from Newhaven we went in and out of the quay three times, because the captain forgot to cast off.

1:00 p.m.
Zut alors, we are being tossed about like *les* corks. I may complain to the captain (if he has not been airlifted home to a secure unit) and suggest he stop driving us into eighty-foot waves. Herr Kamyer, dithering champion for the German nation and part-time fool, has just lost his footing and fallen into the ladies' loos.

1:15 p.m.

In the restaurant there is a notice that says, *"Soupe du jour,"* so Rosie said to the French waiter, "Can I have *le soupe du* yesterday, please?" But no one got it.

1:30 p.m.

Staggering around on the decks in gale-force winds.

I could see Captain Mad up in his wheelhouse thing.

1:32 p.m.

The only way to stay upright is to hold the flagpole at the back of the boat.

1:35 p.m.

Why does he keep staring at me? I'm just clinging on to this French flag because I want to live to see Frogland.

Just then the boat lurched violently, and that's when it came off in my hand.

2:30 p.m.

Madame Slack, who until then had been attached

to Gorgey Henri for most of the voyage (like a Slack limpet), decided to make a big international thing out of the flag removing incident.

She gibbered in *le* Frog to Captain Mad, who had come down to the deck (hopefully leaving someone who could drive in his place). They did a lot of pointing and shouting and shrugging.

Incidentally, why has Madame Slack got two huge handbags? She keeps Sellotape and a ruler in one and a hankie in the other. Should someone like that be in charge of the youth of today? Is France a nation of handbag fetishists, I wonder? As I said to Jas, "Even Henri has got a little hand-bag."

Rosie said, "You are definitely going to have to walk the gangplank. *Au revoir, mon amie.*"

"What makes you think Captain Mad could find a gangplank? I'll be amazed if he can find France." But I said it quietly. I didn't want to start the shrugging again.

In the end, Madame Slack called me stupid about a zillion times, which could have upset me a lot, but I know I am really full of geniosity.

I had to apologize to Captain Mad. In French.

4:45 p.m.

Still in this sodding boat, bobbing up and down in the Atlantic or wherever it is we are now.

Suddenly Rosie said, "Land! I can see land, thank the Lord!" and got down on her knees. Which was quite funny. It could be Iceland, though, for all we know.

Captain Mad came on the PA system and said, "Ladeez and jentlemen, ve are now approaching Dieppe."

I said to the gang, "With a bit of luck, he'll manage to dock by tomorrow evening."

9:00 p.m.

Miraculously survived the ferry journey and caught the train to Paris. I think the driver might have been wearing a beret, but we still managed to arrive at Hôtel Gare du Nord in *le* gay Paree! Right in the middle of everything.

The lady behind the desk said, "Welcome, I will show you to your rrruuuuuuums." I thought French people were actually being funny when they put on their accent, but they aren't being funny, they are being French. That, as I said to Jas, is why I *aime* them so much.

Gorgey Henri has let the ace gang be in the same room together! How fab is he? Usually we get split up in class, but the six of us are back together again. Yes!!! *Les* girls have arrived. It's a really groovy room as well. I have a bed by the window. I lay down on it and said, "Aaahhh, this is the sort of life I will be leading from now on."

Rosie said, "What? Sharing a room with five other women? Are you setting up a lezzie farm?" I had to duff her rather savagely over the head with my pillow.

Jas had brought the photo of Tom and her at Seaworld and she put it on the table by the side of her bed.

Ellen tried to sneak a book under her pillow, but I saw it. "What's that?" I asked.

"Oh, it's just a bit of homework I brought with me."

Rosie fished it out and read out the title. "It's called *Black Lace Shoulder*, a story of passion on the high seas." Now we know what sort of homework she is doing: snogging research. It was a semi-naughty book. I flicked through it and found a bit to read to the rest of the gang.

"'He captivated women with his fierce, proud

face, his lean, well-exercised body and his aura of sexuality, wild as that of a stallion.'"

Rosie said, "That's like Sven."

Jas said, "What, he's like a stallion?"

"Yes."

I said, "A stallion in loons."

Rosie said, *"Mais oui."*

"*Quel* number have you got up to now with *le* stallion in loons on the scoring system?" I asked.

"Eight." Upper-body fondling indoors. All of our eyes drifted towards Rosie's basoomas, which, it has to be said, are not gigantic.

Ellen said, "Is it, does it . . . I mean, are your, erm, nungas . . . getting bigger?"

Rosie looked down the front of her T-shirt. "I think they are a bit. Not as much as Georgia's, though."

Oh no, here we go. I thought my new nunga-nunga holder had stopped this sort of talk. To change the subject I said to Ellen, "What number have you got up to with Dave?"

She went all red. "Oh, well, you know, he's like really a good, well, kisser."

Yes, as it happens, I do know that he's a really good kisser.

Rosie was all interested now. "Has he touched anything?"

Ellen was about to explode from redness. "Well, he stroked my hair."

We haven't even bothered to put hair-stroking on our snogging scale. If we had, it would have been minus one.

Out of our bedroom window we can see the streets of Paris and the French-type *garçons*. Some of them look quite groovy, but their trousers are a bit too short. Perhaps this is the French way. I said, "Look, people are wearing berets and they're not even going to school. Unless they still go to school at ninety-four."

saturday january 22nd
saturday in paris
9:30 a.m.

Oh *j'aime* Paris muchly. For brekkie we had hot chocolate and croissants. All the French kids dipped their croissants into their hot chocolate. How cool is that? Yummy scrumboes.

We set off with Gorgey Henri for the Eiffel Tower. I was singing "Fallink in luff again, never vanted to . . ." until Rosie pointed out that Marlene Dietrich sang that and she was by no means a French person.

up the eiffel tower
11:00 a.m.

Jas and I got split up somehow from the rest of the gang. Well, mainly because Jas was dithering around making me take a photo of her with some French pigeons. How anyone would know they were French pigeons, I don't know. I said to her, "We will have to draw little stripey T-shirts on them when we get the prints back."

Anyway, the others had gone on ahead and we got trapped just in front of a group of French schoolboys of about nine years old. They spent the million years it took climbing the steps looking up our skirts.

Jas was OK because she had her holiday knickers on (same gigantic ones as her daywear in England, but with a frilly bit round the gusset). I, however, had normals on, and so I tried to walk up the stairs with my legs together, which is not easy. Every time I looked behind me I could see the little boys ogling like ogles on ogle tablets.

When we eventually got to the top, Jas said, "It's your fault; you should have worn sensible knickers."

"Jas, *fermez la bouche* or I will *fermer* it for you."

oo la-la la gay paree
2:00 p.m.
We walked along the banks of the Seine in the winter sunshine. There were musicians and so on playing, and a bird market. I wanted to take a chaffinch or some lovebirds home with me, but I knew that they'd only last two minutes if Angus got a snack attack in the middle of the night. As we passed a bloke playing a saxophone underneath one of the arches, he put down the sax and started doing a juggling thing with his hands. It was a bit peculiar, though, because, as I said to Jas, "He hasn't got any balls."

Rosie said, "Ooer . . ." which set us off on the uncontrollable laughing fandango.

Jas said, "He must be doing a sort of mime thing." Mime juggling? In the end, unfortunately, we realized he was actually pretending to juggle my breasts. I am the first to admit that I can be paranoid about my nungas, but in this case it was clear even to Jas that he was a perv. He pointed at my nungas and made a sort of leering, licking smile and then continued his pretend juggling. How disgusting!

Am I never to be free from the tyranny of my basoomas? I buttoned my coat up as tightly as possible.

la nuit extravaganza

Henri took us down *rue* St. Denis in the evening and said, "Zis is where the ladeez of the night ply their trade."

Jas said, "I can't see any ladies of the night; all I can see are a load of prostitutes." She astonishes me with her hilarious stupidosity sometimes.

Actually, it should have been called "*rue de* Bummer*," because all the prozzies looked exactly like the Bummer twins. Only less spotty.

It isn't even just Henri who has a handbag, lots of *les français* men have little handbags. And no one laughs. Weird. I may buy one for Dad as a souvenir.

sunday january 23rd

Herr Kamyer has reached dizzying heights of giddiness since he's been in Paris, even going so far as to wear leisure slacks and a cardigan with a koala on it. Jas said kindly, "Perhaps it's a Christmas gift from his mum." But I don't think so. I think he knitted it himself. And I think he is proud of it.

1:00 p.m.

Jas and Rosie keep nipping off to phone Tom and Sven every five minutes.

I would phone Robbie, but I don't really know what to say to him. What if he asks me what I have been doing? What would I say? "I pulled off a French flag, some boys looked up my skirt and finally a bloke with a saxophone juggled my breasts." I wouldn't mean to say any of that, but I know I would blurt it out.

2:15 p.m.

Herr Kamyer has been showing us how to ask for things in shops. I know how to do this already: all you do is ask Gorgey Henri to go and ask for whatever it is you want in the shop. He does, after all, know the language. However, Herr Kamyer thinks we should learn stuff, so he keeps going up to French people and asking for things, which is hilarious in the extreme as: a) no one has a clue what he is talking about and b) they wouldn't give him anything anyway, because he is not French.

Oh, I tell a lie. He did manage to get something. He went into the tourist information center for a map. "I vill be back in a moment, girls, *mit der* map and ve vill proceed to the Champs Elysées."

He came out ten minutes later dithering like a loon with a souvenir walking stick but no map. As I pointed out to Jools, "The tragic thing is that they speak English in the tourist information center."

plunging into the seine
photo opportunity
We tried the "Just step back a bit, Herr Kamyer, I can't get all your cardigan in" tactic on the banks of the Seine. But Herr Kamyer looked back before he moved so he did not plunge into the Seine. And now we really do have a photo of Herr Kamyer in his cardigan.

notre dame

4:00 p.m.

Very gothic. No sign of hunchbacks, though. So . . .
with a marvelous display of imaginosity (and also
after Herr Kamyer, Henri and Madame Slack had
gone into the cathedral) the ace gang got into their
hunchback gear (haversacks under coats). We
were getting ready, shuffling around and yelling,
"The bells, the bells," but then Jas and I stepped
onto a bit of green grass verge to take a photo of
the ace gang being hunchbacks against the
romantic backdrop of Notre Dame (*très* historic).
Suddenly all hell broke loose. Whistles went off
and some absolute loon started yelling through a
loudspeaker in French at us. Then we were surrounded by blokes in uniforms. I thought we were
going to be taken to the Bastille.

I said to Jas, "What have we done? Ask one of
them."

She said, "You came top in French, you ask."
Unfortunately, I had come top in French only to
annoy Madame Slack. I had learned twenty-five
words and then made sure I answered every question using only those words.

Just then Henri came running back to save us.

He started yelling and shrugging his shoulders, and soon everyone was shrugging shoulders. Even the bloke selling bird food. I don't know what he had to do with it.

I turned to the gang. "Wait for a big group shrug and then run like the wind into Notre Dame for sanctuary. We must beg the priests to save us."

It all got sorted out in the end. The French loon patrol turned out to be park keepers. Sort of like park Elvises. Apparently you are not allowed to step on their grass, because it drives them insane.

Madame Slack gave her world famous "Once again a few bad apples have spoilt the reputation of England" lecture and gave us all bad conduct medals. I mean marks.

I said to Jas, "You would think that she would encourage us to bring history to life, but oh no, *au contraire*, we are pilloried on the spike of . . . er . . . life."

9:30 p.m.

Henri took us out to a restaurant tonight. It was really groovy, apart from some old drunk at the piano who kept moaning on about *"Je ne regrette rien."* Ellen asked, "What is he going on about?"

I said, "He's saying in French that he doesn't regret a thing, which he quite clearly should. He should regret having started this song, for one thing."

Henri said he was a famous French singer. Good Lord.

Very very funny evening. There was a notice on our table saying what you could have to eat. It said "Frogs' legs" at the top. When the waiter came he spoke English (sort of). "Good evening, mademoiselle, what can I get you?"

I said, "*S'cusez moi*, have you got frogs' legs?"

He smiled. "Yes, m'selle."

So I said, "Well, hop off and get me a sandwich, then."

We laughed for about a million years. Even the waiter thought it was funny(ish). However, Madame Slack heard what had happened and said we were "giddy."

monday january 24th
last morning in gay paree
Sitting by myself in a café because the ace gang have gone off to look at some French boys. I even ordered a cup of coffee for myself. And a croissant.

Well, actually, it looks more like an egg sandwich (because it is an egg sandwich), but at least it's not a walking stick.

pompidou centre
midday
You can't move for white-faced loons in the area around the Centre. Some of them just stand still for ages and ages, painted all white like a statue. Then when you are really bored from looking at them, they slowly move a finger, or lift a leg, and then go back to being still. And people throw coins in their hats for that. I said to Rosie, "What is the point of mime artists? Why don't they just tell you what they want?"

Then I noticed that a gorgey *garçon* was watching me watching the white-faced loons. I kept catching him looking at me. He was cute. *Très* cute. And his trousers were relatively normal. And he wasn't wearing a beret. And he was handbag-free.

He caught my eye and smiled quite a dreamy smile. He was very intense-looking, with incredibly dark curly hair. However, I am a red bottom–free zone and I was just about to ignore him when he went off.

Ah well. *C'est la guerre*, as they say here, although what the railway station has to do with anything, I don't know. (Or is that *gâre*? Oh, I don't know. As I say to Madame Slack, French is a foreign language to me.)

five minutes later

The gorgey French boy came back and brought me a red rose!! He said, "For the most beeootiful girl," kissed my hand and then went off into the crowd.

Honestly.

The ace gang were dead impressed. We discussed it for ages. It didn't fit into the snogging scale anywhere. And it wasn't a "see you later." Was I supposed to follow him? Should I have done something erotic with the rose?

As I have said with huge wisdomosity many times, boys the world over are a bloody mystery.

au revoir

We got on the train and said *"Auf Wiedersehen"* to the city of romance. We have our memories to take home with us. More importantly, we also have our HUGE comedy berets.

We found them in a souvenir shop in the station that sold musical Eiffel Towers, nuddy-pants cancan dancers and other sophisticated gifts. The berets are gigantic and they are wired around the rim, so that they stick out about a foot from your head. They are quite hilarious in the extreme. We each got one. I can't wait to wear them to school. They make the lunchpack berets seem traditional by comparison.

When we got on the train, Madame Slack went off to the teachers' compartment, probably to chat with Gorgey Henri about handbags they had known and loved. We took the opportunity to try on our new berets. All six of us leaned out of our carriage window wearing our gigantic berets as the train pulled out. We were yelling *"AU REVOIR, PARIS! WE LOVE YOU ALL!!!"*

And guess what? The people on the platform all waved and cheered. They were shouting, *"Bonne chance!"* I think.

I asked Jas, as we tucked into our cheesy snacks for the journey, "Do you think that the French-type people think we really like our berets?"

She said, "No, I think they think we are English people and therefore not normal."

"How could they think that?" asked Rosie.

Then I noticed that Rosie was wearing a false mustache as well as her beret.

on the ferry heading home

Uneventful trip home because we had a normal captain (i.e., English).

Also we had chips. A LOT.

I was quite overcome when we saw the white cliffs of Dover, until I realized we weren't going to Dover and they are just some crappy old white cliffs of somewhere else.

midnight

Arrived home to my loving family. As I came up the drive, Angus shot over the wall and gave me a playful bite on the ankle as he passed. I opened the door and yelled, "*C'est moi!* Your daughter is home again, crack open the fatted calf and—"

Angus had pushed his way in first and Dad started yelling. "Get that bloody cat out! This house is full of fleas."

I said sternly to Angus, "Angus, stay out of the house, it is full of fleas!" But the Loonleader didn't think it was funny. Even though it was.

12:10 a.m.

Libby was pleased to see me, at least. She woke up when I came in and said, "Heggo, Gingey."

She made me a card with a drawing of a cat band on the front. Angus is the lead singer, although why he is upside down, I don't know. The audience is little mice and voles in disco wear.

By the time I had unpacked my bag, Libby had fallen back to sleep in my bed with her "fwends." She is so lovely when she is sleeping, and I gave her a kiss on her cheek. I wonder how I will get on without her when I go to America. It made me feel a bit weepy, actually. I must have boat lag.

Just as I was dropping off into snoozeland, Mutti came in. I think she might have had a couple of glasses of *vino tinto*, because she looked a bit flushed.

"Hello darling, welcome back. How was France?"

"Fantastique."

"This came for you." And she handed me a letter. In the Sex God's handwriting!! Wow and wowzee wow!

Mutti came and sat on my bed.

"So, did you have a fab time?"

"*Oui. Très sportif.* Night-night."

"Did you see the Eiffel Tower? It's amazing at night, isn't it? Was it all lit up?"

Oh, good grief. I know she was being a nice mutti and everything, but I wanted to read my Sex God notelet. I said kindly, "Mum, I'm a bit boat-lagged. I'll tell you all about it in the morning."

She touched Libby's cheek and then she touched mine.

"Don't grow up too fast, love." She looked all tearful.

What is the matter with grown-ups? They are always banging on about how childish you are and telling you to grow up and so on, and then when you do, they start blubbering.

After she'd left I ripped open my letter.

Dear Georgia,
Welcome home, snog queen. I'm really looking forward to seeing you. I've thought about you all weekend and I wanted to tell you that I like everything about you. Your hair, your gorgeous mouth. The way I say "good-bye" and you say "I'm away laughing on a fast camel."

See you Tuesday.
Lots of love,
Robbie

Phwoar. I put the letter under my pillow. My very first love letter.

1:OO a.m.
Well, unless you count that one that Mark Big Gob sent me, which looked like he had written it with a stick.

1:O5 a.m.
Dave the Laugh sent me quite a nice letter when Wet Lindsay deliberately hit me on the ankle with her hockey stick. Actually, the reason I say "I'm away laughing on a fast camel" instead of "good-bye" is because of him.

And "nippy noodles."

1:10 a.m.
And "poo parlor division" instead of "loo."

tuesday january 25th

Exhausted, but up like a startled earwig at 8:15 A.M., thanks to Libby blowing her new bugle in my ear. What complete fool had bought her that? Dad, obviously.

stalag 14

I wore my beret proudly this morning (not the huge one, as I didn't want to get a reprimand first thing). I wore my beret *à la française* on the side of my head. When I saw Hawkeye, I said, "*Bonjour Madame*, I *aime* a lot your *très bonne* outfit *ce matin*."

"Just get into Assembly and try to be normal for once." That's nice, isn't it? You try to add a little bit of beautosity and humorosity into a dull world and that is the thanks you get.

As we slouched past Elvis's hut, I nudged Jas. "Elvis has got a bell! How ludicrously sad is that?" He has a bell on the outside of his hut and a sign

above it that says: "Ring the bell for the caretaker."
Hahahahahaha.

assembly

Slim in tip-top jelly form this morning, in her attractive elephant-tent dress. We were all still in *la belle* France mood, saying "Ah, *bonjour*" and nodding at one another a lot and shrugging.

Slim ordered, "Silence, at once. And stop shuffling around like silly geese. I have something very serious to tell you. I am sorry to say that the whole school has been very badly let down by a few bad apples. Girls from this school have been involved in a criminal act. And I intend to make an example of them by punishing them in the severest manner."

All of the ace gang looked at one another. God's slippers, what had we done now? Surely Madame Slack hadn't told Slim about the hunchback incident? Or the accidental French flag fiasco?

Hawkeye was glaring at us as we shuffled around. Slim went on. "Two girls have been arrested for shoplifting in town. Charges are to be made."

All of us went Yessssss! (inwardly). The Bummers had finally come to the end of their reign of terror. Yesss!!!

But then we noticed a dog in the ointment. The Bummers were in the row in front of us, looking as tarty and spotty as normal, and also . . . not bothered.

Slim continued. "The two girls are Monica Dickens and Pamela Green. They are, as of today, expelled from school. I trust this will be a warning to any girl who imagines that crime has no consequences."

We were all amazed at the news. I kept saying to the others, "Nauseating P. Green? And ADM? Shoplifting?"

Jools said, "Nauseating P. Green can hardly see the end of her nose. She would be a crap shoplifter. She'd have to ask a shop assistant to point things out to her."

She is not wrong.

Weird to think that behind those huge glasses lurked a mistress criminal.

I said, "And ADM? She came to a school dance in ankle socks once. That is not shoplifting wear."

break

Behind the sports hall we all huddled together under our coats discussing the scandalosa.

Rosie said, "I can't believe Nauseating P. Green actually went shoplifting in a gang with ADM."

I said, "Do you remember when ADM owned up to Miss Stamp about not having had a shower after games last term? And no one had even noticed that she hadn't. Miss Stamp didn't notice. In fact, I don't think she had actually noticed that ADM had even been doing games. That is not the attitude of a mistress criminal. That is the attitude of an astonishingly dim person. Which is what she is."

"I was never very nice to them," said Jas. "I feel bad now. I wonder if we can visit them in jail and maybe take them things . . . you know, knitted things and so on. Oranges."

I said, "Jas, they are not in the Crimean War. They don't need you to knit balaclavas. They won't go to jail."

Jas was rambling on, "Well, Slim said they were expelled and bad apples and so forth and—"

"Jas, can I say something?"

"What?"

"Shut up."

"Well, I—"

"That is not shutting up, Jas, that is keeping on talking rubbish."

"But—"

We could have kept that up for centuries, but then the Bummers walked around the corner. Jackie Bummer said, "Clear off, tiny tots, we want to have a fag and you are sitting in our ashtray."

Jools (bravely, but stupidly) said, "This is just ground, anyone's ground, it's not—"

Alison came over and got hold of her hair, "You are *in* our ashtray, so why don't you get *out* of our ashtray."

We grumbled and groaned as we collected our things. I hate them, I hate them. As the Bummers lit up their fags, Jackie said, "Sad about the criminal element in this school, isn't it?"

In a fit of stupidosity, I said, "Yes, well, why don't you leave, then?" To which Jackie answered, "Careful, Big Nose, as a severe duffing often offends." Then she flicked her cigarette ash onto my head and said, "Oh, whoops."

I had to wash my hair with soap in the loos and

then dry it upside down under the hand dryer. Fortunately, I had my mega-duty hair gel with me. Otherwise there would have been a Coco the Clown incident.

maths

It's a bit funny not having P. Green's head bobbing around at the front of the class. "I miss her," said Rosie. "It's not the same firing elastic bands with no target." She is all heart.

Still, I can't spend any more time thinking about other people. It's only two hours until I meet the Sex God. It's double blodge after this, so providing I don't have to do anything disgusting with pond life, I will be able to get my nails done and foundation on, and possibly mascara, if I crouch down at the back.

double blodge

I thought of an hilarious biology joke (which is not easy). I wrote to the gang in a gang note: "Lockjaw means never having to say you're sorry."

They did their famous cross-eyed sign of approval.

Also, I have made a lovely new furry friend (no, not Jas). It's a pickled vole. There are all kinds of disgusting things pickled in jars in the blodge lab, but this is a really cute vole that has its little paws up so that it looks like it is waving at you.

I wave back. I may call it Rover. Rover the vole.

last bell

in the loos

Mucho excitemondo. My hand was shaking when I was doing my eye shadow. I very nearly put Sex Shimmer all over my face, which is not attractive. I made Jas wait for me to walk out to the gate. I said, "So, Jazzy Knickers, what are you up to tonight? Whilst I am seeing my boyfriend?"

She was sitting on the sink looking at her sideways reflection. "I've got quite nice cheeks, haven't I?"

"Jas, you've got adorable cheeks. One on each side of your nose. Couldn't be better."

She thought I meant it. "Tom is doing his irrigation project and I'm doing my German homework tonight. It's due in. You should do yours—Herr Kamyer will have a nervy spaz if you don't."

"Jas, as I have said many, many times . . . never

put off until tomorrow what you can avoid alto-
gether."

Jas was still admiring her cheeks. "Well, you
say that, but what will you feel like when you go to
Germany and you can't say anything?"

"I'm not going to go to Germany."

"You might, though."

"Well, I won't."

That shut her up for a minute.

"But say you had to."

"Why, what for? I don't like pickled cabbage."

"What if Robbie had to go there for a gig?
You'd feel like a *dumschnitzel*."

Actually she did have a point.

4:20 p.m.

We walked out across the yard to the gates. I
made Jas shield me, just in case any of the
Oberführers were around and noticed that I was
all made up. Since the shoplifting fiasco all the
staff and prefects are on high alert. Miss Stamp
even told Melanie Andrews off because she
didn't have a name tag in her sports knickers. I
really, really don't want to imagine how she found
that out.

Rosie, Jools and Ellen were loitering without intent near Mr. Attwood's hut, so we all linked up. Robbie was leaning on the gate. Phwoar!! I could feel his Sex-Goddy vibes even by Mr. Attwood's special bell. But then I noticed that he was not alone. He was talking to Tom and Dave the Laugh and Rollo! Ellen, Jas and Jools nearly fell over with shock. They had no makeup on. Also Ellen had mistakenly put her beret on because she couldn't be arsed to open up her haversack. Emergency, emergency!!!

Ellen snatched off her beret and said, "OhmyGod, ohmyGod, what shall I do?"

In the end Rosie and I formed a sort of defensive wall behind which Ellen and Jas and Jools applied emergency lippy and rolled over their skirts. Rosie and I had to pretend to be swapping books. I was laughing attractively and so was Rosie, as if we were casually unaware that we had three mates crouching behind us. Jas said from near my ankles, "What are they doing? Can they see us?"

"They're just talking."

Rosie said, "We're going to have to pretend to notice them in a minute, are you ready?" Then the three of them leapt up like leaping things and we all walked up to the gates in a state of casualosity (and lip-glossiness).

Robbie looked marvy. He gave me his dreamy smile and pushed his hair back. "Hello."

I was in Ditherland. It's bad enough when it's just me and him, but in front of the lads and, in particular, in front of Dave the Laugh, I turn into Herr Kamyer in a skirt (i.e., a prat).

I was completely out-dithered by Ellen, however, who I thought might start doing Highland dancing, she was hopping about so much. Tom was nuzzling Jas and she was all red and smiley and dim. How come boys don't go spazoid? They all seemed very cool. I noticed (even though I didn't care) that although Dave the Laugh said hi to Ellen and kissed her cheek, he didn't do any nuzzling. In fact he gave me a look.

It was a "Hello, red-bottomed minx, we meet again"–type look.

my bedroom
9:00 p.m.

I had a dreamy time hanging around with the Sex God. I made all kinds of excuses about wanting to get things from all the shops so that people would see us together. I waved at loads of people, even if I didn't know them very well. I even waved at Mr. Across the Road as he staggered out of the pet shop with two tons of kitty litter. He was so surprised, his bottom nearly dropped off.

Robbie said, "Shopping is over, now it's time for snogging." Then we went and had *le* snog *par excellence* out by the racecourse.

midnight

I wonder if Jas is right for once. Maybe Nauseating P. Green will have to go to the naughty girls' prison. Like in *Prisoner: Cell Block H*. She might get duffed up every day by sadists. Much the same as school, really.

Shut up, brain.

I care too much for people. I am a bit like Jesus. Only not so heavily bearded.

wednesday january 26th

stalag 14

On our way to the Art room we had a quick burst of "Let's go down the disco" in the corridor until we nearly crashed into Nauseating P. Green's mum. She was crying as she went into Slim's office.

Oh, poo.

break

Hiding in the games cupboard. It's full of hockey sticks, but at least it is not minus fifteen degrees like it is outside.

Kate Richardson told me that Jackie Bummer has got ten leather coats, all different colors. And Jackie was also showing off and saying that she and Alison made Nauseating P. Green and ADM go and do their shoplifting for them. Like in *Oliver Twist* . . . or is it *David Copperfield*? Anyway, one of those really depressing stories about tiny orphans with Fagin in it. They frightened P. Green and ADM into going into shops and putting leather coats on under their own coats and walking out of the shop and then handing them over to the Bummers. They said that if they didn't get six each they would do something horrible to P. Green's hamsters. They even gave them a special tool to get the security labels off.

Rosie said, "Well, why did they get caught, then?"

I explained, "Because P. Green tried to steal six coats at once. She put them all on under her own coat and then got trapped in the revolving door as she tried to get out."

1:00 a.m.

On the bright side, Mutti says I can have some new boots. To wear to the gig that my boyfriend is playing at on Saturday at the Buddha Lounge.

1:10 a.m.

Did I mention that there is a gig on Saturday that my boyfriend is playing at? Once again I can expose myself as girlfriend of a Sex God. Ooer.

thursday january 27th

german

Herr Kamyer was telling us about the Müller family from our German textbook—about Klaus going camping and getting his *kocher* out. Klaus always uses his *kocher* to *koch* his *spanferkel* (suckling pig). Jas was annoying me by doing a quiz in *Cosmo*. Not an interesting quiz about what kind of skin you have or whether you are a sex bomb or not. It's to find out what your natural body clock is. Whether you should stay up late and get up late, or whether you should get up early and go to bed early.

Who cares? Jas does. She wrote me a note: "I like to get up early and that makes me a Lark-type person. Tom likes to get up early as well, so he's a Lark and not an Owl, and that makes us get on really well. I wonder what the German for 'lark' is?"

I wrote back: "Larken." But she doesn't believe me.

I ended up doing the stupid boring quiz because it insinuated itself into my brain. I am very impressionable, which is why people should be very careful about what they bother me with. For instance, when we did *Treasure Island* I developed a limp. Anyway, it turns out that I am a moderate Owl. On our way to Maths I said to Jas, "That means that, although I like to go to bed late and get up late, I am not very fond of field mice."

She said, "Your eyes are a bit owly, sort of bulgey."

"Oh dear, now the little Lark is going to get a duffing from the moderate Owl." And then I biffed her over the head with my Science overall. She said I had to stop, because I was making her fringe go all wonky. And no one wants that.

break

I have been made hockey captain!!! Honestly, at this rate I will become a regular citizen and possibly start doing voluntary work with the elderly mad! Er no, forget that bit. I've just remembered the last time I went round to Granddad's and accidentally went into his secret money drawer to borrow a few pounds for essentials. Chewing gum and so on. He had set his false teeth open as a trap. When I opened the drawer they slammed shut.

Even though he is supposed to be deaf, Granddad heard his false teeth bang shut from the bottom of his garden. He laughed so much I thought I might have to call the emergency services. But I contented myself by hiding his pipe.

Anyway, back to my triumph on the pitch. Miss Stamp announced that I would be captain. The ace gang were all doing the "Let's go down the disco" dance as celebration, until Miss Stamp told them to pull themselves together and get into the showers. Which quite literally put a dampener on things.

When we were dressed and going off to English, Miss Stamp took me to one side and said, "You have the makings of quite a good captain, Georgia. Make sure your attitude matches your hockey skills."

I haven't the faintest idea what she is on about. I said to Rosie, "Is she implying that I have insufficient maturiosity?"

Rosie said, "I don't know . . . but . . . let's go down the disco!"

We did our special disco inferno dancing across the playing fields. Elvis was lurching around in his overalls. "What are you doing now? Messing about, playing the giddy goat."

I tried to explain pleasantly to the old maniac that we were in girlish high spirits. Pointless, though. He just went mumbling off.

"In my new capacity as hockey captain," I said, "I may have him confined to his hut for the foreseeable future."

in the front room
7:00 p.m.
Vati said, "I'm going to start going to the gym three

times a week to get in peak physical condition for our football matches." I didn't laugh. He started doing a sit-up in the front room. Good grief.

I went off into the kitchen in search of something to eat. Oh yummy, a yogurt without mold on it! Mum does not take her nurturing role very seriously. But if I complain she'll only say something ridiculous, like "I'm at work all day. Why don't *you* make something?"

When I went back into the front room, Dad was back lying on the sofa watching TV. I asked him, "How many sit-ups did you do?"

"Well, I think it's a mistake to rush into things."

"Just the one, then?"

He pretended to be interested in some gardening program.

7:30 p.m.

Mum came in from her girls' aerobics all red and giddy. She said to Vati, "Don't get up, Bob, try and rest yourself." But I don't think she meant it. I followed her into the kitchen in the hope that she might have some food hidden in her leotard. She did have a tin of beans, as it happens, so we tucked in.

"It's very very like Paris in our home," I told her.

She wasn't paying any attention—just being red and adjusting her bra. Then she burbled on. "We had such a laugh tonight, Gee. Prue and Sandy went to this singles bar the other night and got off with a couple of Russian sailors. Sandy said Ivan could only say *Nyet* but that he was a really good snogger."

I just looked at her.

"Mum, that is disgusting."

"Why?"

"Because, well, they are mothers."

"I know, but they haven't got husbands anymore. They are single women again who have children."

"I know, but . . ."

She'd gone off on one, though. "Do you think that anyone over twenty-five should just stay in forever?"

"Yes."

"You're being ridiculous."

"I am not."

"You're a teenage prude."

I was thinking, A prude, am I? You wouldn't say that if you knew the amount of lip nibbling I had done. I have been practically eaten alive by boys! But I didn't say it.

8:30 p.m.

In the bath, contemplating my life as the girlfriend of a Sex God and also tip-top hockey captain.

And also why nunga-nungas float. What is the point of that? Perhaps in prehistoric days they were used as life belts in times of flood. But if that was the case, why did they bother with Noah's Ark? Mrs. Noah and all the women could have just floated about and everyone else could have climbed on board.

Then I heard raised voices. Libby started shouting, "Fight, fight!"

Vati was yelling, "I don't watch television all the time . . . and what if I did, what's wrong with that?"

Mum yelled back, "It's boring—that's what's wrong with it!"

"Well let's talk about bloody aerobics, then. Go on, tell me how many times you wiggled your arse in time to the music!"

"Boring pig!"

And then Libby started yelling, "Bad piggy, bad piggy!!"

Sacré bloody *bleu*. I am going to be an orphan soon. Ah well.

friday january 28th

breakfast

This not talking to each other thing is driving me to the brink of bonkerosity. How am I supposed to experience growing up if the so-called grown-ups are making *me* be the most grown-up?

Mum said to me, "Would you ask your father if he would mind looking after his daughter Liberty tomorrow evening, as I have a pressing social engagement?"

Oh, good Lord. I said to Dad, who was half an inch away fiddling with his beard, "Dad, would you mind looking after your daughter Liberty tomorrow evening, which is, incidentally, when I shall be at a pressing social engagement myself, because Mutti also has a pressing social engagement, apparently."

Dad went all red and trousery. He said, "This is ballocks."

I said to Mum, "He said this is ballocks."

And Dad said, "Don't bloody swear. It's not clever."

And I said, "And he said, don't bloody swear, it's not clever."

Dad started to say, "Don't be so bl—" and then

345

he stopped and I looked at him in a helpful way and said, "And he said, don't be so bl—" But he walked out and slammed the door.

Mum said, "He's so childish." Which is true, but I think it's ironic that she should say it when she is wearing a T-shirt that says "Go Girl" and fluffy mules.

saturday january 29th
Up at the crack of 8:00 A.M. for pregig preparations.

Vati was up as well in his ludicrous football shorts. He was being all "masculine." Mum was still ignoring him, but I said, "Good-bye, Vati. This may be the last time I see you fully limbed."

He chucked me under my chin and said, "I'm in my prime, Georgia, they won't know what hit them." Then he strode off like he thought he was David Beckham. Which I think he does.

I said to Mum, "Vati is very very like David Beckham, isn't he? Apart from being porky, heavily bearded and crap at football."

She just tutted and did that basooma-adjusting thing she does.

When I came out of the bathroom wrapped in a towel Mum was staring at me. Surely she couldn't tell that I had used her strictly forbidden skin stuff?

"What?" I said.

"Your elbows stick out a lot."

What fresh hell? Sticky-out elbows??? I said, "What are you talking about?"

She was prodding my arms. "Well, they do, don't they? I've never noticed them sticking out like that before. Look at mine. They aren't like yours. Do you think you've dislocated them playing hockey or something?"

Dislocated my elbows? I stormed off to my room to inspect them. Perfectly ordinary elbows. Maybe a bit sticky-outy, though.

Phoned Jas. "Jas, do you think my elbows stick out?"

She was, as usual, chewing something, probably her fringe. "They've always been a bit odd-looking."

Thank you, Nurse Jas. She's too self-obsessed to bother with my elbows. She just raved on about how she and Tom have joined the Ramblers'

Association. She's not kidding. She could ramble on for England. I didn't know there was a special association for it.

lunchtime
in my bedroom

I am having some relaxing "me" time. And me time means groovy music and an eye mask. Libby is making some earmuffs for the kittykats, out of some cotton wool, I think.

1:30 p.m.

Mum came in and went ballisticisimus. The cotton wool earmuffs for the kittykats are made from her new packet of tampons. She huffed off with what was left and accused me of selfishosity for not noticing. I yelled after her, "Mum, it is very hard to notice anything when you have tea bags on your eyes."

She came back in again to take Libby down for her bath and said, "I think we should get those elbows looked at."

What is she rambling on about? Get them looked at by whom? An elbowologist, no doubt.

On the funny side, I have just looked up

"elbow" in German and it is *Ellbogen*.

Campingfahrt means not, as you might imagine, an unfortunate incident with Libby in a tent. . . . It means "camping trip." I think I have a natural talent for languages.

6:30 p.m.

Mucho excitemondo and jelly knickers activity. I am a vision in black, wearing my new and groovoid boots.

7:00 p.m.

Met the gang at the usual place to go to the gig. Sven had his special flares on. They have a battery in them and little lightbulbs all the way down the seams. When he presses the battery his trousers light up. He really is bonkers. And huge.

When we got to the door of the Buddha Lounge he said to the door guy, "Got evening, I am Sven and these are my chicks. Let us in, my trousers want to boogie." And Rosie isn't a bit embarrassed.

We all went immediately to the loos. It was the usual scrum in there. Ellen was sooooo nervous (again), like a jelly bean on a trampoline. She kept going into a ditherspaz, saying, "I really, really rate Dave, you know."

We said, "We know."

"But I really, you know, like him."

"WE KNOW!!!"

Out in the club it was heaving. We found a little corner to use as gang headquarters and had a good eyeball around. All the lads were by the bar, Dave the L (hmmm, cool shirt), Rollo, Tom, and a bunch of their friends. Oh, and Mark Big Gob was there with his rough mates. I hadn't seen him since the telephone box incident. He deliberately looked at my nungas and licked his lips. I pity his poor tiny midget girlfriend. At least my basoomas are nicely protected in their Christmas holder. Mutti said she got it specially because it had "extra-firm control."

Then, from behind the stage, The Stiff Dylans came out to start their set. Groovy pajamas. Everyone went wild. The Sex God looked around and saw me (just casually flicking my hair back and exuding sophisticosity). He smiled at me and then blew me a kiss. Oh, yes! In front of everyone. Oh, yes and *bon*!

10:00 p.m.

Dancefest *extraordinaire*. Top fun all night. As I may have said before, Dave the Laugh is . . . er . . . a laugh. And also quite a cool dancer. Ellen doesn't really like dancing, so when she had gone off to the ladies' he made me do the conga with him. He made me do it to "Oh No, It's Me Again," which is one the Sex God composed that's on my Chrimbo compilation tape. It's a slow number and really serious about someone (van Gogh, I think) who wakes up and looks at himself in the mirror and says, "Oh no, it's me again," which is depressing. But not to Dave the Laugh, who thought it was a conga opportunity. Robbie was singing with his eyes closed (hmmm, very moody), but then during the slow guitar break he looked up and I think he caught sight of me and Dave conga dancing. He didn't look full of happi-nosity. In fact, he looked a bit miffed.

I stopped doing the conga then, but Dave shouted at me, "Don't stop mid-conga; it's very bad for my cong."

What in the name of Elton John's codpiece is he on about? He's naughty, though. When we were dancing he let his hands sort of drift onto my bottom. I could feel it slightly flushing. Down, bottom, down.

Ellen still wasn't back from the loo, so we went across to the bar to get a cold drink. He said, "I think I have got the General Horn."

I said, "What is that?"

He explained that "having the Horn" means fancying people. And it's got various stages. "You can have the Specific Horn, when you fancy one person. Then if it gets worse you get the General Horn, which is when you fancy loads of people. But worst of all is the Cosmic Horn."

He was really making me laugh and feel funny at the same time, but I couldn't help asking, "What in the name of Lucifer's bottom is the Cosmic Horn?"

"That is when you fancy everything and everyone in the universe."

Blimey.

Ellen came over then and grabbed Dave's arm. She said, all girlie, "Dave, do you fancy going outside? I'm a bit hot."

Dave sort of hesitated and looked at me in a peculiar way and then said, "Me too." And they went off. Ellen is sooo keen on him, she has no pridosity.

I said to Jas (and Tom, as they are like Siamese twins. I wonder what happens when she goes to the loo?), "Honestly, Ellen is really uncool about Dave. She practically stalks him."

Jas said, "You stalked Robbie."

I laughed in an attractive way. "Oh Jas, I did not stalk him. . . ."

Jas rambled on like an unstoppable loon. "And you made me assistant stalker. Also, do you remember when you made me go round to Wet Lindsay's house and we went and looked in her bedroom window and saw her in her thong?"

Tom said, "You went round to Lindsay's house and looked in her window? I didn't know that! Does Robbie know?"

I quickly said, "Tom, have you ever had the Cosmic Horn?"

Just then The Stiff Dylans finished their set and came off stage. I went off to find Robbie for a snog break, but it was hopeless. There were loads of girls all crowded around him in the dressing room, and I couldn't get near.

He said over the top of their heads, "I'll walk you home at the end, don't leave."

midnight

Outside the Buddha Lounge. Jas asked, "Is your vati picking you up?"

"No," I told her. "I've got a special prison pass, which means that I am allowed to get home by myself. Mostly because Mum is out and Dad can't walk after playing football with the 'lads.' They only lost thirteen to zero."

The gang set off, a band of merry snoggers, and I was left outside by myself.

12:15 a.m.

Brr, quite nippy noodles. Where is he?

I went and looked in through the doors, Robbie was talking to six girls: the rest of the band's girlfriends, Sam, Mia and India, and another three. I recognized a couple of them because they used to be in the sixth form and had gone off to London to fashion college or something. Perhaps that explained why one (Petra) was wearing a Tibetan bonnet with earflaps. Petra had long blond hair that poked out of her bonnet (very Tibetan . . . not). She was swishing it about like, er, a swishing thing. Robbie was laughing with them. But as I always say, She who laughs last . . . er . . . doesn't always get the joke.

Why was he talking to them? Perhaps he was doing PR for his career. Or perhaps they were like those groupies I read about that used to hang around boys in groups and make little statues of their manly parts out of plaster of Paris. I didn't see any bags of plaster, though. Although one of them did have a haversack. The plaster might be in there. Just then Robbie saw me and said, "Georgia, hi."

Petra looked round and said (in a bonnetty way), "Oh hi, Georgia. Long time no dig. How are you? How's Stalag 14? Not wearing your beret?" And she laughed in a common way.

Robbie looked a bit uncomfortable and said quite quickly, "Well, nice to see you all again. See you later. Come on, Georgia."

Hahahaha and double hahaha. That shut Petra up. She looked amazed to see me and Robbie walk off together.

Robbie was a bit quiet on the way home, but when we walked through the park he got hold of me and kissed me for a really long time. I only remembered to start breathing halfway through, so I nearly passed out.

It was like a snoggers' rave in the park. Every bush was full of them. Mark Big Gob was there with his tiny little girlfriend. And it was very dark, but I am almost sure that he picked her up and put her on a tree stump to snog her. Either that or her legs get very fat towards the ankles.

When we got to my gate, Robbie said, "Petra has just come back from backpacking round India and Nepal."

I said, "Oh, that explains the earflaps."

The Sex God pinched my nose. "What am I going to do with you?"

"Take me to Hamburger-a-gogo land with you."

"Hmm, I wonder what your dad would say to that."

"He'd say 'bye and God bless all who sail in you." SG didn't look like he believed me. Or knew what in the name of arse I was talking about.

1:00 a.m.
Libby was still up when I got in. She had her pajama top on but her bottom was flowing free and wild. She is not what you would call inhibited, which is a pity. She was giving Teddy a late-night

haircut. Mum said when I came in, "Come on, Libbs, it's very late and your big sister is home now. Time for bed."

Libby didn't even look up, she just said, in an alarmingly grown-up voice, "Not now, dear, I'm busy."

2:00 a.m.

Kissed the back of my hand good-night. I think I am becoming a champion snogger. As Peter Dyer said when I went for snogging lessons, I apply just the right sort of pressure, not too pressing and not too giving. Much like my nature, I like to think.

In a way, it's a shame not to share my special snogging talents far and wide.

3:00 a.m.

What am I talking about? I love the Sex God, end of bottom. I mean end of story.

3:15 a.m.

Looked out my window. Angus and Naomi are on the wall. . . . Do cats snog? Perhaps they have a cat snogging scale.

3:30 a.m.

Do owls snog?

SHUT UP, BRAIN, SHUT UP. This is all Dave the Laugh's fault with his Cosmic Horn talk.

monday january 31st

Met Jas at her gate. She showed me her Ramblers' Association badge. Honestly. Apparently you go off with other half-wits and wander around the countryside looking at things. I said to her, "The gig was groovy bananas, wasn't it?"

"Yeah, fabby."

"Jas, don't you ever, you know . . . get the Horn for anyone else besides Tom?"

"No. I am not like you. Promiscuous."

"Jas, I'm not promiscuous."

"Well, you flirt with Dave the Laugh."

"Well, I . . ."

"In fact, you snog Dave the Laugh . . . and I bet you would snog Gorgey Henri if he asked you."

"Well . . . I . . ." For once she had a sort of point.

The ace gang all wore enormous berets this morning to remind us of our visit to *la belle* France. It seems about six hundred years ago. We have decided to commemorate the occasion by having a National Hunchback Day. Maybe we will wait till things cool down a bit at Stalag 14 first, though.

When we got near the school gates we took the comedy berets off and had our ordinary ones underneath. (From comedy to tragedy in one movement!) So hahahaha to the Oberführers. We are too full of cleverosity for them.

As we were walking past Hawkeye something really horriblimus happened. Nauseating P. Green was standing near the gates! She looked like she had been blubbering for about a million years. I smiled at her and she started to come over to us. Oh, good grief. Then Hawkeye saw her and said, "Pamela Green, you are not to come anywhere near this school again. You are a complete disgrace."

P. Green started blinking and stuttering. "But Mrs. Heaton, I . . . I didn't . . . it wasn't me, I . . ."

Hawkeye just snapped at us. "Come on, you girls, get into school NOW!" I wonder if she was a Doberman in a previous life.

cloakroom

I said to Jas, "Nauseating P. Green is obviously a twit of the first water but I do feel sorry for her."

Jas said, "I wonder if we should . . . er . . . go and see someone about it."

Rosie said, "And then get the duffing-up of a lifetime from the Bummers?"

Hmm, she had a point.

Still.

games

Brrrrrrrrrrrrr. Miss Stamp has had us doing hockey maneuvers in minus five hundred and forty.

As we shivered I said to Jas, "Even seals would stay in their little seal homes on days like this. They would stay snuggly tucked up knitting and chatting."

Jas got interested in the seals. She's a bit obsessed with sea creatures, I think. "Do you think they have their own language? I wonder what sort of thing they talk about?"

"They talk about the great seal package holidays they have been on. Greenland by night, Antarctica weekend breaks, two nights on a top-class iceberg and as much krill as you can eat."

This is the life. Charging around on a frozen pitch, whacking concrete balls at each other with sticks. Once you got the feeling back in your bum it was quite good fun, actually. I was tearing up and down the pitch like David Beckham (without the shaved head and manly parts, of course, but with the consummate ball skills). Well, until I accidentally whacked Jas on the knee (above the shin pad) with a ball.

It was her fault, really. I whacked a really good goal in the net but Mrs. Slow Knickers didn't get out of the way in time (probably because she was weighed down by her enormous sports pantibus). As she hobbled off she was moaning and groaning and blaming me. "You're mad, Georgia, hitting balls around like . . . like . . ."

I said, helpfully, "Like a brilliant hockey captain?"

"No, not like that."

"Well, like what?"

She was red as a loon. I gave her my famous world-renowned affectionate hug, but she pushed me off and said, "Like . . . a promiscuous HOOLIGAN."

Oooooooh. Now she had really upset me.

lunchtime

Lad alert!!! Lad alert!!! Dave the Laugh was at the school gates. He looked in a bit of a funny mood. Normally he is all smiley and sort of cocky, but he wasn't smiling. And he looked a bit tense. He is really nice-looking. If I didn't have the Sex God I would definitely want to go out with him. Especially as Tom told me that Dave made a huge banner and hung it on top of their school, and it said, "For Sale." Which anyone can see is vair vair funny. By the time I got to gang headquarters (first floor loos), Ellen was being Dithering Queen *extraordinaire*. She was saying, "Oh, oh, what shall I do? What shall I do?"

Jas said, "Just go and talk to him. He's come to see you. That's really nice." Then she went all dreamy and dim. "Tom sometimes just gets an urge to see me and he comes to meet me on the—"

I said, "Veggie van?"

She didn't even look at me. She just continued to talk to Ellen as if I hadn't said anything vair vair hilarious. "He comes to see me on the spur of the moment." Then she gave me her worst look (scary bananas) and limped off.

I called after her, "You know I love you, Jas. Why are you not touching me with a barge pole? And eschewing me with a firm hand? And *ignorez-vous*ing me?" She still didn't pay any attention.

After about a million years of applying lip gloss, Ellen went out to meet Dave the L.

We all watched from the loo windows whilst they talked. I said to Jools, "He didn't snog her when he saw her, did he?"

Rosie was doing her toenails; she had bits of soap between each toe to stop the polish going smeary. I must remember not to use the soap ever again.

Anyway, Rosie said, "Sven always snogs me when he first sees me. In fact he snogs me pretty much all the time. Even when he is eating."

We all said, "Erlack!"

Dave and Ellen went behind the bike shed and we couldn't see what was happening. I was sort of glad about that somehow, because even though I had a boyfriend, was ecstatic, in seventh heaven, couldn't be happier, never thought about another boy for a second, had set aside my red bottom with a firm hand, only had the Specific Horn with no sign of the General Horn at all, I didn't really like to see Dave the Laugh snogging other people. I don't know why.

maths

Ellen was blubbing in Maths. She was sniffling next to Jas and I could see that she was telling her what had happened, but as Jas is even *ignorez-vous*ing my notes, I couldn't find out anything. Then Ellen put her hand up and said she felt ill and could she go to sick bay.

I know I often feel like blubbing during Maths, but I thought she was being a bit over the top having to go to sick bay. Mind you we were doing pi, and I may have said this many times before, but didn't the ancient Greeks have anything better to do than measure things? Or leap out of baths, yelling, *"Eureka!"*

When Miss Stamp (quarter lesbian, quarter sports Oberführer and also quarter Maths teacher . . . hang on, that only makes her a three-quarter person . . . ah well) asked us why Archimedes shouted *"Eureka!"* when his bath overflowed, I said it was because *eureka* is Greek for "Bloody hell, this bath is hot!!!" Which may well be the first ancient Greek joke.

World news breaking! Dave has dumped Ellen!! And Ellen is not a happy dumpee. In the Chemistry lab loos Ellen was nearly hysterical. Her eyes were all swollen like mice eyes. She was gulping and trying to talk, and then blubbing again. Nurse Jas was hugging her.

Finally Ellen managed to say, "He, he, said he first realized at the . . . at the . . . fish party that he . . . that he . . . that he . . ." Sniffle, sniffle, gulp.

I thought, I'm ever so peckish. I wonder if it would be really unfeeling if I just nibbled on my Mars bar?

But then Ellen managed to go on. "I mean, I said to him . . . 'Is it something I've done?' And he said . . . he said . . . 'No, you're a great girl, it's something I've done, not you. It's a sort of General Horn–type thing.' What does he mean? What has he done? What General Horn thing?"

Oh God. Oh Goddy God God.

The others were nodding, but Jas was nodding and looking at me. Like a wise old owl in a skirt. But with arms instead of wings. And no beak.

Then the bell went. Phew.

4:30 p.m.

On the way home, Jas walked really quickly ahead of me, like she had something stuck up her bottom. I nearly had to jog to get alongside her. I put my arm around her and she sped up even more, so that we were both jogging along.

I said, "Jas, Jas, my little pal, I'm sorry about bonking you on your knee. Do you want me to kiss it? Or carry you home? I will. I will do anything if you will be my little pal again."

Jas stopped. "All right, don't drop me, though." So I had to carry her home. All the way home. And she is not light—her knickers alone must weigh about half a stone.

I was nearly dead by the time we reached her gate. I tried to put her down, but she said, "This is the gate, not my bed." So I had to carry her right to the door. She unlocked the door still in my arms, whilst my head practically fell off with redness, and then I had to carry her upstairs to her bedroom.

It did make us laugh, though. As we were lying on her bed with a squillion of her soft toys, I said, "Jas, have you forgiven me now?"

"Polish my Ramblers' badge." So I had to polish

the badge. Then she said, "I might be preparing myself to forgive you."

I fed her a cheesy whatsit and she munched on it. Then she said, "But will Ellen forgive you?"

"What do you mean? For what?"

"For snogging her boyfriend and . . . for . . . for allowing your red bottom to rule the roost."

"Jas, my bottom is not a chicken."

"You know what I mean."

"Don't start all that 'you know what I mean' business."

"Yes, but you do know what I mean."

my room

Jas thinks that I should tell Ellen what happened *vis-à-vis* Dave the Laugh, because then she will know that he is a serial snogger and lip nibbler . . . or whatever . . . and then she will not pine for him.

Hmmm. She might not pine for him, but she might pull my head off.

Mum came bustling in. "Are you ready?"

"For what? Nuclear war? World peace? Tea? A surprise inheritance?"

"Dr. Clooney . . . er, I mean Dr. Gilhooley."

"Gorgey though he is, Mum, why would I be ready for him?"

5:00 p.m.

I had a quick look at my *Ellbogen*. I haven't thought about them much lately because of all the other emergencies that have been happening. They are a bit odd-looking, actually, when you get them naked. And I won't be able to go around wearing long sleeves for the rest of my life, especially in California. And what about the press when I go to premieres and stuff with Robbie? I don't want headlines pointing my elbows out to the world: "Sex God and Weird Girl with Sticky-out Elbows Go to Top Restaurant."

As we entered the Valley of the Unwell (Dr. Clooney's waiting room), I said to Mum quietly, "What can he do about them anyway?" I said it quietly because the room was, as usual, full of the mentally deranged.

Dr. Clooney is quite gorgeous. Blue-eyed, dark and sort of sexy. He makes Mum go in a terrible tizz, all flushed and basoomy. He said, "How can I help?"

Mum pulled up my sleeves exposing my elbows and said, "Her elbows stick out."

Dr. Clooney laughed for about a million years. He said, "Honestly, I would pay you two girls to come to my surgery every day." Then he walked over to examine my elbows.

Dr. Clooney smiled at me. Phwoar!! "Georgia is a racehorse."

What in the name of Miss Stamp's mustache and matching eyebrows is he talking about?

He went on. "She's got long limbs and not much fat on her body, so her elbows seem to be more boney and exposed than someone who has a different body shape. As she grows they'll be less noticeable."

I thought Mum was going to snog him on the spot. "Oh, thank you, Doctor, it was such a worry. Anyway, how have you been doing? Done any dancing lately?"

On the way home I said to Mum, "What did you mean, done any dancing lately?"

Mum went all red and delirious. "Well, I've just, you know, seen him out sometimes, when I've been with the girls . . . dancing, and . . ."

"Yes . . . and . . . ?"

"Well, he's very fit." Oh, dear God. My own mother is displaying alarming signs of the General Horn.

9:00 p.m.

On the plus side, the *Ellbogen* mystery is solved. . . . I am a racehorse.

10:00 p.m.

Rosie phoned. "Georgia. Something really awful has happened."

"Has your hair gone all sticky-up? I think mine has."

"No, it's not that."

"Lurker alert?"

"No, worse."

"Blimey. You're not having a baby Sven, are you?"

"Sven is being sent back to Swedenland. He has to help out with his family farm, or whatever they have over there."

"Is it a reindeer farm?"

"GEORGIA, I DON'T KNOW and I don't care!!!"

Rosie is sheer desperadoes. She says if Sven goes to Swedenland, she goes too. I said, "Well, you'd better find out where it is first. You drew the wheat belt across the Irish Sea in our last geoggers test."

tuesday february 1st
breakfast
8:05 a.m.

This is ridiculous—Mum and Dad are still not speaking. Normally I would be glad of the silence, except it means they both speak to me and ask me things. Like, "So, what's number one this week in the pop charts?" How sad is that?

stalag 14

It's like the Valley of the Damned. Rosie is moping around, Jools has had a fight with Rollo, and Ellen is sniffling around the place like a sniffler *extraordinaire*. You only have to say to her, "Do you fancy one of my cheesy whatsits?" and she runs off to the loos blubbing. And Jas keeps looking at me. Looking and looking.

I said to her, "You should be careful, Jas, one of the first formers was in a staring competition last week and she stared for so long that her eyes went dry and she had to go to hospital to have them watered."

She just sniffed. It is a very very good job that I am full of cheeriosity. Also a tip-top hockey captain.

r.e.

Rosie sent me a note. "I've found out where Swedenland is. I'm going to go after Sven and get a job and make new Sweden-type friends."

I wrote back: "Is there much call for fifteen-year-old snoggers in Swedenland?"

She looked at me when she got the note and did her famous impression of a cross-eyed loon. Then she wrote: "Anyway, what will YOU do in Hamburger-a-gogo land for a job? Your very amusing impression of a lockjaw germ, or . . . er . . . that's it."

evening

Same bat time. Same bat place.

Libby was applying some of Mutti's face powder and lipstick to Angus whilst he sat on my bed. And he didn't seem to mind. In fact, he was purring. Becoming a furry vati has made him alarmingly mellow. Or a transvestite.

Robbie has gone off for some interview thing. He didn't really explain what it was about. Popstar stuff, I suppose. Rosie is very very wrong if she thinks I will not be able to do anything in Hamburger-a-gogo land. I could form a girlfriends' hockey eleven and play my way across America.

wednesday february 2nd

Hockey tournament today with me at the helm. But more to the point, Wet Lindsay has resigned from the team. HURRAH! She says it is a protest against me being hockey captain, because I am a facsimile of a sham and have the attitude of a juvenile pea. Useless stick insect ankle molester.

6:30 p.m.

Cracking victory!!! The most amazing day. We played six matches and won all six! I scored in each match, and even though I do say it myself . . . I AM A HOCKEY GENIUS!!!

I had to give a speech when I accepted the cup for our school. It was my chance to show the world and, in particular, the heavily mustachioed Miss Stamp that I am full of wisdomosity and maturios-

ity and *gravitas* (not "gravy ass," as Rosie thought).
I said, "I would just like to say that I owe this victory
to many people. To my team, to my school, to my
mum and dad for having me, to the ancient Britons
for giving me my proud heritage, to the early cave-
men, without whom none of us would have got here,
as they invented the wheel . . ."

Miss Stamp was about to implode but she
couldn't do anything because the head of All
Saints School seemed to think I was being *très
amusant* and clapped A LOT at the end of my
speech.

thursday february 3rd
stalag 14
Hahahahaha. Slim had to mention my name in
Assembly and congratulate me!!!

Hawkeye looked like she had poo in her mouth
(which she probably did). Slim, as usual, was in a
ludicrously bad mood. Her chins were trembling in
time to the hymns. She said, "Despite what I have
said before, certain elements in this school con-
tinue to think they can carry on flouting school
rules. Mr. Attwood misplaced his cap a day or two
ago and found it today, burnt to a cinder. This is my

final warning to you all: Be very, very careful of your behavior, as all misdemeanors will be treated very seriously."

As we ambled off to English, I said, "Mr. Attwood probably set fire to his own hat on purpose. He hates us because we are young and lively."

Jas said, "And because we drop skeletons on him."

"Well, yes . . ."

"And the locusts ate his overalls. . . ."

"Yes, well there is . . ."

"And he tripped over his—"

"Jas, shut up."

r.e.

Rosie has been living in Glum City all day since her beloved Sven got in his Viking boat (Olau Lines ferry) and went off to Swedenland today. He has only gone for one month, but she insists that she is going to go and live in Swedenland with him for that month. Miss Wilson was telling us about her unhappy childhood, so I took the opportunity to draw some fashion items for Rosie to take with her to the Nordic wastes. I drew her

wearing furry glasses and a nose warmer. I even
did a vair vair funny drawing of her in a fur bikini,
but she could hardly be bothered to join in, even
when we started our traditional R.E. humming.
(We all start humming really softly and at the
same time carry on as normal so that you can't
tell we are humming. Or where the humming is
coming from.) Miss Wilson thinks it might be the
radiators. It drives Miss Wilson round the prover-
bial bend . . . not so far to go in her case.

break

In sheer desperadoes to cheer Rosie up, I had a
moment of my usual geniosity. We were slouching
along past Elvis's hut with its stupid sign that
says: "Ring the bell for the caretaker." I said to
RoRo, "*Un moment, mon* pally." Then I went and
rang his bell.

He came looning to his door, like the grumpi-
est, most mad man in the universe, which he is. He
glared at me and then said, "What do you want?"

I said, pointing to his sign, "What I want to
know, Mr. Attwood, is why you can't ring your own
bell."

Anyway, he didn't get it. He was rambling on

and I was just about to slope politely off, when Wet Lindsay came round the corner. She was ogling us like an ogler with stick legs, which she is.

Elvis was so red I thought his head might explode, but sadly, it didn't. He was shouting, "It's always you, messing about, coming in my hut. You let those bloody locusts eat my spare overalls. . . ."

I tried to be reasonable with the old maniac. "Mr. Attwood, Elvis, I wasn't to know that the locusts would eat your overalls. I merely thought they would like a little fly around in the blodge lab after being cooped up in their cage."

Mr. Attwood was still yelling. ". . . and I bet it was you who burnt my cap!"

Oh, for heaven's sake.

maths

I was just peacefully buffing my half-moons, when Hawkeye put her head round the door. She barked, "My office, now!!!"

hawkeye's office

Oh *sacré* bloody *bleu*. Hawkeye was livid as a loon. She was all rigid with indignosity. "I am sick to death of this, Georgia Nicolson. You have a perfectly good brain and a few talents, and you INSIST on squandering them in silly, childish pranks and unkindnesses. When Miss Stamp told me that she had chosen you as hockey captain, I had grave doubts. I still sometimes get headaches from your ridiculous display at the tennis championships last year."

Oh Blimey O'Reilly's vest and pants, what is it with teachers? Do they make lists of things that happened ages and ages ago and just hang around waiting for something else to add to them? Why doesn't she read some of the books I read? Let things go . . . relax, don't sweat the small stuff, talk to dolphins, go with the flow . . . etc.

Hawkeye hadn't finished. "However, these latest so-called jokes have confirmed what I said to her: that you have a silly attitude and are a poor example to both your peers and, more especially, the young and impressionable girls in this school. You are relieved of your duties as hockey captain forthwith."

I started to try to say something, but I felt a funny prickling feeling in my throat. I had to hand back my captain's badge. And what is more, I am on gardening duty with Mr. Attwood for a month!

When I came out of Hawkeye's interrogation

room, Wet Lindsay was smirking around. I bet she snitched on me. I didn't dignify her by saying anything. I have more pridosity than that.

Rosie was waiting for me around the corner. "Was it the forty lashes or has she just cut your basoomas off as a warning to others?"

"She's sacked me from being hockey captain."

RoRo put her arm around me.

my bedroom
11:17 p.m.
I wanted to phone the Sex God and tell him about the hockey captain fiasco, and I was going to. But I wasn't sure whether he would think that the "Ring the bell for the caretaker" thing was *très amusant* or the act of a twit.

midnight
I bet Dave the Laugh would think it was . . . er . . . a laugh.

Why am I thinking about him?

friday february 4th
lunch
I didn't feel much like talking and the gang kept

being nice to me, which was a bit strange. So I went off by myself to think. What was it Billy Shakespeare said? "And as we walk on down the road, our shadow taller than our souls . . ." Oh no, that was Rolf Harris doing his version of "Stairway to Heaven."

How crap was that?

The gang were following me around at a distance. Like stalkers in school uniforms.

I really loved being captain, though. Oh, double poo.

Even when you are the girlfriend of a Sex God things can go wrong. And anyway, what is the point of being the girlfriend of someone if every time you want to tell him something you can't? That is like being the ungirlfriend of someone. That is what I am: an ungirlfriend.

And not hockey captain. And with quite sticky-out elbows.

I moped around to the back of the tennis courts and a voice shouted out, "Has naughty Big Nose been in trouble with the scary teacher?" The Bummers were sitting having a fag on a pile of coats.

Oh, joy. The *pièce de résistance*. *Merde*, poo and triple bum.

Alison Bummer had a draw on her fag and then went off into a sort of hacking coughing fit.

I said, "Still in tip-top physical condition then, Alison, I'm pleased to see."

Alison gave me a very unattractive look (which is actually the only look she has). And I was just walking off when I heard a little voice say, "Can I get out now? It's almost end of break and my knees are really hurting."

Jackie said, "I'd like to let you out, but I haven't finished my fag yet." And I realized the Bummers had some poor little first formers underneath the coats on chair duty.

I turned back. "Let them out, you two."

Jackie pretended to be really scared. "Oh, OK then, Georgia, because we are sooooooo very very frightened of you."

Alison joined in. "Yes, you might hurt us with your enormous nose."

I looked at them and I thought, Right, that is it. I have been pushed to the brink of my tether. My hockey career might be over, but there is still something I can do for England. (And no I did not mean leave it.)

I marched back so quickly to school that the stalkers had to almost run to keep up with me.

They did catch me just as I was going into Slim's outer sanctum. "Gee, what are you doing?" Jas asked.

I said, "I'm going to tell Slim about Nauseating P. Green and the Bummers."

Everyone said, "OhmyGod!!!"

Jools said, "They will kill you if they find out."

Rosie said, "Slim might not trust you because of all the trouble you've been in."

I said, with great dignosity, "I will have to take my chances, then."

Then this really weird thing happened. Jas said, "I'm going to come in with you and tell what I know as well." So I hugged her. She tried to get away from me and spoiled the moment by saying, "Well . . . you know . . . erm . . . I mean, I am a member of the Ramblers' Association and . . ."

She would have rambled on, but Rosie said, "Yes, I'll come in as well. I will be on a reindeer farm by summer anyway, so what do I have to lose?"

All the ace gang said they would come to tell Slim with me. Even Ellen stopped sniffling long enough to join us. We were like the Six Samurai or whatever it is. We could ride around the countryside wronging rights and so on.

Then Slim appeared like a wardrobe in a dress and I slightly changed my mind.

4:30 p.m.
Well, we did it. We snitched on the Bummers and they have been immediately suspended from school and the police went straight round to their houses. God knows what will happen next.

6:00 p.m.
I'll tell you what happened next. Nauseating P. Green and her mum came round to my house. OhmyGod, they know where I live!!! They were blubbing and carrying on in an alarming way.

Nauseating P. Green brought Hammy, her hamster, round to celebrate, which was a bit of a mistake because Angus took him off to play hide and seek with Naomi and the kids. But we managed to find Hammy in the end and I think his fur may grow back.

The P. Greens left after several centuries of excruciating boredom and goldfishiness. But sadly it didn't end there. I have become a heroine in my own lunchtime.

Vati said, "I am really, really proud of you, my love." I thought he was going to start blubbing.

Mum was hugging me. In fact, they both forgot they were not speaking to each other and they were BOTH hugging me. Then Libby joined in with Teddy and scuba-diving Barbie. I never thought the day would dawn when I would be the victim of a group hug.

I may never do another nice thing in my life—it really isn't worth it.

9:00 p.m.

Robbie rang. I started to tell him about my day. "Hi Robbie, honestly, WHAT a day I've had. Well, guess what happened. The Bummers were sitting on some first formers and—"

Robbie interrupted me. "Georgia, look, I have to see you tomorrow, it's quite serious."

I said, "Have you broken a plectrum?"
But he didn't laugh.

midnight
Oh God. What fresh hell now?

Go Forth, Georgia, and Use Your Red Bottom Wisely

saturday february 5th

I am meeting the Sex God at the bottom of the clock tower. Libby wanted to come with me and ran off with my makeup bag. She ran into the bathroom and held my bag over the loo, saying, "Me come."

I had no time to negotiate, so . . . I just lied. "OK, go and get your welligogs on."

She ambled off to get them and I snatched my makeup bag and escaped through the door. There will be hell to pay when I get home. In fact, I will be surprised if there is a home left by the time I get back.

I had to apply my makeup crouching behind our garden wall. I could see Mr. Across the Road looking at me. He should do some voluntary work—perhaps he could be a seeing-eye dog or something.

11:00 a.m.

Robbie was already at the clock tower when I got there. As soon as I arrived he pulled me to him, which was a bit of a shame as he was wearing a coat with quite big buttons and one went right up my nose. I didn't say anything, though.

He said, "Let's walk to the park. I want to go to that place where we first sat together. Do you remember?"

Oooh, how *romantico*. He sang his first song to me there with my head on his knees. (He was sitting down at the time, otherwise I would have looked ridiculous.)

On the way there Robbie didn't say anything. It makes me really nervy when people don't speak. Dad says it's because I don't have much going on in my own head, which is hilarious coming from someone who knows all the words to "New York, New York."

When we got to the exact spot where we first kissed, Robbie looked at me. "Georgia, there isn't an easy way of saying this, but I'm going to have to go away."

I said, "Hahahahaha . . . I know, to Hamburger-a-gogo . . . and I'm coming too. I've been practicing saying 'Have a nice day,' and I can very nearly say it without throwing up." I rambled on, but he stopped me.

"Georgia, love, I'm not going to Los Angeles. That interview I went to was for a placement on an ecological farm in New Zealand. And I've got it. I'm going to go live there for a year. It will be really, really hard to leave you, but I know it's the right thing to do."

"A placement . . . a . . . in . . . a . . . Kiwi-a-gogo . . . Maoris . . . sheep . . . the . . . it . . . I . . ."

in bed
crying
a lot
How can this be happening to me? After all I've been through. The Sex God said he realized it was a shallow, hollow facsimile of a sham to be a pop-star.

I said, "We could recycle our caviar tins."

But he was serious. I should have known when he turned up on his bike that something had gone horribly wrong.

1:30 p.m.

Kiwi-a-gogo land. Loads of sheep and bearded loons. And I am sure that the men would be just as bad.

Robbie flies off to Whakatane next week.

Next week.

Perhaps I am being paid back for having the Cosmic Horn.

1:35 p.m.

Robbie said maybe I could come over for a holiday when he was settled in. I cried and cried and tried to persuade him not to go, but he said this weird thing. He said, "Georgia, you know how much I like you, but you are only young, and I'm only young and we have to have some time to grow up before we settle down." And even though I was really really blubby, I felt a funny kind of reliefiosity.

4:00 p.m.

Phoned Jas and told her. She said "OhmyGod" about a million times. Then she came round and stayed overnight with me. She said I could wear her Ramblers' badge, but I said no, thank you.

In the middle of the night, in the dark, I said to

her, "Jas, do you know what is weird?"

"What?"

"Well, you know I am on the brink of tragicosity and everything, but . . . well, I've got this sort of weird . . . weird . . ."

"What?"

"I'll tell you if you stop saying 'what.'"

I could hear her chewing in the dark. What had she found to chew?

"I've got this weird feeling of reliefiosity."

And she said, "What, like when you need a poo and then you have a poo?"

sunday february 6th

I've spoken to Robbie. He is upset, but he is definitely going.

He cried on the telephone.

5:30 p.m.

I am absolutely full of tragicosity. I went for a walk down to the square where the gang usually hangs out. I feel lonely as a clud.

Not lonely as a clud for long, because I bumped into Dave the Laugh, on his way to play snooker.

He said, "Hello, groovster. How are you?"

I said, "A bit on the poo and *merde* side, to be honest."

"Yeah, me too. Do you fancy going down to the park and hanging out for a bit?"

He's really nice actually, almost normal, in fact, for a boy. He is upset that Ellen is upset, but he says it wouldn't be right to keep going out with her just because he felt sorry for her.

I said, "You are quite literally full of wisdomosity."

I told him about the Robbie fandango.

He smiled at me. "So then, Sex Queen, you are not going to go to Los Angeles, you are going to go to Whakatane and raise elks with Robbie?"

in my room
10:00 p.m.

Everyone is out. Mutti and Vati have gone out on a "date" and Libby is staying at her friend Josh's for the night.

Dave the Laugh and I talked for ages. About life and the universe and everything. Yes, we did. And then . . . we SNOGGED again!!! I can't believe it!!! I am like Jekyll and Whatsit in babydoll pajamas.

10:05 p.m.

I must have the Cosmic Horn because of spring (even though it is February).

Dave the Laugh said we are only teenagers and we haven't been teenagers before, so how can we know what we are supposed to do.

He's right, although I haven't a clue what he is talking about. He said we should just live live live for the moment!!! Blow our Cosmic Horn and be done with it.

10:07 p.m.

I must do something. I feel like I am going to explode.

10:10 p.m.

Phoned Jas. "Jas."

"Oui."

"Do you ever get the urge?"

"Pardon?"

"You know, to flow free and wild."

She was thinking. "Well, sometimes when Tom and I are alone in the house together."

"Yes . . . ?"

"We flick each other with flannels."

"Jas, you keep talking on the telephone and I will send out for help."

"It's good fun . . . what you do is—"

"Jas, Jas, guess what I am doing now."

"Are you dancing?"

"Yes I am, my strange little pal. But what am I dancing in?"

"A bowl?"

"Jas, don't be silly. Concentrate. Try to get an image of me flowing wild and free."

"Are you dancing in . . . your P.E. knickers?"

"*Non* . . . I am DANCING IN MY NUDDY-PANTS!!!"

And we both laughed like loons on loon tablets.

I danced for ages round the house in my nuddy-pants. Also, I did this brilliant thing—I danced in the front window just for a second whilst Mr. Across the Road was drawing his curtains. He will never be sure if he saw a mirage or not.

That is the kind of person I am.

Not really the kind of person who goes and raises elks in Whakatane.

the end

midnight

Looking out of my bedroom window. (Partially dressed.)

I can see Angus, with a few of his sons and daughters, making an escape tunnel through Mr. and Mrs. Across the Road's hedge. He's still blowing his horn, even though he has no horn to blow.

Surely God wouldn't have invented red-bottomosity unless he was trying to tell me something. Perhaps He is saying, "Go forth, Georgia, and use your red bottom wisely."

That will be it. So I can snuggle down now, safe in the sanctity of my own unique bottomosity.

Hang on a minute, who is that? By the lamppost? Oh, it's Mark Big Gob with his latest girlfriend, walking home. He must have dumped the midget and moved on to bigger things, because this one at least reaches his waist. Still, I cannot point the finger of shame at him. None of us is perfect. Although I don't think it's entirely necessary for his mouth to be as big as it is. He is like part bloke, part blue whale.

1:00 a.m.

Still looking out the window.

Perhaps I could have Dave the Laugh as an unserious boyfriend, and for diplomatic world relations–type stuff, also have that gorgey French boy who gave me the rose in gay Paree.

Hmmm. Here come Mutti and Vati, back from their night out.

So, I could have the Cosmic Horn for now. And I could save the Sex God for later!!

Perfect. Providing he doesn't get a Kiwi accent and start snogging sheep.

Mutti and Vati have got out of their car and although they are holding each other up, they are still not fighting, so all is still well with the world.

Hang on a minute. They're not holding each other up, they are snogging.

That is so sad. And disgusting.

So all's well that ends well in God's land.

I'll just say good-night to the stars. Good-night stars.

And the moon. Good-night moon, you gorgeous,

big, round, yellow, sexy thing.

Phew, I really have got the Cosmic Horn badly.

THE OFFICIAL AND PROPER END.
PROBABLY.

Glossary

billio • From the Australian outback. A billycan was something Aborigines boiled their goodies up in, or whatever it is they eat. Anyway, billio means boiling things up. Therefore, "my cheeks ached like billio" means—er—very achy. I don't know why we say it. It's a mystery, like many things. But that's the beauty of life.

Boboland • As I have explained many, many times English is a lovely and exciting language full of sophisticosity. To go to sleep is "to go to bobos," so if you go to bed you are going to Boboland. It is an Elizabethan expression (oh, OK then, Libby made it up and she can be unreasonably violent if you don't join in with her).

Boxing Day • The day after Chrimboli Day (Christmas Day—keep up).

It is called Boxing Day because that is the day you are supposed to open your presents. You don't do it on Baby Jesus's birthday because that is when he is opening his presents (symbolically). How pleased he must have been to get some frankincense (not).

bum-oley • Quite literally bottom hole. I'm sorry but you did ask. Say it proudly (with a cheery smile and a Spanish accent).

Changing of the Guards • Outside of Her Maj's pad (Buckingham Palace or Buck House as we call it) there are a load of blokes marching about with bearskins on their heads. They are guarding her against—er—stuff—the French, probably. After a bit they get tired and droopy and have to be changed for new ones.

Chrimbo/Chrimboli • Christmas Day, really, but as you know, time is money.

Churchill Square • A shopping center (mall) named after Sir Winston Churchill who won World War II. (Although my grandad said he won the war by parachuting into Germany and landing on Hitler's motorbike and overcoming him with native cunning and superior military skills. What you have to take into consideration is that my grandad is bonkers).

Cliff Richard's Y-Fronts • Y-Fronts are boys' knickers, but they are not worn by any boy you would want to know. Cliff Richard is a living legend (who is now a Lord—or is it a Lady?).

clud • This is short for cloud. Lots of really long boring poems and so on can be made much snappier by abbreviating words. So Tennyson's poem called "Daffodils" (or "Daffs") has the immortal line "I wandered lonely as a clud."

Ditto Rom and Jul. Or Ham. Or Merc. Of Ven.

coach • Er . . . bus. Oh, I get it. You think that "coach" is like a trainer-type person! Oh, I see now. You thought we climbed onto a person for our trip to gay Paree. No wonder you were on the edge of bamboozlement. You see in England coach means a bus as well as a trainer. It's a bit confusing. But we are allowed to say what we like because we made up English in the first place.

conk • Nose. This is very interesting historically. A very long time ago (1066)—even before my grandad was born—a bloke called William the Conqueror (French) came to England and shot our King Harold in the eye. Typical. And people wonder why we don't like the French much. Anyway, William had a big nose and so to get our own back we called him William the Big Conkerer. If you see what I mean. I hope you do because I am exhausting myself with my hilariosity and historiosity.

David Beckham • Of course you know who David Beckham is. He is the sensationally vain English football captain. He is married to Posh Spice. But we love the little scallywag (don't start pretending you don't know what scallywag means).

DIY • Quite literally "Do It Yourself!" Rude when you think about it. Instead of getting someone competent to do things around the house (you know, like a trained electrician or a builder or a plumber), some vatis choose to do DIY. Always with disastrous results. (For example, my bedroom ceiling has footprints in it because my vati decided he would go up on the roof and replace a few tiles. Hopeless.)

duffing up • Duffing up is the female equivalent of beating up. It is not so violent and usually involves a lot of pushing with the occasional pinch.

duff • useless

Edith Piaf • Some French woman who used to sing *"Je ne regrette rien,"* which means she didn't regret anything. Which is ironic as she was only four foot high and French.

first footing • Traditional Och Aye land madness. On the stroke of midnight on December 31st some complete fool (a vati) knocks on your door and gives you a lump of coal. No one knows why. Ask the Scottish folk. And whilst you are at it, ask them about sporrans. And deep fried pizza.

first former • Kids of about eleven who have just started "big" school. They have shiny innocent faces, very tempting to slap.

form • A form is what we call a class at English secondary schools. It is probably a Latin expression. Probably from the Latin *formus ignoramus.*

fringe • Goofy short bit of hair that comes down to your eyebrows. Someone told me that American-type people call them "bangs" but this is so ridiculously strange that it's not worth thinking about. Some people can look very stylish with a fringe (i.e., me) while others look goofy (Jas). The Beatles started it apparently. One of them had a German girlfriend, and she cut their hair with a pudding bowl and the rest is history.

geoggers • Geoggers is short for geography. Ditto blodge (biology) and lunck (lunch).

gusset • Do you really not know what a gusset is? I do.

horn • When you "have the horn" it's the same as "having the big red bottom."

Isle of Man • A ridiculous island in the sea in between Scotland and Ireland. You travel on a boat full of mad people being tossed about like a cork. Then you get there and it's full of people from Liverpool and the most exciting thing about it is that the cats don't have tails. Honestly.

Kiwi-a-gogo land • New Zealand. "A-gogo land" can be used to liven up the otherwise really boring names of other countries. America, for instance, is Hamburger-a-gogo land. Mexico is Mariachi-a-gogo land and France is Frogs'-legs-a-gogo land.

Maths • Mathematics.

Michael Parkinson • He interviews people on a TV chat show. He has very nice gray hair and shiny suits. Like a badger. But without the big digging paws. As far as I know.

nicked • stolen

nippy noodles • Instead of saying "Good heavens, it's quite cold this morning," you say "Cor—nippy noodles!!" English is an exciting and growing language. It is. Believe me. Just leave it at that. Accept it.

nub • The heart of the matter. You can also say gist and thrust. This is from the name for the center of a wheel where the spokes come out. Or do I mean hub? Who cares. I feel a dance coming on.

nuddy-pants • Quite literally nude-colored pants, and you know what nude-colored pants are? They are no pants. So if you are in your nuddy-pants you are in your no pants, i.e., you are naked.

nunga-nungas • Basoomas. Girl's breasty business. Ellen's brother calls them nunga-nungas because he says that if you get hold of a girl's breast and pull it out and then let it go—it goes *nunga-nunga-nunga*. As I have said many, many times with great wisdomosity, there is something really wrong with boys.

Old Bill • The police, a.k.a. "the filth" or "our brave lads in blue." Depending on whether they can hear you or not.

piggies • Pigtails. Or "bunches," I think you call them. Like two little side ponytails in your hair. Only we think they look like pigtails. English people are obsessed with pigs; that is our strange beauty.

porkies • Amusing(ish) Cockney rhyming slang. Pork pies = lies. Which is of course shortened to porkies. Oh, that isn't shorter, is it? Well, you can't have everything.

prat • A prat is a gormless oik. You make a prat of your-self by mistakenly putting both legs down one knicker leg or by playing air guitar at pop concerts.

rate • To fancy someone. Like I fancy (or rate) the Sex God. And I certainly do fancy the SG as anyone with the brains of an earwig (i.e., not Jas) would know by now. Phew—even writing about him in the glossary has made me go all jelloid. And stupidoid.

R.E. • Religious education.

Rolf Harris • An Australian "entertainer" (not). Rolf has a huge beard and glasses. He plays the didgeridoo, which says everything in my book. He sadly has had a number of hit records, which means he is never off TV and will not go back to Australia. (His "records" are called "Tie Me Kangaroo Down, Sport," etc.)

sledging • Something you do in nippy noodles season. When it snows thickly enough to cover the ground you leap onto a bit of wood that has runners on it. Then you lie on the board (sledge) and skim, skim like a bird across the snow. In theory. In practice you leap onto the sledge and crash immediately into a tree.

spondulicks • A Sudanese term for money. Possibly. The reason we use it is because in olden days English people used to go to other countries where the weather was nicer (i.e., everywhere) and say to the leaders of these other countries:

"Hello, what extremely nice weather you are having,

do you like our flag?" And the other (not English) people would say: "Yes, it's very nice, is it a Union Jack?" And the old English people would reply: "Yes. Where is your flag?" And they would say: "We haven't got one actually." And we'd say: "Oh dear. That means you have to give your country to us then."

That is how we became world leaders and also how we got foreign words in our language.

By the way, it is a very good job that I have historosity at my fingertips; otherwise certain people (i.e., you) would feel hopelessly dim.

sporrans • Ah, I'm glad you asked me about this because it lets me illustrate my huge knowledgosity about Och Aye land. Sporrans are bits of old sheep that Scotsmen wear over their kilts, at the front, like little furry aprons. Please don't ask me why. I feel a nervy spaz coming on.

Water Board • A bunch of blokes who look after the nation's reservoirs and water supply.

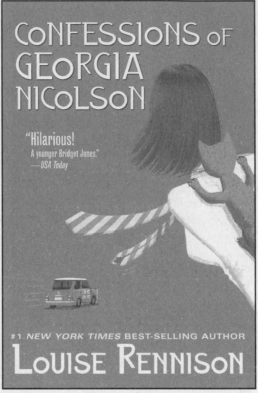